"Those looking for an emotional roller-coaster ride will be rewarded."
—*Publishers Weekly*

"Combine Lucinda Berry's deep understanding of the complexities of the human mind with her immense talent for storytelling and you have *The Secrets of Us*, an intense psychological thriller that kept my heart racing until the shocking, jaw-dropping conclusion. Bravo!"
—T.R. Ragan, *New York Times* bestselling author

"*The Secrets of Us* is an unputdownable page-turner with two compelling female protagonists that will keep readers on their toes. Fantastic!"
—Cate Holahan, *USA Today* bestselling author of *One Little Secret*

"Lucinda Berry's *The Secrets of Us* is a tense psychological thriller that explores the dark corners of the mind and turns a mind can take when it harbors secret guilt. The interplay between sisters Krystal and Nichole and their hidden past is gradually revealed, and in the end, the plot twists keep coming. Right and wrong can be ambivalent, and this story explores all shades of gray, from their dysfunctional family to an old childhood friend to a husband who may or may not be too good to be true. Berry's background as a clinical psychologist shines in this novel with a character so disturbed they spend time in seclusion lockdown at a psychiatric ward. Don't miss this one!"
—Debbie Herbert, *USA Today* and Amazon Charts bestselling author

"*The Secrets of Us* is an utterly gripping, raw, and heartbreaking story of two sisters. Berry's flawlessly placed clues and psychological expertise grab you from the first word, not letting go until the last. Compelling, intricate, and shocking, this inventive thriller cleverly weaves from past to present with stunning precision. I was absolutely enthralled."
—Samantha M. Bailey, *USA Today* and #1 national bestselling author of *Woman on the Edge*

"The past and present collide with explosive consequences in this addictive, twisty thriller from an author at the top of her game. *The Secrets of Us* grips from the first page and doesn't let go until the final shocking twist."
—Lisa Gray, bestselling author of *Dark Highway*

THE BEST OF FRIENDS

"A mother's worst nightmare on the page. For those who dare."
—*Kirkus Reviews*

"*The Best of Friends* gripped me from the stunning opening to the emotional, explosive ending. In this moving novel, Berry creates a beautifully crafted study of secrets and grief among a tight-knit group of friends and of how far a mother will go to discover the truth and protect her children."
—Heather Gudenkauf, *New York Times* bestselling author of *The Weight of Silence* and *This Is How I Lied*

"In *The Best of Friends*, Berry starts with a heart-stopping bang—the dreaded middle-of-the-night phone call—and then delivers a dark and gritty tale that unfolds twist by devastating twist. Intense, terrifying, and at times utterly heartbreaking. Absolutely unputdownable."
—Kimberly Belle, international bestselling author of *Dear Wife* and *Stranger in the Lake*

THE PERFECT CHILD

"I am a compulsive reader of literary novels . . . but there was one book that kept me reading, the sort of novel I can't put down . . . *The Perfect Child*, by Lucinda Berry. It speaks to the fear of every parent: What if your child was a psychopath? This novel takes it a step further. A couple, desperate for a child, has the chance to adopt a beautiful little girl who, they are told, has been abused. They're told it might take a while for her to learn to behave and trust people. She can be sweet and loving, and in public she is adorable. But in private—well, I won't give away what happens. But needless to say, it's chilling."

—Gina Kolata, *New York Times*

"A mesmerizing, unbearably tense thriller that will have you looking over your shoulder and sleeping with one eye open. This creepy, serpentine tale explores the darkest corners of parenthood and the profoundly unsettling lengths one will go to, to keep a family together—no matter the consequences. Electrifying and atmospheric, this dark gem of a novel is one I couldn't put down."

—Heather Gudenkauf, *New York Times* bestselling author

"A deep, dark, and dangerously addictive read. All-absorbing to the very end!"

—Minka Kent, *Washington Post* bestselling author

OFF
THE
DEEP
END

OTHER TITLES BY LUCINDA BERRY

OFF THE DEEP END

A THRILLER

LUCINDA BERRY

Published by Thomas & Mercer, Seattle

www.apub.com

Amazon, the Amazon logo, and Thomas & Mercer are trademarks of Amazon.com, Inc., or its affiliates.

ISBN-13: 9781662506208
ISBN-10: 1662506201

Cover design by Damon Freeman

Printed in the United States of America

To Amber Rae. Once upon a time, we drove around a lake, and I've been writing this story ever since.

PROLOGUE

My eyes snapped open.

Pitch black surrounded me.

I can't see. I can't breathe. I can't move.

Dark water pummeled me, violently shoving its way up my nose, into my mouth, down my throat—everywhere. So cold. Piercing pain shot through my body like a thousand needles stabbing every cell. Bleeding my insides.

Twisted metal shards.

Loud, angry cracks shattered and multiplied around me. Filling my ears like the rushing water. The blaring car horn.

Panic triggered a scream—*Gabe!*—forcing more water down my throat. I gasped and choked as I flailed and kicked, desperately trying to find him, but it was impossible. The dark water swirled and spun around me like an angry monster, pushing its way up to my chin and shoving me under before I had a chance to breathe. My chest seized.

I couldn't see anything, the murky water thick with weeds. Dark shadows. The horn. *Make it stop.*

I frantically swiped at the water. He had to be here. He had to be. *Don't panic,* I mentally shouted at myself, trying to conserve the energy I'd need to get us to the surface. I twisted left, right, back again. And then I felt something.

Fingers.

Reaching. Clawing. Scratching wildly at my arm.

Gabe! An inaudible scream so loud it blurred the edge of my vision. I reached for his hand and grabbed his wrist. He clung to me, digging his fingernails into my forearm. I jerked him and tried to swim up. Our heads cracked against the top of the SUV within seconds.

Gabe's panicked grip tightened on my arm. I flipped the other direction and kicked at the window as hard as I could. Nothing. I kicked again. Then, again and again, using both feet, until it finally burst. Water rushed in like a just-released fire hydrant, and I clung to Gabe's wrist until the torrent passed.

My lungs screamed at me to breathe, but I ignored them and pressed forward, desperately trying to swim. It was like swimming through sand, and I couldn't see more than a few inches in front of me. The water was so hard to push through.

Which way was up? I frantically scanned left to right, up, down, but I couldn't tell which way to go. There was no time. I kicked and swam blind. My clothes clung to me, weighing me down. My pulse throbbed in my temples. Yellow spots danced in front of my eyes. A kick and another scissor kick. One more. Two. Then, a final push and we were almost there. I could see the night sky.

I crashed through the surface of the water. Coughing. Choking. Gasping for breath. I pulled Gabe to freedom next to me with the last bit of strength I had left. He inched his way onto the ice and flopped on his side. I turned to look at him. My hair already frozen to my head.

It took a second for my brain to register what I was seeing.

Oh my God.

Gabe's friend Isaac stared back at me with wide terror-filled eyes as he took huge gulping breaths. *I pulled out Isaac. Oh my God. I pulled out Isaac.* That was his hand. His body thrashing behind me. Gabe was still down there!

I shoved Isaac off me and hurtled headfirst back into the freezing lake water. Within seconds, the darkness covered me again. I plunged down, trying to make my way back to the SUV, but my muscles were mush. None of my body worked right. Marshmallow arms. Heavy legs. Insides on fire, but I wouldn't stop until I found him. I pressed on, following the sound of the horn still coming from the vehicle. A few more seconds and I was there, feeling my way along the SUV, frantically searching for a door handle, but all I felt was slick metal. I tried to punch through one of the windows, but it didn't budge. I banged on it with both fists, but it was like it was made of plexiglass.

Where is he? I pounded on the car again. And again. Why wouldn't it break this time? I heaved myself against it. Still nothing.

Uncontrollable shivering seized my body. Teeth chattered so hard they bit the inside of my cheeks. The metallic taste of blood filled my mouth and dripped down my throat. My chest throbbed with the need to breathe, but I'd lost sight of the surface again. That was okay. Was that Gabe? Over there? Under that star?

Oh, look—there were fireworks. Now those were nice. Really nice. I liked the purple.

"I'm here, Gabe. Mama's right here," I called out, taking the water into my lungs and reaching for him.

Then, floating.

CASE #72946

PATIENT: JULIET (JULES) HART

What doesn't kill you makes you stronger. That's the happy horseshit he's spent the last ten minutes trying to feed me as he sits on the other side of the small table in his tweed blazer with his carefully crossed legs. It's the stupidest saying ever. Sometimes, what doesn't kill you simply doesn't kill you, and you spend all your time wishing it had. Escaping death isn't any kind of a prize when you'd rather not be on the planet. But he's trying to bond with me the way all shrinks do when they meet you for the first time. They can't help themselves. It's called building rapport, and it's the first thing they teach students in graduate school. I should know—I used to be one, but that was another lifetime ago.

He pushes his clear-framed glasses up his nose and gives me an encouraging smile, about to ask me another question, but I jump in before he has a chance to do so. "What'd you say your name was again?"

"Dr. Stephens," he says, not skipping a beat, "but you can call me Ryan."

I hold myself back from shaking my head at him. What a rookie mistake. His attempt at connection and intimacy takes away the tiny power differential he had, and he needed the credibility of *doctor* in front of his name. A doctorate in forensic psychology trumps my master's degree in marriage and family therapy, but he just stepped himself down to my equal. That's not a position he wants to be in if he wants to get anywhere with me. But what can you expect? He's clearly fresh out of college. A "try-hard," like Gabe and his friends used to say. I almost burst out laughing because it's exactly what Gabe would say if he saw him sitting there in front of me right now, and I know exactly how he'd look when he said it too—giant blue eyes sparkling with mischief and a lopsided grin. The image quickly flashes through me, leaving me shattered and on the edge of tears. Grief's like that. Months ago, I would've crumbled into tears, inconsolable, interview officially over.

But time marches on, right? Another one of those stupid sayings I hate.

At least Dr. Stephens—there's no way I'm calling him Ryan—is better than the psychiatrists on the locked unit at the state security hospital in Willmar. Those doctors didn't even look at you while they rapid-fired their questions at you. Their eyes stayed glued on the charts in front of them the entire time, quickly checking off their required boxes so they could move on to the next patient on their list. They only cared about whether you'd managed to smuggle in or create a weapon to hurt yourself or someone else with. At first, I thought they were being a bit melodramatic about the whole thing, but it happened on the regular. Someone was always slicing open their inner thigh with a paper clip they'd managed to snag from the nurse's station when nobody was looking or attacking someone else with a piece of a broken chair leg.

Dr. Stephens sits closer to me than any of those other doctors ever got. They rarely sat when they visited your room during rounds. They usually just stood in the doorways with their arms crossed, doing their best to keep you in front of them at all times while someone else watched their backs. They had to be on alert constantly since certain patients had a disgusting habit of throwing feces at them if they got a chance. You had to be really out of your mind to throw feces, and I almost gagged the first time I saw someone do it. Most of the time, the people on the ward that were that crazy were easy to spot, but I'd been fooled more than once. It makes sense that those doctors had given up hope and stopped seeing anyone in front of them as anything other than a number on a chart. But not Dr. Stephens—crazy people haven't hardened him yet.

"How long has it been since the accident?" he asks, breaking into my thoughts. It's a stupid question. He already knows everything about me. I'm sure he spent all night studying my charts like he was getting ready to take a final exam. He's got type A personality written all over him.

"Which one?" I joke, but he doesn't laugh or look like he thinks it's funny at all despite his boyish, playful face. This is going to be hard to do if he doesn't have a sense of humor.

"Since you lost your son," he clarifies.

The air tightens in the room like it does every time someone brings it up. "Ten months."

"That must be so hard." His face shifts into sadness, attempting to mirror my feelings.

"Hard?" I nod my head at him dramatically. "Yeah, you could say it's been hard. Kinda like being gutted while you're still alive, you know? Like you didn't get the proper anesthetic for surgery and you can feel it all happening. That's—"

He holds his hand up, interrupting me. "I'm sorry. I get it. That was insensitive." He moves his hand into a peaceful gesture and slowly brings it back down to rest on the table. "I'm just trying to get to know you."

"We both know that's not what you're doing."

He cocks his head to the side. "Fair enough."

"Can we get to what you're really doing here?" It's not like I don't already know. The entire town is crawling with law enforcement personnel and volunteer search teams looking for Isaac. People from all over the state have joined the search for him. He disappeared six days ago while he was taking their family dog out for a walk. It was only a matter of time before someone showed up to ask me questions about it.

Ruth Ann, one of the resident staff members at Samaritan House, pulled me out of group therapy twenty minutes ago. "There's some kind of detective here about the missing boy, and he'd like to speak with you. Would you mind?" She said it like I had a say in the matter, but we both knew that wasn't true. I forfeited having a say in my life a long time ago. I happily agreed to meet with him, but my attitude was as fake as her request. I was compliant for the same reason I agreed to do everything around here—it was required of me if I wanted to stay out of the security hospital, and I do. More than anything. I'm never going back to that terrible place.

"I want to talk to you about Isaac," Dr. Stephens breaks in, interrupting my thoughts again. All anyone ever wanted to talk about was Gabe. It might be a nice change of pace to talk about Isaac. "We're hoping you might have information that could be helpful to the case."

"I'm not sure how helpful I can be, but I'll do my best." I stretch across the small table separating us. "What do you want to know?"

"Why don't you take me back to the beginning?"

ONE

AMBER GREER

"How'd it go?" I whipped open the front door and grabbed Detective Hawkins by the shirt before he had a chance to knock, then pulled him inside. "What did Jules say?"

My husband, Mark, didn't even look up from his spot on the couch in the family room. He sat with his hands folded on his lap and stared at the TV on the wall in front of him without actually watching what was playing on the screen. That was what he did whenever things got too intense with the investigation. He just shut down like there was a switch inside him that someone had turned off. He'd been that way since Isaac had gone missing six days ago.

Six grueling days since our world got flipped upside down again. It hadn't even righted itself since the last time. This couldn't be happening. It wasn't fair. How many bad things could happen to a person? Wasn't there some kind of limit on the number of traumatic events you could experience in a lifetime? The universe needed to back off and leave us alone.

Detective Hawkins stepped through the entryway and headed into the family room so Mark could be a part of the conversation too. Although it hardly mattered because Mark didn't have much of anything to say to anyone at the moment. He just sat there like a big dummy doing nothing in a way that infuriated me. Like whatever was happening, we were just supposed to sit back and take it.

I'd totally gone nuts on him last night. I hadn't lost it on him like that since I was pregnant and hormone crazed, but his detachment and emotional disconnection during all this was infuriating. He'd shut down hour by hour as the clock ticked further and further away from the last time Isaac had left the house. He wasn't even bothering to go through the motions anymore except when he was upset. He was over the top then. I couldn't take it. I wasn't cut out for any of this.

"Hi, Mark," Detective Hawkins said, sticking his hand out to greet him. When the sheriff told me they were bringing in some hotshot from the twin cities to lead the case, I'd expected someone big and commanding to assume the role, so Detective Hawkins had taken me by surprise, and I was still trying to adjust. Although he was commanding, he certainly wasn't big. He wasn't much taller than me, which wasn't saying a lot since I was barely five four. Everything about him was average—his height, his build, his face—except for his eyes. Those were one of a kind. He had piercing blue hawk eyes. They took one look at you and penetrated your soul. No wonder he was a detective.

Mark raised his arm and slowly shook Detective Hawkins's hand like it weighed ten pounds. All his movements were slow and sluggish. He laid his hands back in his lap after he'd finished like the simple social interaction had sucked the remaining life energy out of him. I stifled my annoyance and focused my questions on Detective Hawkins.

"Where did she say she was the night Isaac went missing? Were you able to speak with any of the staff at the house? Can they verify that? Do you think they'll be cooperative?" I asked, my words tumbling out of me so fast they fell on top of each other. I just had so many questions, and I'd been holding them inside all day. Talking to Mark about them was useless. Our discussions only ended in fights.

Detective Hawkins shook his head and held up his hands, motioning for me to slow down. "That's not how these kinds of interviews work. They take time. Sometimes a lot of time."

"I don't understand why. All the psychologist has to do is ask her where she was the night Isaac went missing. Then check to see if she's lying. That's more than probable cause to get you into her room." It wasn't that complicated. I'd been a die-hard *Dateline* fan for twenty years, and they always stressed how important the first seventy-two hours were after a person disappeared. It'd been way longer than that since Isaac had gone missing, and they were wasting valuable time. Jules had him. I knew she did.

He shook his head again. "Being interviewed by a forensic psychologist is not like being interrogated by the police or a detective. It's a completely different process when you're dealing with someone so mentally unstable. You have to be so careful."

"Okay, well, then, can't *you* at least interview her in the meantime?" They should've been interviewing her since day one, and we'd be a lot further along than this, but they hadn't listened to any of my input about the investigation even though it was my son we were looking for. I swore that half the time, they treated me like I'd done something wrong.

Detective Hawkins gently placed his hand on my arm and pointed to the spot on the couch next to Mark. "Why don't you take a seat?"

I brushed his hand off. "I'm good, thanks." Sitting next to Mark was the last thing I wanted to do. I didn't want any of his negative energy to rub off on me. We had to stay positive through this. "So, what did she say?"

"Nothing yet, but they're just getting started. He's only been with her for a few hours. I imagine they'll take a break soon and then get back to it. Like I said, these things take time, and I know that it's hard, but you're just going to have to be patient," he said in a gentle voice.

"Patient?" I screeched. "I'm supposed to be patient when some lunatic has my son?" I glared at him, and he stared back at me, unmoved by my emotions. His steely eyes didn't flinch. His gaze was unwavering on mine like he was doing some strange Jedi mind trick to get me to calm down, and somehow, it worked despite my intentions.

He waited another beat before clearing his throat and continuing, "While Dr. Stephens is with Mrs. Hart and we're monitoring the phones for any activity, I thought the three of us might be able to follow up on a few things." I didn't like the way his tone of voice shifted or that he wanted me to sit down for whatever he wanted to discuss. I crossed my arms against my chest and waited for him to continue. He was silent for another second just to make sure I wasn't going to sit. "Our agents received clearance to start going through Isaac's phone, and they've noticed something interesting that I wanted to talk to the two of you about."

Mark immediately came alive like he'd been sleeping and suddenly jolted awake. He jumped off the couch and hurried to join us. He was in the same sweatpants and T-shirt he'd been in for the past five days. He smelled like it too. "What is it? What'd you find?" He ran his hands through his greasy dark hair.

Detective Hawkins pretended not to notice his smell or his disheveled appearance. "It's not so much what they found as to what they didn't find." He gave us both a knowing look, but I had no idea what he was talking about. From the look on Mark's face, he didn't either.

Thankfully, I'd sent our younger daughter, Katie, to my mom's house for a few days even though I hadn't wanted to let her go at first. None of us had been separated since it had happened, but I was glad my mom had talked me into it. Katie needed a break from all the intensity, and I wasn't sure I wanted her to hear whatever Detective Hawkins was about to say. I wasn't sure I wanted to hear it, either, by the grave expression stamped on his face.

"I don't have teenagers myself, but I've been through enough of their phones over the years to know that they're always packed full of stuff. Everything they're doing. What they're getting into. You want to know what's going on in a teenager's life?" He cocked his head to the side and raised his eyebrows. "Look in their phone."

What'd they found in Isaac's phone? My knees weakened. I eyed the couch, wishing I'd taken Detective Hawkins up on his offer to sit. Of course, I looked in both of my kids' phones. That had been part of the deal when we got them for them. We'd made that clear from day one: *These are not your phones, they're ours, and as such, we have a right to them whenever we choose.* They'd both kicked and screamed, but faced with the prospect of having us monitor their phones or no phones at all, they'd each chosen the latter and begrudgingly consented to the rules. But I hadn't been through Isaac's phone in weeks. He never left it alone, and I was too afraid he'd get upset if I asked him if I could go through it. I wasn't usually like that, but the slightest provocation could set him off into one of his rage fits, and once he'd crossed over that line, there wasn't any getting him back until he'd spiraled through it, ending in the same awful pit of shame he always did.

He never used to be that way. He was my calm and steady one. Katie was the one whose emotions bounced around and skyrocketed all over the place. She could laugh with you in one breath and hiss at you in the next. But Isaac? He was a rock. He'd come out of the womb that way. Steady. Strong. Consistent. Unbothered by anything happening around him.

Not now.

I felt like I didn't know who he was, and honestly, that scared me more than anything else. In the same way, Detective Hawkins's expression scared me as he explained, "Isaac doesn't have any activity on his phone from the past three weeks. He hasn't called or texted anyone. He—"

Relief flooded my body, and I interrupted before he could go any further. "That's because he never goes anywhere or talks to anyone anymore. I keep telling his therapist that, but she doesn't listen. We can barely get him to leave the house. The only thing that got him outside was walking Duke. We always made him walk Duke—" My throat caught, and my eyes darted to Mark. That look. The other one.

Mark narrowed his eyes to slits. "Yes, Isaac never went anywhere, and she made him walk Duke every night to get out of the house." There was no mistaking the venom in the word *she*.

He blamed me for this. That had been clear since the beginning of this nightmare. He blamed me for this in the same way he blamed me for Isaac having been in the car with the Harts that terrible night, as if it was my fault that Katie's dance rehearsal had run late and I'd had to ask Jules to pick up Isaac for me. I glared back at him. I wouldn't have had to call another mom to help me with pickup if I had a husband who ever lifted a hand to help with them when I needed it the most.

"Yes, well, regardless of that, there isn't any activity on his phone whatsoever. It's more than just not texting or FaceTiming anyone. He hasn't played any video games. Hasn't watched any YouTube. His Snapchat history is empty. All his streaks are gone. He hasn't been on TikTok. No Instagram. I mean, there's nothing there. It's the cleanest teenager's phone I've ever seen, and I've been at this for a long time. It's almost like he hadn't touched the thing."

"But that's impossible. I saw him on it," Mark said, shaking his head in disbelief. I'd seen him on his phone plenty of times in the past few weeks, too, and it was the same phone they'd found on Clarks' Road yesterday. Exactly a mile and a half from our house.

"Is it possible he had another phone?" Detective Hawkins asked, shifting his gaze back and forth between us.

I shook my head. "Absolutely not," I said at the same time Mark said, "It could be."

I whipped around to face Mark. "What do you mean it's possible he might've had another phone?"

He shrugged, and his eyes filled with annoyance at my response. "He's quite capable of getting another phone on his own, Amber. I don't know why you insist on treating him like he's still a child."

"Really? Just when would he have gotten that phone?" I put my hands on my hips. "All the times he went out?" He knew as well as I did that Isaac had all but stopped going out unless he was with us, and only then because we forced him to go. He rarely ever went anywhere alone unless it was to walk Duke. "Or he ordered it? But we all know who gets the packages and mail around here." I couldn't help the subtle dig. It was true. He didn't help with the household duties any more than he helped with the kids. "Also, you're forgetting one important thing—even if he got another phone, he'd still have to pay for it, and we would've seen that on one of his accounts." Each kid had a debit card linked to our account, and they both had Apple Pay, so we could see all their purchases. "Isaac definitely didn't have another phone."

"He could've—"

Detective Hawkins interrupted, jumping in before we spiraled into a bigger argument. "It's certainly plausible that he erased all of his history going back three weeks, but that would take a long time to do and require some serious work on his part. You'd only do it if there was a really good reason for it, and"—he gave a small hands-only shrug—"you know what that looks like."

"What do you mean?" I asked.

"It looks like he might have something to hide."

"What could he be hiding? He doesn't—"

Mark cut me off. "What does any of this matter, anyway?" he asked angrily. "Who cares if Isaac was hiding anything? None of that makes a single bit of difference. They found his phone on the side of the road yesterday just like those other boys', and if you don't do something soon to find him, we all know what they find next. Can we not waste time on this phone nonsense, please?"

CASE #72946

PATIENT: JULIET (JULES) HART

"How long have you known the Greer family?" Dr. Stephens asks, nudging me along with a question after it takes me too long to get started on the story.

"Practically forever," I say, which is exactly why it's impossible to know where to begin in the telling of all this. Dr. Stephens tilts his head to the side and raises his eyebrows at me, clearly not interested in anything less than specific facts. I quickly do the math in my head. "I guess almost seventeen years? Their family moved to Chatsworth Lane the summer after we did."

Chatsworth Lane was a gorgeous housing community on the east side of Falcon Lake in southern Minnesota where we'd built our forever home. The streets were filled with beautiful custom houses on massive lots surrounded by amazing schools and sprawling neighborhoods. It's the only reason people lived on that side of town. The entire reason Shane and I had moved to Falcon Lake in the first place. Falcon Lake was a small town exactly forty-five minutes away from Minneapolis, so it gave you the best of both worlds. Chatsworth Lane was one of the prettiest streets in town. The maples formed a gorgeous braided arch over it, and we residents all chipped in to help decorate them with Christmas lights every year.

The Greers had always lived three doors down from us, so it would've been nice and really convenient for our families to be close. I'd been dreaming about living on the same street as my best friend since I was a little girl, and I grew up playing house with all my friends that way. We'd pretend our husbands would go off to work while we'd raise the children and keep our respective houses running smoothly together, leaning on each other for help and support. It sounded so 1950s house-wife, and it was, but I was perfectly content with the arrangement. It seemed liked a lovely life.

"Oh my God, I can't believe you're just going to throw away every-thing women have worked so hard to gain," my younger sister, Carrie, would retort every time I brought it up around her when we were teenagers.

"I should be able to be a housewife if I want to." Always my first line of defense. "That's a valid choice too."

Carrie would storm out of my bedroom after that. She couldn't stand the term *housewife*. She still couldn't, but that's what it was, and I didn't think I should have to feel bad about letting someone else have a career while I took care of the children. There was nothing wrong with a woman wanting to stay home with the children and letting someone else be the breadwinner. If all choices were okay—and that was the point, wasn't it?—then that had to be an acceptable option too. I still feel the same way even after all these years. Even after how opposite everything turned out.

"Were your families close?" Dr. Stephens asks, bringing me back to the present.

"We should've been, but we weren't. I tried really hard to make it happen in the beginning, though. Amber must've thought I was trying to make her gain ten pounds with all the cookies and brownies I kept bringing over. I started before the construction crew had even broken ground."

He lets out a tiny laugh. It's the first time he's shown any real emotion, and it stops my story midstride. I like his smile. He should do it more often. I force myself to focus. "Anyway, we were both newly married, and neither of us had kids yet, but we were on the same track, you know? Marriage. House. Baby. That's how it went. It's how you did things if you wanted to set them up right, and I did. I've always been a perfectionist and a planner. So it made sense that we'd be two of those super close families who practically did everything together, but the timing was never right."

"What do you mean?"

The light in the corner won't stop giving off an annoying buzz, and it's starting to give me one of my headaches. I don't know how much longer I'm going to be able to keep it together for this interview. "Despite the similarities between us and living on the same street, we never became friends. Our paths rarely crossed unless it was in the grocery store or in our respective cars at the intersection at the end of the block. Amber worked as a flight attendant, so she was gone for weeks at a time, and Mark worked in the city, so he was rarely around either. Those were the days before kids, so me and Shane were still really into going out on the weekends, and they preferred staying in whenever they got a chance to actually be home." He nods like he's genuinely interested, and I can't tell if it's real or not, but it's the first time in a long time that anyone has really seemed like they were listening to me and not just looking at me like they felt sorry for me or like I was some kind of unknown crazy they'd never met before. It's easy to keep going even though the prick has started at my temples. "Every time we ran into each other, it was always the same thing: 'We should get together for drinks! Let's have dinner soon.' But we never did. It was just something we said to each other. Part of our routine. And then we had kids. Well, they had kids. We just had Gabe. Not that we didn't want more kids," I quickly explain like I do every time people find out Gabe is an only child and I feel the need to apologize for it. People act like it's child abuse not giving him a sibling. "Anyway, from the very beginning, our kids were on different routines. Gabe was up shortly after five every morning, which meant we were part of the early-morning crew, and we did all our activities before eleven. Isaac was the total opposite. He was up half the night and slept most of the morning. By the time they were getting out of the house, our day was more than halfway over. Then, she ended up not going back to work after her maternity leave was over, and I went back to work full time before mine ended because Shane lost his job." I shudder at the memory. Those were hard days. Juggling a baby and work on top of Shane's depressed mood. Doesn't seem so bad now, though. I'd give anything for one of those rough days. I bet Shane would too.

Grief hasn't torn our small family apart. It's shredded it to pieces. When you have only one child, your entire world revolves around them. And Gabe was our life. We both wanted other kids, and we'd tried really hard to get pregnant again, but for whatever reason, we never could, and once I hit early menopause at thirty-seven—that was it. We didn't bother trying anymore. We both secretly hoped we'd be one of those couples we'd heard about so many times in our fertility groups who got pregnant after they'd given up all hope and stopped trying. Sadly, that didn't happen either.

I wonder if Shane will visit me today after what happened yesterday. I've never seen him so angry. He acted like I was committing some kind of cardinal sin showing up on the doorstep of my own house.

"What are you doing here?" He whipped open the front door and raced down the sidewalk to catch me in the driveway before I was even halfway to the walk. I hadn't expected him to be home. He was supposed to be at work. I didn't want to see him any more than he wanted to see me.

"What are *you* doing here?" I fired back, instantly defensive too.

"I just decided to come home on my lunch break." He ran his hands through his hair. His shirt was unbuttoned at the top and untucked. He wasn't wearing shoes.

"It's almost two." I rolled my eyes. He'd probably called in sick again. "You're going to lose your job if you're not careful." I stepped around him and headed toward the house.

He quickly grabbed my arm and pulled me back, trying to stop me. "I'm not sure you should go in there right now. Do your counselors know you're here?" he asked, doing his best to sound concerned. But he didn't seem concerned at all to me. Just nervous as his eyes darted around me and behind me at the house.

"Of course they know I'm here," I snapped, doing my best to sound convincing, but I was lying. I wasn't allowed on home visits unless they were scheduled in advance and preapproved by my primary therapist, but I'd woken up that morning obsessed with Gabe's old baby blanket. I couldn't get it out of my head that all his things were losing his smell, and then I spun into a panic about what would happen if I forgot what he smelled like. That's why I had to go home for the blanket no matter what. He'd had it since he was a baby, and it was laden with his scent. I wanted to put it in a sealed bag to keep it inside. That's all I wanted to do. I wasn't trying to cause any trouble. This wasn't like last time. "Look, I just want to grab something out of Gabe's room. I'll make it really fast. I know exactly where it is."

"No, now's not a good time." He stepped to the side, directly in front of me, now blocking the sidewalk with his body.

"That's my house." I pointed at it behind him. "I'm allowed to go inside my own house."

"You lost that privilege when you walked out on it," he said like the house was some kind of child I'd abandoned.

"Are you serious right now?" I yelled loud enough for the neighbors to hear, but I didn't care. They already thought I was crazy. Everyone did. "I left because I couldn't stand the continual reminders of Gabe staring me in the face. It was like losing him all over again, and you know why?" I didn't wait for him to answer before I went on, pummeling him with my words. "When I lived here after Gabe was gone, there was one tiny second every morning when I opened my eyes where it was beautiful and life was still the same. And then in the next half second, the crushing blow that he was gone. It was like finding out he died every single day, and I couldn't live through it another time. I just couldn't. But that doesn't happen when I stay somewhere else. When I wake up in my room at Samaritan House, I know he's gone from the moment I'm conscious, and as painful as that is, it doesn't compare to thinking he's there and losing him all over again."

His face was still hardened. Nothing I said had made any kind of an impact on him. He was still spread out across the sidewalk with his legs wide and his arms crossed against his puffed-out chest like he was security at the front door of a club.

"Why are you being so cruel? When did you get so mean?" Tears streaked down my face, and then, suddenly, it dawned on me. How could I have been so stupid? "She's here, isn't she?" I pointed at the house. "That's why you don't want me to come inside, isn't it?" Horror filled my insides at the realization that there was another woman in my house. And not just any woman. One who was sleeping with my husband. One who had stepped in and taken over my life.

"Mrs. Hart?" Dr. Stephens snaps his fingers, instantly crashing me into the present moment.

"Oh, I'm sorry," I say, but I'm not. It's not my fault they dope me up on so much medication I forget half my sentences midway through and my thoughts have a way of taking off and wandering wherever they want to go.

"You were saying that your family and the Greers weren't close?" he prods.

"Yeah, right." I nod my agreement, getting back to where we were at. "Our families weren't close even though we lived on the same street.

Don't get me wrong. We were always friendly, and there were plenty of times, especially when the kids were younger, when we helped lug them back and forth from preschool or ran milk over because they were out of it. But we weren't intimate. She was never someone I'd call if I was having a bad day or to meet me for a spur-of-the-moment glass of wine at Cantini's. You know what I mean? We weren't that kind of friends. Neither were our kids."

"Gabe and Isaac weren't close?" A brief flash of surprise across his face before he quickly erases it.

I shake my head.

"But you were giving him a ride home that night?"

"Yeah. They had an away game at Jefferson, and the bus was late getting back in. Amber got stuck at her daughter's dance class, so she texted and asked if I could pick up Isaac."

"Is that something you did often? Give Isaac rides?"

"Like I said, when they were younger, we did it a lot more. We didn't do it as much lately, but definitely when one of us got in a pinch."

"When was the last time you gave him a ride home prior to the accident?"

I search my memory, trying to remember. "Probably last year. Maybe the year before?" Why was he circling around this? What could he possibly be looking for in it? But before I have a chance to dig any deeper, he pops his next question.

"I know you've already been through this lots of times, but do you think you could take me through the accident?"

"Which one?" I joke again like I did last time. He doesn't think it's funny this time either. I can see him making a mental therapy note about me: *treatment resistant*. That's how they conceptualize me since I'm a repeat offender. I don't have to sit in on any of their consultations or get my hands on my chart to know that's how their descriptions of me have changed over time. All his graduate students are probably chomping at the bit to get a chance to consult on my case. I would've been all over it, too—a former therapist has a total mental breakdown after her child's death and is being questioned in a missing person's case. There are probably at least three students outside this door right now trying to listen.

"Does humor make it easier for you?"

"I mean, not really. Maybe if anyone in the room was laughing, that might make me feel a little better about it." I can't help myself. He's just so uptight. His shirt is buttoned all the way up to the collar. Who buttons their shirt that far?

"Okay," he says, rubbing his chin with one hand. "Do you want to try again to tell me about the accident?"

"I don't understand how hearing about the accident helps you find Isaac Greer."

"I understand this must be hard for you to talk about."

"That's not why."

His face is set. He doesn't believe me at all. I don't believe myself either. Talking about your son's death never gets easier.

"Okay, well, I'm sure there's a report about it written up some-where, probably in multiple places, but I guess you need to hear it from me." I give him an annoyed look so he doesn't miss that I'm not a fan of where he's leading, but that's where they all go. I just hate this constant retelling and rehashing, but I live a life where my feelings no longer matter. "That night was a perfect combination of everything that could go wrong going wrong. You know what I mean?" We've all had those kinds of days. The ones where nothing goes right. A perfect storm? That's what happened to us. "We were driving around the lake and rounding Paradise Point right before we were going to turn off at Chatsworth. It was really dark because it was super cloudy and the moon was barely a slit. And I was tired. Exhausted, really. I'd had eight clients that day." How many times had I told Gabe that driving tired was the same as driving drunk? But what was I supposed to do? Not get the boys? That's not how it works. I push the thoughts away. Bring my attention back to the present. "They were on their phones—Gabe in the back seat, Isaac on the passenger side. I was rounding the peak and then, suddenly, a deer jumped right out in front of me. He came out of nowhere, and I swerved to miss him. Both front tires caught on the black ice, sending us spinning and flying. The momentum pitched us straight over the edge and into the water."

The memory flashes through me, unbidden, like it's happening all over again.

I slammed on the brakes, and the car spun sideways. Then, it was as if a huge hand grabbed us and flung us into the frozen lake like our car was a Matchbox toy. It wasn't anything like an amusement park ride right before the fall. It was silent and still. Nobody screamed. If they did, I didn't hear it. Maybe the sound got turned off. The only thing I felt or experienced was sheer soul-sucking terror as we plunged.

I didn't remember hitting the ice or crashing into the lake. My next memory was opening my eyes while the car sank down into the murky water. It was the annihilating cold that shocked me back to consciousness. A freezing on the inside that made my organs burn and my bones instantly brittle. There wasn't a part of me that wasn't painfully cold. I shiver unconsciously at the memory and rub my hands against my arms, trying to get warm, even though Dr. Stephens has the heat turned up in the room. It doesn't matter, though. I'm always cold now.

He reaches down to his briefcase and pops it open, then pulls a folder out. He makes a dramatic production of thumbing through it before coming to a stop a few pages in. "It says here that you suffered a broken rib from Isaac doing CPR on you?" He raises his eyebrows, mystified as to how that came to be, except if he keeps going, the entire incident is probably spelled out right there in the following pages. He wants to hear it from me, though, and just as I predicted, he tilts his head to the side and asks, "Can you tell me a little bit more about that?"

TWO

AMBER GREER

I followed Mark into the kitchen. He wasn't getting away from me that easily. Not after the stunt he'd just pulled with Detective Hawkins. "They were onto something with Isaac's phone, and you know it. How dare you just shut it down like that?"

Detective Hawkins had quickly agreed with Mark that he was right. It didn't matter all that much about the empty phone when there were other more pressing issues hanging over our head, like monitoring every single park within a five-mile radius of Falcon Lake because in another forty-eight hours, if all things followed the same pattern as the other boys, a package with the clothes Isaac had been wearing the night he went missing would be dropped in a tightly sealed cardboard box at a local park. The clothes inside would be freshly laundered and neatly folded. They'd left Brady's box with his clothes on a picnic bench in Windsor Park. Josh's was left behind the dugout at Campton Fields. At least Mark and I had a pattern. Some form of structure to this madness. Their parents never had a pattern.

Mark opened the cupboard above the sink and took out a glass like he wasn't the least bit irritated or perturbed by what had just gone down in the family room. My question hung in the air for a few more seconds before falling unanswered.

"Isaac erased his phone, and that means something," I said not willing to let him dismiss me like that. I couldn't contain my anger. Our son was missing. It was our job to do everything we could to find him. Follow every lead. Examine each possibility even if it was unlikely. We couldn't just lock our eyes on one lead and follow only that direction. We had to look everywhere. Uncover every stone. This was one of them. So was Jules.

He shrugged and didn't bother turning around to look at me while he spoke. "Yes, I suppose it does. He might've erased everything on it, but I'm still going with the theory that he had another phone, so he just wasn't using that one."

"Okay, right? So, then something *was* going on. Just like Detective Hawkins hinted at. What was Isaac hiding? That's where more of the investigative team's energy needs to be focused." Thankfully, they were going to be able to recover the deleted texts and the other stuff on his phone, but unfortunately, the red tape in front of that process was thick, and it wasn't going to be done anytime soon. "Even if it's going to be a while before they get his texts back, why don't they circle back through his friends again or go through his computer?" I was grasping at straws, but I had to grab something.

His back stiffened. He moved to the sink and turned on the faucet, then waited for the water to get cold. It always took forever because of the broken tank valve, and we'd been meaning to get it fixed for months. "Isaac doesn't have friends anymore. You know that as well as I do."

His words hurt even though they were true. Isaac was an introvert and had always preferred being by himself. He'd always liked to have just a few close friends, but he'd pulled away from all of them after the accident. It wasn't like they hadn't tried to stay friends. His best friend, Jordan, still made an effort. I saw last week that he'd sent Isaac three game requests that had gone unanswered. That was why Jules made me so furious. She acted like I was so lucky and fortunate to have had my son's life spared, and I was—I didn't want to ever appear or sound ungrateful—but I'd lost my son that day too. Isaac had come back from that lake forever changed. I shifted my gaze back to Mark. He had finally turned around.

His shoulders slumped forward in defeat. He was unshaved, and his eyes were bleary and bloodshot like he'd been drinking for three days straight. He wore an expression I'd never seen in our twenty-one years of marriage, and I thought I'd seen them all.

"I'm not doing this with you again tonight. I'm just not." His voice was flat. No emotion.

"Doing what? All I'm trying to do is figure out what happened to our son."

He let out a slow, deep breath. "I'm tired of going round and round in these meaningless circles with you. We both know what happened to him."

"No, we don't." I ferociously shook my head. "We have no idea what happened to him. I—"

"Yes, we do." He spoke on top of me. I tried to interrupt him, but he raised his hands to shush me. "We know exactly what happened to him, Amber. The same thing that happened to Brady and Josh."

"That's not true. We can't know that for sure." My voice shook. I gripped the island with both hands like I might fall off the earth if I didn't.

"Yes, we can, and we do." He nodded, almost patronizingly, at me. "We're pretty much as close as you can get to being positive about it. Everything follows the exact same pattern of the other boys. That man—"

"Shut up! Stop talking like that!" I slapped the granite countertop. "Why do you always have to go there?" I yelled, stepping around the island and over to him. "You always go there! Why do you always do that? It's like you've already given up hope. Like he's already dead." I wanted to punch him in the face. My hands shook at my sides. "We can find him. We can. We still have time, especially if Jules has him. She's not smart. Not like the man who took those other boys. She's not a real criminal. Just disturbed, and we can get to her, I know we can."

His mouth formed a thin line. His jaw was set firm as he locked eyes with me. "They found his phone yesterday, Amber. Come on. You know what happens next."

"No. Just no." Fury and denial flooded my system.

"I get not wanting to believe it at first, I do, believe me. But yesterday they found his phone tossed on the side of the road just like the others." He took another step closer to me. "I'm sorry, Amber, but that sicko has our boy."

"No, he doesn't. He doesn't." I gave my head a sharp jerk with every word like that would negate it even more. "You don't know that. You don't. No one does." I put my hands over my ears so I didn't have to hear what he said next. I'd already heard it. I wasn't hearing it again. What happened to those boys had nothing to do with my son, even if it might look like it did. She was a copycat. Playing a game with me. Taking him away from me because I'd taken him away from her. "Jules has something to do with this. She's behind it. I know she is."

"Really? What happened to him then?" Mark pulled my hands off my ears. His nose flared in and out with each breath. I pushed him back. He was getting too close.

"I don't know exactly what happened to Isaac, but Jules had something to do with it." I wish I had something more to give him or the police, but even if I didn't, he was forgetting the most important fact—the one that made all the difference. "We file a restraining order on her, and a week later our son goes missing? You're trying to tell me that's a coincidence? Come on, Mark."

CASE #72946

PATIENT: JULIET (JULES) HART

"Tell you more about Isaac giving me CPR? You want me to tell you about that?" I'm taken aback by Dr. Stephens's questions about Isaac, even though he's the reason we're here.

Nobody ever focuses on Isaac rescuing me, and I've spent a lot of time processing that night. That's all any of the therapists and counselors want to do with me in our sessions, as if I'm just one good cry away from getting over the whole thing. Do they really think that's possible? The only people who get over losing kids are the ones who don't have any.

I cock my head, studying Dr. Stephens closely. Does he really not know what happened with Isaac pulling me out of the lake that night? Why does he think it's important? Where's he going with all this? His face is impossible to read. Maybe it's because he's so young. He's got such a boyish face. No matter what I say or what he reads about me in those pages, his face stays stuck on indifferent. Or maybe he's always this aloof?

I glance at the clock on the wall behind him: 3:10 p.m. This can't go on much longer, can it? I adjust myself in my seat and try to look like a normal person—willing and compliant—which isn't easy to do when every part of me is itching to get out of here and run screaming in the other direction. It's hard to rein yourself back in after you've gotten so used to giving in to your impulses. "There's not really much to tell. I pulled Isaac out first, so I had to go back in for Gabe." My throat catches. This is the hard part. Every time. All I can hear whenever I retell it is Shane's voice screaming at me during one of our nastiest fights. Where we did more damage with our words than any fist ever could.

"How could you grab Isaac before Gabe?" He hurled the question at me.

There it was. Finally. The judgment and blame had been there all along. Festering. Poisoning. Boiling underneath the skin, and he'd finally released it.

What kind of a mother saved another boy's life over their own son's?

The answer was simple—I didn't know that's what I was doing. If I'd realized that I was pulling Isaac to the surface and not Gabe, I would've let go of his hand. I've relived that moment thousands of times. I force the memories back. The sooner I get through this, the sooner I get out of here. I pull my head up and try to focus on Dr. Stephens.

"Isaac went in the water to rescue me after I didn't come back up, and he had to pull me out. Apparently, I was blue and had stopped breathing, so he gave me CPR."

The space from that part of the night still remains blank, no matter how hard I've tried to pull something about it from my memory. The last thing I remember is giving in to the fact that I was going to drown. As soon as I knew it was going to be impossible to find Gabe, and that even if I managed to find him, I'd never make it back up to the surface, I quickly decided there was no way I was going to let him die down there alone. None. And even though I couldn't see him, I could feel him. So I just gave in to it. There wasn't anything scary about it. It was actually quite nice—this weightless, peaceful feeling came over me, and the cold was gone, fiery heat left in its place.

The doctors say it doesn't stay that way. That once the severe stages of hypothermia hit, the mind short-circuits and dives off the rails. Same with the body. Instead of feeling cold, your body feels like it's being burned alive. I'm lucky. My brain protected me from all that trauma and blocked it out without me even having to try.

My next memory after my moment of surrender is waking up at Falcon Lake Hospital. The sounds of beeping machines and the hiss of the weird pump next to my bed broke into my consciousness, forcing me awake. My eyelids were so heavy, and my limbs ached. The sheet on top of my body was heavy, too heavy for me to move. Everything smelled like toilet-bowl cleaner.

I slowly turned my head to the side. The movement sent excruciating pain throughout my entire body and left me nauseous. My eyes slowly took in my surroundings while I tried not to move my head—the small stainless steel sink and the paper towels, the beeping machines monitoring my vitals, and all the wires attached to me. Something had gone horribly wrong, but I didn't know what. There was still nothing.

I'd give anything to go back to that nothing now. That last moment when everything was the same. When Gabe still lived and walked and breathed on this planet. Where my perfect life was still my perfect life.

But the next shift of my head changed everything.

Shane sat curled up in a chair a few feet from my hospital bed. At first, I thought he was sleeping, but as I looked closer, it became clear he wasn't. His eyes were glazed over, and he was just staring at the wall inches from his face like he was mesmerized by the design on it even though there was nothing there.

"Shane?" My voice came out as a raspy whisper.

He whipped around. He took me in but didn't speak. Just gaped at me wide eyed. Was I still dreaming? My head throbbed, making me even more nauseous.

"Shane?" I called a second time, trying to snap him out of whatever weird trance he'd disappeared into. My throat was swollen and irritated.

He got up slowly like an old man twice his age, and the three steps to my bed seemed to take forever. His eyes swept the room, refusing to look at me.

And in that instant, it all came flooding back to me—driving the boys home after their basketball game, the deer that had jumped in my way. The lake. The freezing cold. So cold. And Gabe.

"Oh my God, where's Gabe?" I sat straight up, jerking all the wires attached to me and sending the IV port crashing into the railing on my bed. Shane grabbed the port before it hit the floor. Everything clattered. "Did they find him? Is he okay?" If they'd gotten to me, maybe they'd gotten to him in time too. My heart sped up at the possibility of seeing my baby.

Shane moved the IV port back to keep it from getting any more tangled up with me and tried to get the other wires away from the rail without hurting me. "Don't move like that. You're going to pull your IV out, and it's so hard for them to get it back in. Please, Jules, just settle down."

But I wouldn't settle down. Not until I knew if Gabe was okay. I moved to throw my legs over the edge of the bed. If he wouldn't tell me where he was, I'd go find him on my own. The movement sent an intense stabbing sensation in my chest and took my breath away. I clutched my side and let out a low moan.

Shane hurriedly wrapped his arms around me and steadied me on the edge of the bed. "Take it easy. You've got to be careful of your rib."

"What's wrong with my rib?" I asked, trying to breathe around the stabbing pain in my side. At least it wasn't a heart attack, even though it felt like it.

"Isaac broke it giving you CPR." He searched my face, trying to gauge what I remembered.

"Isaac gave me CPR? Why'd he do that?"

And why was I here? I was supposed to be disappearing on the bottom of the lake with Gabe. The only thing I recalled from Isaac was the way his face looked when I pulled him out of the water—shocked and afraid, barely breathing.

I drag myself from the memory. I don't want to keep going. Not to what comes next. I pull my focus from then to now, back to Dr. Stephens.

"Apparently, Isaac dove in after me when it took too long for me to come up. He said that he counted to sixty. That's how many seconds he gave me before heading down there to help. The only reason either of us could find the car was because the horn was stuck. The horn led him to the car the same way that it did me. He grabbed me and swam with me to the surface." I rattle the facts off as quickly as I can to get it over with.

Dr. Stephens makes a weird sound with his throat. "Well, not exactly. According to Isaac, you fought with him when he tried to rescue you." He gives me a suspicious look like I've done something wrong or that it says something about me pathologically, but he's digging down the wrong hole.

"I'm sorry, but if you want me to explain why I did the things I did when I was unconscious, I'm just not going to be able to do it." He clearly hasn't done his homework. Severe hypothermia makes people turn combative and aggressive. They take their clothes off too. It's called paradoxical undressing.

"It says here that the two of you were close?" He says it like a question. "That you"—he makes air quotes so there's no mistaking he's reading directly from the chart—"'grew enmeshed and dependent on one another.' Would you agree with that assessment?"

"We were close. I wouldn't say we were enmeshed or dependent, though." There's no way he's going to understand what it's like between Isaac and me. Unless you've stared death in the eye with another person in the way we have, you just don't get it. You have a shared experience impossible to put into words. "You wouldn't understand our relationship."

"Try me."

I shook my head. "Unless you've been through trauma like we have, you don't get it."

"What makes you think I haven't?"

My eyebrows went up. So did my head.

"Do you think people get into the type of work that I do without having some kind of trauma in their own background? Believe me, I've got my own story." His eyes are fiery and lit. He's telling the truth. I've got an amazing gut sense for when people are lying. It made me a great therapist and a hard-to-fool mom. "So, why don't you take a risk and see if I might be able to understand in a way that others haven't been able to. Besides, what do you have to lose?"

"There's nothing more to lose. I've already lost it all."

"Okay, then, what's the big deal?" He lifts his hands, palms up. "Let's hear it. When did you start getting close to Isaac?"

"After the accident." Doesn't that go without saying? I hate that he asks questions with answers he already knows.

"Which accident?" he asks, clearly pleased that he's successfully volleyed my own joke back at me. I appreciate the sentiment, but I don't feel like laughing anymore.

"The second one." I cross my arms on my chest.

"You mean after you put your car in front of a train and somehow managed to survive?" he asks, clearly impressed, like I had something to do with my escaping death, but that part wasn't on me. I was only responsible for putting my car on the tracks.

I nod, trying to ignore the throbbing in my temples. "Yeah, that one."

THREE

AMBER GREER

There was a formal order signed by a judge saying Jules couldn't come within fifty feet of Isaac or any other member of our family. That was the reason the investigators even had their eyes on her in the first place or took my accusations about her involvement seriously at all. Mark wanted to pretend like that piece didn't belong in the puzzle, though. That somehow, even though Isaac disappeared a week after we filed it, the two things weren't related.

"And do you remember why the judge signed off on the restraining order, Mark?" I faced off with him in the kitchen, refusing to let it go. I wouldn't allow him to treat me like I was some hysterical woman spouting theories that had no basis in fact.

Isaac had finally broken off their relationship, and she'd called fifty-two times in one hour that day, begging and crying to talk to him. First on his phone. Then on mine. Each message grew more desperate and frightening than the last until she filled up his voice mail box. She went on and on with her rants about the universal order of things and their place in it, how she desperately needed to talk to him because she'd finally figured out their purpose. She had the answer—the thing that would make everything okay. She kept saying that over and over again.

"Answer to what?" I asked Isaac after we'd listened to her latest message, where she'd derailed into full-on sobbing at the end.

He shrugged and shook his head like he felt sorry for her. "I don't know. I don't understand half of what she's talking about, Mom. I just pretend like I do."

I turned off my phone and made him turn off his phone, too, thinking that would put a stop to things, but then she showed up at our house even more worked up than she'd been on the phone. I told Isaac she'd go away if we just ignored her, but she was relentless.

"Isaac! Isaac, are you in there?" She pounded on the door with both fists. The sound reverberated throughout the house. "Please just open the door. We need to talk. It will only take a minute. Just a minute, I swear. I have to see you."

Mark was away at a conference in Boulder and wouldn't be back for another three days, so he was missing all the drama. Isaac and Katie weren't, though. They sat at the top of the stairs listening and watching it all go down. The security cameras on the front porch had her meltdown on full display.

She'd looked much worse before, especially in the days following Gabe's death, but I was more frightened of her that day than I'd ever been. Before, she'd looked pathetic and pitiful like the only person she was capable of hurting was herself, but she'd put herself back together again after the last hospitalization and was staying in some kind of group home across town. She looked like the president of the PTA, and something about that was scarier. She was so desperate.

I couldn't let her inside. I was afraid of what she'd do.

Finally, after she'd been going on and on for over ten minutes, I stood on the other side of the door and tried to coax her to leave. "Jules, honey." I used the same voice I used when I needed to bribe my kids to do something. "Please, just go. I know this is hard. I know you're going through an unbelievably difficult time, but your relationship with my son is not okay. It's totally inappropriate. Now please just go away."

"You don't understand. You don't understand, Amber. It's not like that," she cried, pressing her face against the door. "You have to let me see him. You have to let me talk to him. Just for a second. It doesn't even have to be that long. I have to know if he's okay."

Anger surged through my veins at the idea that there was something wrong with him that only she could take care of. "He's perfectly okay where he's at. He's with his mother."

She kicked the bottom of the door, startling me and making me jump back. "Please, Amber. Just let me inside. Let me talk to him. Don't be this way. Why are you doing this to me?" She pressed her face against the door again and let out the most pitiful cry. "I have to know how he's doing. I just want to know he's okay. I have to see him. That's all. After that I'll go. I promise."

I turned around to see how it was affecting Katie and Isaac. Katie's face was a mixture of fear and fascination. She'd never seen someone so beaten down and broken. Isaac looked stricken, like he was doing everything he could not to burst into tears. He rose slowly from his position on the landing at the top of the stairs and started making his way down to where I stood in the entryway. I motioned for him to stop.

"I should just talk to her. She'll be fine if I talk to her," he whispered. There was so much pity and compassion for her laced in his eyes that I melted on the spot at what a sweet boy he was despite everything he'd been through.

I shook my head at him while Jules kept begging from behind the door.

"Please, please." She sobbed even harder, tugging at my heartstrings and having a powerful effect on Isaac. "All I want is to see his face. That's all. Then I'll go. I promise. Please."

Isaac's body crumpled, and he clutched his stomach like it hurt. He stepped forward, almost within her sight, and I pushed him back so she wouldn't see him.

"I'm sorry, you have to go, Jules. Please just go," I pleaded. He wasn't strong enough to resist her on his own. I couldn't blame him. She was so desperate and sad.

"You have to let me see him!" she screamed, and suddenly, her fist jutted through the window on the door. The glass shattered. For a second, nobody moved. The flesh of her forearm opened, spilling beads of blood on the floor, and I leapt into motion.

"Don't move!" I yelled, but it was too late. She was already pushing her arm farther through the hole, trying to reach the handle.

"I'm fine," she snapped, being careful not to catch any part of her skin on the jagged edges. The movement made the blood spurt, then gush. Katie let out a deep groan and went white. She hated the sight of blood.

"You have to hold still," I ordered as every movement only made the flow harder, but she wasn't interested in stopping the blood. She only cared about getting inside my house—getting to Isaac. She reached around for the handle to let herself in.

"Call 911!" I yelled at Isaac as I slapped her hand away, desperately trying to keep her outside.

She lost it on the police when they came for her after the paramedics had bandaged her up and momentarily stopped the bleeding.

"Get away from me! Don't touch me!" She screamed like a rabid dog we had had in the neighborhood once. She wasn't foaming at the mouth, but she flung as much spit as if she were while she screamed at them to get off her and all sorts of other obscenities. She cried about being punished, how there wasn't any God. Only the devil and he'd taken over her life.

"What did I do that was so bad?" she'd wailed at the officers as they'd finally wrestled her into one of the squad cars. "Tell me! Please, tell me. What did I do?"

They should've brought her to the psychiatric hospital that night and locked her up, but they didn't. That's why she kept getting away with everything. People felt sorry for her. You couldn't help it. She was living proof you could go mad from grief, which was terrifying because it preyed on every parent's worst fear. And since most of us were parents ourselves, we couldn't say for sure that we wouldn't do the same thing if we lost our child. So everyone let her slide. Even the police. They brought her to her mom's that night after she got stitched up instead of keeping her in the hospital where she belonged. Where she probably still belonged.

The next day she showed up at Isaac's school and caused a scene there. Two days later, she mailed him a knot of her hair. Just the hair. There was no note. No letter. No nothing, but it was stamped with her return address, so there was no mistaking it was her. She hadn't wanted to keep her identity a secret. We had no idea what the hair signified, but either way, both Mark and I agreed we'd never seen anything so creepy. It was a bunny-on-the-stove kind of a moment. We had recently finished filling out all the paperwork detailing our reasoning and complaints regarding the restraining order, but Mark was dragging his feet about submitting it to the court. He didn't want to create more stress for her, but I was adamant, and this only solidified how serious my concerns were. It was finally the tipping point for him too.

How could he possibly believe that filing the restraining order and Isaac's disappearance weren't related?

But he did.

He was standing in front of me in the kitchen and shaking his head like nothing I'd said to this point had penetrated him. Like all the things that had happened with her before this were insignificant.

"Isaac went missing at the exact same time of night that all those other boys went missing." He stuck one finger out, then added another, holding them up in my face so there was no mistaking his numbered points. "He was walking the dog just like they were walking their dogs, and yesterday?" He paused dramatically before continuing and putting up his third finger. "His phone showed up in a ditch on a backcountry road just like theirs did."

"Why are you so unwilling to consider another possibility?" He couldn't be mad at me for doing the same thing he was doing.

"Because it doesn't matter. How many times do I have to tell you that it doesn't matter?" He worked his jaw, trying hard to maintain his composure, but he was struggling.

"Yes, it does," I stressed. "How can you even say that? The boys were kept alive right up until the point they were dropped. The medical examiner's report confirms it, so if Jules has him and she's following the same pattern, then there's still time to get him, and every single minute counts."

"You think I don't know that?"

"Then why aren't you doing more? Why are you just sitting on the couch like it's already happened? Yes, that's how it ended for those boys, but we didn't know who those boys were with. We know her. We can get to her. Somebody can. And if they can't get to her, then they've got to figure out whatever clues she left around her so that we can find him."

"We don't know if it's her. We have no idea who it is." He shook his head. "But that's not the point. Whether it's the same person that's got him or whatever's happening is a copycat by her or somebody else—it just doesn't make a difference. Either way, the outcome is the same."

He didn't need to say what the outcome was. We both knew. So did the entire country.

"Don't talk like that," I shouted, like him saying it out loud had the power to make it happen. I had never been one of those people who believed your words had the power to manifest your destiny, but I wasn't taking any chances on speaking those things out loud and making them true just in case.

"Like what? A realist?" He stuck his chin out.

"You're not being a realist. You're being pigheaded," I flung at him and shoved him away from me. I wanted him out of my kitchen. Out of my space. This house.

He grabbed my wrist before I could push past him and pulled me back toward him. He put one of his hands on each arm and got right up in my face. "That bastard took our boy, Amber. He took our boy the same way he took those other boys. The exact same way. The only reason you've concocted this story with Jules is because you don't want him to be with a killer. You know if he's with Jules, then he's at least somewhat safe because she would never hurt him. She's a nutjob, but she would never hurt him."

I jerked away and shoved him off me. "That's not true! That's not true!"

But there was a small chance it was.

CASE #72946

PATIENT: JULIET (JULES) HART

"I still don't understand why people get so disturbed when they find out I parked my car on the railroad tracks and waited for the train to hit me." Which it did within minutes. Dragged the car almost a full mile before coming to a complete stop. "All I did was what every parent said they would do if they lost a child," I explain to Dr. Stephens, but he doesn't understand. How could he? He probably doesn't even have kids.

"I wouldn't be able to live if something happened to Ruthy," my best friend, Amanda, said when her baby was suddenly struck with a skyrocketing fever that they couldn't locate a cause for. We all nodded as we huddled around her in the emergency room, passing her endless cups of coffee and stale doughnuts while we waited for the news, agreeing that we wouldn't be able to live if something happened to our children either.

That's exactly how I felt. Living in a world without Gabe was like living in a world with no color. No air. Lots of mothers had other children, who finally allowed them to reach somewhere deep inside themselves to find a way to go on. I understood that motivation. I got it. I did. If I had another child, there was no doubt in my mind that I'd find a way to put the fractured pieces of my psyche back together again and move forward. Trouble was, I didn't.

I had no reason to go on. Even Shane wasn't enough to keep me from putting myself on those tracks outside Kwik Trip on Easter morning, which is probably part of the reason why he hates me so much now. You couldn't have been more perfectly positioned than I was to get the job done. And it worked. That train smacked me in a perfect T, pushing the car down the tracks. I cracked my head on the windshield and knocked myself out pretty good. It left a three-inch scar across my forehead, a continual reminder of what I'd done. But I'd healed from my other physical injuries without any permanent damage. Everyone else called it the train accident, but something isn't an accident when you do it on purpose.

"We don't know how she survived," the doctors said over and over again each time they led a new attending into my hospital room. "Her car was flattened. The paramedics needed to use the Jaws of Life to get her out. Nobody expected to find her alive. Let alone this." They'd always motion to where my very much alive body sat upright in the hospital bed, despite the traction holding up my right arm and both legs in full casts, as if I was the closest thing they'd ever see to a miracle.

A walking, talking miracle—that's what they called it on the KDWB morning show.

Local Woman Escapes Death Twice

She Must Be Highly Favored

Those were just the headlines from the newspapers and magazines. I was social media famous for a while too. Lots of memes were created in my honor. My favorite was a picture of me walking out of the hospital after the train accident with a cat photoshopped in next to me. The bubble above my head read, "You ain't got nothing on me."

I'm supposed to feel lucky that my life got spared twice. But I don't. Not even close. I'm just really pissed off. It's like a cruel cosmic joke. I must've done something awful in a past life to deserve this kind of unrelenting karmic punishment. Or maybe God just hates me.

But that's not what all the therapists and counselors that regulate my life have to say—think of yourself as a survivor. That's the advice they throw at me in the group therapy sessions. Still mandatory by the courts if I want to stay out of the hospital, which I do. Pretty much the one thing keeping me going right now is making sure I never go back to that place. Locked psychiatric wards are as scary as I'd always imagined. I haven't spent much time in psychiatric facilities even though I was a therapist, but my work never put me anywhere near them. I only did outpatient counseling, and I'd had the same private practice for over ten years.

Every scary thing I'd ever seen or read about psych wards was true. But it was so much more than the physical facilities themselves, although those weren't great either. It was being stripped of all my rights. They can do that after they've labeled you unstable and a threat to yourself. The scariest part was how easy it'd been for them to strip them away. Maybe being treated like an animal turns you into one. Has anyone ever thought of that?

How do you expect someone like me, who's never had anything bad happen to them, to react when their child dies? Putting your car on the train tracks sounds pretty reasonable then. How do I get Dr. Stephens to see that?

"I know you've seen all the stuff written about me in the last eight months, and I get that I look like a complete train wreck—" I burst out laughing. I didn't even mean to say that. It just came out. Totally inappropriate—all of it—but I can't help it. He doesn't crack a smile. I quickly regain my composure so I don't look totally insensitive. "Anyway, you can't expect people like me to go through something like that and not fall apart."

He picks up on my choice of words immediately. "What do you mean by 'people like you'?"

"The ones that have had an easy life. I've never had anything bad happen to me ever. Nothing. The worst thing?" I pause for a second, building up the suspense. "I didn't get into my first-ranked college. I'm not even kidding. That was the worst thing, and even then, it wasn't so bad, because you know why?" I don't wait for him to answer. "That's where I met Shane. If I hadn't gone to Moorhead, then I never would've met my husband. So even the one bad thing that happened to me turned out to be the best thing for me. That's the world I used to live in. The world before all this." I motioned around us, the brown metal door and the concrete floors. The peeling paint on the dingy walls. "You're not equipped to go from nothing bad ever happening to you to the worst thing that could possibly occur happening to you. It's like being hurled into the deep end of a pool when you don't know how to swim. That's what it feels like. And all of it is dark. As if every light in the universe has been turned off."

"That must be so difficult." He clasps his hands in front of himself. Concern lines his forehead.

"It's not just that. There are people who are born to do hard things. They have a grit and determination on the inside of them. I'm not one of those people, Dr. Stephens." I raise my head, locking eyes with his so he doesn't miss my next point. "I'm a wimp. I have no fight in me. I give up when things are hard. Like you know how most kids struggle when they're learning how to ride a bike?"

He nods.

"All kids fall when they first get on. They fall down and get up over and over again until they finally figure it out. Not me." I shake my head. "When I was seven, I got a new bike with purple streamers for my birthday and was super excited to learn how to ride it. My dad was the one to teach me, and he did everything right. He held the back of my seat while we made our way down the street, timed it perfectly until the let-go spot, and then let go. I took off wobbling and tumbled on the asphalt within seconds. I skinned both knees pretty badly. Do you know what I did?" Another one of my questions that I don't wait for him to answer. "I never rode my bike again. I put my new bike away and didn't touch it after that. I still can't ride a bike."

His forehead wrinkles even deeper. I'm not what he expected. His supervisor must not have prepared him for this. Then, I quickly realize—he is the supervisor. Suddenly, I feel so old, and all I want to do is go back to my room and crawl into bed. This day has drained me. We've been here for hours.

"So, do you think we could circle back to Isaac? You still haven't told me how the two of you grew close." His eyes are red. He must be tired too. That's how I used to feel when I had a day with back-to-back clients. Other people's problems are exhausting.

I glance at the clock. "It's almost ten o'clock, do you think we could get back to talking about Isaac tomorrow?"

He reluctantly agrees.

FOUR

AMBER GREER

I lay next to Mark in our bed even though it was barely after nine and still early. We'd done the same thing last night after our fight in the kitchen ended in a stalemate. We'd hardly spoken all day, like we had an unspoken agreement to go to our respective corners and cool down. He'd headed to our bedroom shortly after our fight last night, and I'd followed him here again tonight since I didn't know what else to do. Sending Katie with my mom yesterday was definitely the right thing to do since my and Mark's tension only added to the stress in the house. I'd never been so grateful to be surrounded by family as I had been through all of this. My mom had been wonderful, and my dad had shown up in surprising ways too.

It felt strange not having Katie in our bed. She had slept with us every night since Isaac disappeared. She'd been sleeping tucked in between us like a Katie sandwich. Normally, Mark would've made a big joke about it, but none of us had laughed since Isaac had gone missing. The house was quiet and still, like it was holding its breath too.

It was impossible not to think about the impact this was going to have on Katie. She'd come back from her swim meet the night Isaac went missing to find her driveway packed with emergency vehicles and her house swarming with police officers. She'd burst into tears immediately and had been terrified ever since. If someone had come for her brother, would they come for her too? How bad were they torturing him?

It wasn't as hard on her during the daytime hours. The fact that her brother might potentially be the third boy to go missing in the last sixteen months had catapulted her into celebrity status. She was thirteen, so even though she was wrecked over her brother, the constant media frenzy and attention outside and playing out across the country provided a decent distraction. But none of that shut out the horrors of the night. Not from any of us.

She was as convinced as Mark that Isaac had been taken by the same man that took the two other local boys—Brady and Josh. Both of them were only fourteen—a year younger than Isaac—and they'd disappeared at night while they were out walking their dogs. The wandering dogs were the red flags that always ended up alerting people to the missing kids. Brady's dog had been hit by a truck trying to dart across Interstate 90. Thankfully, it had only broken his leg. It could've been much worse. It was incomprehensibly worse for Brady.

Five days after Brady had gone missing, his cell phone was found ditched on a country road, and three days after that, the clothes he had been wearing when he went missing showed up at Windsor Park. They were freshly cleaned and neatly folded in a sealed cardboard box. Nobody had seen or noticed anything out of the ordinary. A biker found his body in a field halfway between Minneapolis and La Crosse six days later. It was exactly two weeks—fourteen days—from the day he had been grabbed to the day they found his body.

He disappeared from a large suburb right outside Minneapolis, and as horrific as it was, you still felt safe because you could blame it on the city. One of the terrible criminals living in the city was responsible for it.

But then three months later, in a small town four hours north of Saint Paul, Josh Hardy took his dog out for a walk and never came home. Unlike Brady's dog, his dog ran straight back home, and Josh's dad knew something was wrong immediately.

And it was.

We all watched in stunned horror as Josh's story played out in the exact same sequence as Brady's. A day-five phone drop at a gas station outside Lexington. Clothes neatly folded and washed in a sealed cardboard box at Campton Fields three days later. And then the body. Laid in a cornfield behind Loyola High School six days after that.

That's when the FBI and local police announced we had a serial killer on our hands who liked adolescent boys. They suspected he was linked to three other similar crimes in Ohio and Illinois where boys had gone missing and been killed in a similar fashion. It looked like he was making his way undetected throughout the Midwest. They labeled him the Dog Snatcher—which never made sense to me, since he was snatching kids and not dogs—but it caught fire in the media, so that's who he became.

They never had any leads. There wasn't a shred of evidence on anything he delivered—phone, clothes, or body. Everything was always spotless and wiped clean. It mystified police and terrified us, especially since the Dog Snatcher was doing all this while everyone was watching. That was the most messed-up part in all of it. He was still getting away with it right under everyone else's noses. He must be feeling invincible. That was dangerous.

Nobody knew what to do, and it wasn't like we could just lock our kids inside even if we wanted to. That wasn't any way to live, so we just went on with our lives as best we could without any kind of answers.

Until Billy.

He lived in a town only ninety miles away, which was entirely too close for any of us to feel safe any longer. Even though he ripped away our last shred of security, he was the first break in the case. Nobody else had ever been grabbed and gotten away.

Billy had been walking home from football practice around sunset when a man came out of the park and approached him with his dog. By then, all our kids had been schooled on what to do if they were approached by a stranger, and Billy was prepared. In fact, if you had to place bets on who was most likely to survive an attack, he was the kid you'd put your money on. Not only was he a black belt in jujitsu, but his mom was a badass prosecutor who taught free self-defense classes on the weekend to women in domestic violence shelters. She'd been dragging Billy to classes with her since he was in elementary school.

The man approached Billy and asked him for a waste bag for his dog, which instantly raised Billy's suspicions, and he bolted. As he raced down Sycamore Street, the man jumped out from the alley and grabbed him from behind. Billy quickly spun and kicked him, then stabbed him in both eyes with his fingers. He sprayed him with the pepper spray that all our kids carried now. Then, he ran screaming for help. He didn't stop until he got home. It was almost two miles.

He was a hero and gave investigators loads of helpful information they'd never had before. Important clues to the pathology of the killer. Our first hints as to what he was like or what his motives might have been. Investigators had always suspected he had a dog because that would make it easier to bond with kids, and their suspicions were confirmed. Billy said it was a cute dog, too, like a puppy. That was likely why the man had never spooked any of the children at first. The kids were too focused on the puppy.

He tried to approach Billy, but the moment he crossed the street, Billy picked up his pace. The Dog Snatcher must've taken a left on Seventh Street and cut through the alleyway because that's where he tried to nab Billy. They interviewed Billy for weeks, and he made all the national headlines.

"Before I knew what was happening, there was a gun smashed into my back," he reported as his mom stood beaming proudly behind him at every press conference. "And then I just did what my mama taught me to do. I jabbed him hard as I could in the eyes and took off running. I screamed at the top of my lungs the whole way."

It was impossible not to be impressed with his bravery. Not only did he give us our first look into the Dog Snatcher's methods, but he gave us the first glimpse into his appearance too. Billy worked diligently with a sketch artist, and within twenty-four hours, we had an idea of what the Dog Snatcher looked like. His face was printed on flyers and spread all over town. It was shown on every news station in the country. His baldness was the most striking feature about him. And it wasn't just that he was bald—there wasn't an ounce of hair on his face either. Not even eyebrows. Investigators explained that getting rid of all his hair was a sophisticated and cunning way not to leave any evidence on his victims or at the scene of the crime. It was likely that his entire body was shaved.

Billy deserved a reward. Without him, we wouldn't know any of that. They should give him the money that they'd raised for Brady and Josh for what he did.

Things with the Dog Snatcher had been quiet ever since. It'd been almost seven months. Everyone had started believing he was gone for good or he'd at least gone into hiding for a while after his failed attempt with Billy. It was rare that we even heard anything about it in the news anymore.

But then seven days ago, my Isaac took Duke out for a walk and never came home.

I got an angry text from my elderly housebound neighbor that Duke was taking a dump in their front yard. Last time Duke had gotten out and gone over there, he'd done the same thing, and she'd shot him with a pellet gun. I'd run over there as fast as I could, and it'd never dawned on me that something might've happened to Isaac, because Duke liked to take off. It was one of his favorite games. But my worry peaked when he wasn't home in an hour. By the time Mark got home from work at six, I was frantic.

They were crucifying us in the media. How could we possibly have let our child go outside by himself? Of all things—to walk a dog? Every headline was another version of the same. They felt sorry for those other boys, but nobody felt sorry for us. Everyone thought we should've known better.

But we couldn't keep our children locked up. What were we supposed to do? Make all teenage boys in the tristate area come inside after dark? We couldn't live our lives in fear. That wasn't any kind of life to live. And besides, the reality was that kids disappeared and went missing every day, and if we thought about the reality of those statistics—the danger kids were always in—we'd never let them out of our sights.

None of that mattered to me, though, because the Dog Snatcher hadn't kidnapped Isaac. If he'd grabbed Isaac, Isaac would've gotten away just like Billy. There was no doubt in my mind. I'd made him take the same self-defense classes Billy took. He got certified, too, and I even made him carry the same brand of pepper spray. I did the exact same things with Katie. She was by his side through it all. They used to practice their holds together in the backyard, trying to see if they could get away from the other. They knew what to expect, but most importantly, they knew how to react if, God forbid, the situation presented itself.

That's why I knew the Dog Snatcher didn't have Isaac despite what it looked like—and it didn't look good. I wasn't delusional. I could see exactly how it looked. The similarities. The evidence. All of it. I was a smart woman. A smart woman and a mother who knew two things: people copied serial killers all the time, and my mother's intuition that told me the Dog Snatcher didn't have my boy and there was still a chance to save him from the person who did.

FIVE

AMBER GREER

I slid out from underneath the covers after realizing I didn't have to do this tonight. I couldn't sleep at night with Isaac gone, but I hadn't been able to get out of bed because of Katie sleeping next to me. Any sound or slight movement on my part startled her, and she woke up immediately. Mark took two Xanax and a shot of whiskey every night before brushing his teeth, and that seemed to work for him, but I couldn't bring myself to use any of that stuff even though the doctor had called in a prescription for Xanax for me too. He probably would've called in heroin if we'd asked.

I eased my feet into my slippers and quietly plodded my way out of our bedroom and down the hall to Isaac's room. It was exactly as it looked the night he'd left. The book he'd been in the middle of reading lay open on his nightstand. The clothes he'd worn to school that day crumpled in a pile on the floor a few steps from his closet. I'd expected his room to be trashed after the police went through it in their search, but nothing was upturned or messy. You couldn't even tell they'd scavenged through it. They'd been delicate and easy with all his things, picking them up and carefully placing them back where they'd found them, but I didn't like that they'd put their fingerprints all over his stuff.

That their hands—not his—were the last ones to touch his things. As quick as that thought hit, I shoved it away. I wouldn't allow myself to think about him in ways that implied he was permanently gone despite what my family thought.

They weren't alone. Everyone assumed Isaac was another one of the Dog Snatcher's victims. He went missing just like they did, and Mark was right, finding his phone the way they had wasn't a good sign. If things followed the same pattern as the others, tomorrow his clothes would show up in a local park somewhere in a tightly sealed box.

I walked over to Isaac's desk and fingered his papers and books, remembering the first night I'd found him suffering in his bedroom after the accident. The only thing he'd asked for after he got out of the hospital was the box from the attic with all his stuffed animals from childhood—the ones he'd slept with until the summer he was twelve. Mark had gladly gotten them for him, and I'd found Isaac curled up in the fetal position on his bed a few nights later with his favorite teddy bear clutched against his chest and the other stuffed animals surrounding him. I'd never seen him look so innocent and broken. Like a baby bird that had fallen out of its nest and been trampled on.

I held myself back from rushing over to him and throwing my arms around him. I took tentative steps to the bed instead. Before the accident, I wouldn't have thought twice about holding him until he felt better, and he would've gladly accepted my comfort. Isaac was no stranger to bad days, especially when it came to the kids at school, and he'd been saying since kindergarten that my hugs held magic juice to make things better. But those days were gone. He'd turned into a feral cat overnight. He recoiled from my touch like it physically hurt him. I explained that to his grief counselor, Theresa, each time we spoke after their sessions and told her how troubling it was, how worried it made me. She said the same thing she always said whenever I expressed my concerns about what a hard time Isaac was having coping.

"He's still in shock," she'd say, like that explained every difficulty no matter what it was. "Everyone processes trauma differently and in their own time. You have to be patient. Give him time."

She was supposed to be an expert, so I believed her in the beginning, but that changed the more time went on and Isaac didn't show any signs of getting better or being okay. He still hadn't. He'd only gotten worse—not better. That was troubling. I couldn't let it go because it just didn't make sense.

Yes, Isaac was in a terrible accident ten months ago, and someone on his basketball team had died, but the reality was that he wasn't that close to Gabe even though they'd grown up around each other since they were babies. They didn't hang in the same circles. They never had. In fact, Gabe had always been kind of mean to Isaac ever since elementary school. Lots of the kids were. For some reason, Isaac had always been a target of their teasing. I tried to avoid playdates or places where Gabe might have been because of how he treated Isaac. It was somehow worse with him because he tolerated Isaac if they were alone, and there were even times he was nice to him, but he was mean to him at school and didn't stand up for him or defend him when he was being picked on. I never talked to anyone about that part because there was no way I'd speak ill of the dead, but it was the truth—Gabe wasn't nice to Isaac. The two of them didn't even like each other.

In a town as small as ours, everyone knew everybody else, and roles were practically assigned at birth. Certain last names always came with special rights and privileges. They carried a level of popularity and prestige whether you'd done anything worthy enough to receive it or not. Our family didn't have the right last name, and we weren't community-grown folk, which automatically put us in the "other" category.

We didn't know small-town culture then and had no idea that's what it would be like when we made the move from the East Coast. We were ready to start building our family, and we loved the idea of leaving the big city behind and settling down into a slower-paced life. It was a perfect location for both our jobs since each of our respective employers had headquarters there. We craved the small-town life, having spent the majority of ours in big cities. We just weren't prepared for some of the unexpected challenges it brought once we started having kids.

Unlike us, the Harts were one of the most well-known families in Falcon Lake. Gabe had all the things Falcon Lake loved—the right last name, the looks, the family, the money, even the talent. The kid was amazing at everything he tried and always had been. He wasn't one of those kids who was gifted in just one particular area. Like they were an amazing soccer player, but they couldn't do anything else, or they could play the guitar by ear but got terrible grades. Gabe wasn't like that at all. He was talented across the spectrum. He won awards for the fastest mile and also took first place in the science fair. He was the star basketball player on the junior varsity team at the same time he was on track to be our grade's valedictorian. It was remarkable stuff, and you couldn't help being impressed by him.

Isaac had never run in his circles. He hadn't sat with his group at sharing time on the rug in kindergarten or ever been one of the kids at Gabe's lunch table throughout all their years at school. Isaac was a shifter and didn't like groups. He never attached himself to a particular one, and he preferred one close friend rather than many. Gabe was the total opposite. He thrived in groups and loved being the center of attention. I rarely ever saw him without a few friends attached to him.

The boys were different when it came to their education too. Isaac had always struggled with schoolwork. A learning disability made school even more challenging for him. He'd always played sports, so they'd been on the same teams, but they were never on the same level. Gabe was a starter, and Isaac was consistently second string.

So, besides the unfortunate luck of being in the car with him that night, Isaac wasn't any closer to Gabe than most people. He wasn't in his inner space. If I had to bet, I'd say they probably didn't say one word to each other the entire drive home. It only happened because I couldn't find anyone else to give him a ride home. Asking Jules for anything with Isaac was always a last resort, but I didn't have a choice that night because I couldn't get a hold of anyone else, and I was stuck in the city with Katie at her dance rehearsal.

That's why I didn't understand why Isaac was still so wrecked. If anything, he should've come back from his near-death experience with a newfound zeal and spark for life. That's what most people did after they'd survived something terrible. They walked around like everything was fresh and brand new again and exuded a sense of appreciation for simply being alive. That never happened with Isaac. Not even close.

I traveled back mentally to a similar incident when I'd found him curled up on his bed. I was searching for something I'd missed. That's how I spent my days and my nights—rewinding footage, digging for clues, and beating myself up for all the things I should've done differently.

"Can I sit?" I had asked, doing my best to sound nonthreatening. He gave a small nod. I sat on the edge of the bed. There were so many questions I wanted to ask him. So many things I wanted to say, but I forced myself to keep quiet because he was finally letting me near him when he was hurting. Even if he wouldn't let me touch him, at least I could be with him on the bed, and he would know he wasn't alone. I just didn't want him to be alone in the awful dark place with his pain. I had no idea how big it was at the time until after a few minutes had passed and he suddenly burst into tears all over again.

"It should've been me, Mom," he said in a choking sob. "It should've been me."

"Oh honey." It took every amount of restraint in me not to wrap my arms around him and hold him tight, but I didn't want to scare him away. Instead, I slowly reached for his ankle and rubbed his lower leg. He didn't flinch. Didn't pull away. "That's absolutely not true."

"It is. It is and you know it. You know it's true," he cried, snot bubbling from his nose and getting all over the pillow. "Everyone wishes it was me. Everyone." His face was contorted into nothing but raw pain.

"No, they don't. Nobody thinks that," I said with as much firmness as I could put in my voice, hoping I sounded convincing. No one had even come close to voicing something like that out loud, but it wasn't lost on anyone that the golden boy was the one who hadn't made it.

He shook his head. "I'm not mad at them. I'm not. It's because they're right. They're right, and everyone knows they're right. Even you." He hurled the last part at me.

"Stop it. Stop saying that," I cried. I wanted to slap those words out of his mouth. "None of that is true. Do you hear me? None of it." I tried to look at him, but he'd covered his face with his arms. "What happened was a terrible tragedy and completely random. Nobody thinks otherwise. Both of your lives matter. You're equally important."

His body shook with sobs. My insides twisted with pain for him as I rubbed his back, and I was so glad when he didn't flinch or shove my hand off but just let me comfort him instead. We sat like that for over an hour before he finally cried himself to sleep.

I had shared what happened with Theresa like I shared everything going on with him back then. They assigned her to us when we left the hospital. Jules had been in the hospital for almost a week, but Isaac was only in overnight for observation. He came back miraculously unflawed. His skin as porcelain smooth as it'd been before the icy plunge.

"Isaac has a lot of survivor guilt." That's how she'd explained his behavior when I'd told her about the first incident and all the ones that came next. I found him curled in the fetal position on his bed like that many times over the next few months, and it broke my heart to pieces every time. It was always the same desperate cry: "It should've been me, Mom."

Theresa kept reassuring me over the following months how common survivor guilt was among people who had experienced a traumatic event, especially one where other people had died. Things like 9/11 and Hurricane Katrina. Wars. Accidents. Cancer. Basically, all the really bad things. You'd expect people to be happy to have made it out alive, but oftentimes that's not what happens, and it certainly wasn't Isaac's experience.

"His is the worst case I've ever seen. I'm having a hard time getting through that," she'd said at their final session. It wasn't supposed to be their final session, but that's when Isaac quit therapy. He flat-out refused to go the following week, and I couldn't exactly carry a six-foot man-child into the car. Mark and I talked about forcing him to go. We discussed lots of ways we might want to intervene, but we just kept telling ourselves time would take care of it and that he'd grow out of the survivor guilt.

We couldn't have been more wrong.

CASE #72946

PATIENT: JULIET (JULES) HART

I can't believe I have to do this again so early. I had no idea when Dr. Stephens and I said goodbye last night that he was going to drag me back in here first thing in the morning. But I understand. It's not like they can wait. They're on a fourteen-day time clock. Every hour matters.

I've never been so grateful to be living in a house with people with severe mental illness. As bizarre and strange as it is, everyone is so wrapped up in their own problems and issues that they don't have time to worry about anyone else's. Some of them aren't even aware that another boy has gone missing. I feel so sorry for those boys.

Dr. Stephens pushes open the door, carrying two cups of coffee. "Sorry I'm late, but I stopped to get these," he says, setting one down on the coffee table and handing the other one to me.

None of the other doctors ever brought me coffee, and I'm so touched. I give him a huge smile. "Thanks so much."

He smiles back. "Don't worry about it. It was the least I could do after keeping you up so late last night." He smiles again. Twice in less than a minute. Today is going to be a good day. He shifts into the same position he was in before—legs crossed, head cocked to the side, ambiguous-but-slightly-caring face. "I say we just jump right back into where we left off yesterday. What do you say?"

I nod my consent like I actually have a choice in all this.

"Great." His voice is peppy. He must be excited, or maybe this is just really good coffee. "You said before that you and Isaac grew close after the train incident. Can you tell me a little bit more about that?"

Did I sound that cheesy when I worked with clients? Like I was reading a therapy script I got from school? I shove my feelings down. They don't matter. Focus. Get this done and get out of here.

I take a sip of my coffee. Dr. Stephens is glued to his chair, hanging on my every word. These are the parts he's been waiting for. Everyone has. "He came to see me in the hospital after, well, you know . . ." I never know how to refer to this part. It makes people so uncomfortable when you say things like that out loud, but then I quickly remember he's a forensic psychologist and thrives on hearing this awful stuff. The more hideous, the better, probably, so I don't bother sugarcoating it. "He came to see me in the hospital after I tried to kill myself on the tracks."

"He did?" His usual blank expression shifts, and for just a split second, he looks surprised. He should be. I've never told anyone that before. Nobody knows about our relationship even though they think they do, and despite how they've painted me in the media—I never went after Isaac. He came to me first.

Nobody visited except my parents and husband, even though I was finally on the level in the hospital program where I could have visitors. Before I turned around, I assumed it was Shane standing in my doorway. After my transfer from Falcon Lake Hospital to the inpatient psychiatric unit at the state security hospital, he never came to see me. Every time we spoke on the phone, he said it was because the place was too depressing and he was trying his best to surround himself with positive things in a world that had gotten so dark. I couldn't blame him. That place was about as depressing as it got.

I was as shocked as anyone to see Isaac in my doorway. I hadn't seen him since Gabe's funeral, and even then, we'd barely said more than two words to each other. Most of that day was a blur. The entire service was recorded, but I've never been able to make myself watch it.

Dr. Stephens interrupts my thoughts like he's walking through the memory with me. "What was he like?"

"Angry."

He balks and lifts his eyebrows. "He was angry?"

It wasn't the response I'd expected from Isaac either. "Yeah." I nod. "He was pretty pissed off."

"With you?" he asks like he still doesn't believe it.

I nod again.

"Why was he angry with you? I don't understand."

I hadn't either, but it didn't take long to find out what had him so upset.

"Hi," I said tentatively as his eyes set on me with a fiery gaze. I hadn't seen anyone but medical personnel, my parents, and Shane for almost four weeks. Having someone other than them in my room felt so strange. For a second, he just stood there staring at me—eyes squinted, arms crossed, and a body wound tight with stress. It was unnerving.

"How could you?" His voice shook so hard with anger that he could barely get the words out.

His question took me by surprise. I had no idea what he was talking about. I scooted to the edge of my bed so I could get closer to him. "What do you mean?"

"We saved each other's lives that day. You saved mine, and I saved yours. And you were just going to throw all of that away? How could you?" He was sweating profusely like he'd run up the eight flights of stairs leading to the unit. His hands trembled as he ran them through his hair. "How could you do that?"

His accusations jarred me. Startled me into myself and inside my body in a way I hadn't been for a long time. I'd never given him a second thought after I'd pulled him out of the lake. Saving his life meant nothing to me. Neither did him saving mine. It never occurred to me that it meant something to him.

I shove the memories down before the emotions swell and focus on explaining things to Dr. Stephens. He's always waiting in the wings.

"My grief was all-consuming. People always say things shook them to their core, but it wasn't like that for me. It was like I'd lost my core, as if I no longer had a center, and I came undone. Totally unraveled. I couldn't see any hope. No light. Only darkness. I couldn't see in front of me, let alone a way out. But for the first time since the accident, when Isaac visited me, I saw a glimpse outside of myself," I say, doing my best to explain the important moment, but I'm not sure I can do it justice. "Before that, I was so wrapped up in my pain and grief that I couldn't see anything or anyone else. Not even Shane, and he'd lost a son too."

"What was different about Isaac?"

I don't have to think about my response to this question. It's one I've spent time with on my own before since I was as surprised as Isaac by what developed between us. "It was the look in his eyes when he talked about what happened to us and the impact it had on him." There was more to it than that. So much more. When Isaac talked about breathing life back into my lips and how much it meant to him, it sent shivers down my spine, made my stomach flutter. I held my breath each time he described how cold my lips were when they came out of the water and his obsession with touching them afterward to see if they were warm. But I don't tell Dr. Stephens that. I keep those pieces to myself. I'm not stupid. He'd definitely make it into something that it wasn't.

"What was it about the look in his eyes that moved you?" he asks next. Interesting that's what he picked from my statement. I would've definitely gone with why our experiences were different, but I'll humor his therapeutic approach.

"He looked like a scared puppy that was lost in a dark hole, and for a second, it brought me out of my own pain. I could see something—someone—outside of myself. It'd been a long time since I'd been able to do that." I lower my head in shame, trying to drown out the sounds of Shane's accusations. "I'm not sure why it wasn't like that with Shane. I'm sure he was in just as much pain as Isaac and—"

Dr. Stephens reaches out and puts his hand on top of mine to stop me. "That's okay. The experience you and Isaac had surrounding Gabe's death was very different than Shane's experience. Very different." He makes sure to emphasize the last statement.

My heart swells with appreciation. He gets it. Nobody else has gotten it before and definitely not Shane. He didn't even try to understand. Just said I was sick in the head.

"The two of you experienced a traumatic event together, and that forms a bond like none other. You know that." He gives me a slight nod, recognizing my education and not wanting to insult me. So thoughtful of him. "Trauma bonding—"

"It's more than that, though," I interrupt before he goes further down the trauma track. "Shane was always so pissed off at me because he didn't think I validated his pain. He said I thought my pain over losing Gabe was greater than his, and he was always trying to get me to admit that it was the same." Just talking about the old argument raises my blood pressure, and I force my voice to stay steady. "But here's the thing: it's not like it was a competition—still isn't—but my pain *is* greater than his because guess what? I was the one driving the car that killed our son. It was my mistake."

"You're not responsible for Gabe's death." He squeezes my hand, but I quickly pull it out from underneath his.

He's said a lot of stupid things since we started meeting together, but this is by far the stupidest, but I'm not surprised. I was just hoping things might be different this time, but he's just like the others. "I was driving the car, and I crashed into the lake, so I'm the one that's responsible."

"You're not responsible for Gabe's death," he repeats himself like a dummy.

It doesn't matter how many times he says it: his proclamations won't make it true. It's not like he's Dorothy from *The Wizard of Oz* and he can tap his ruby-red slippers together three times and be home. That's not how it works. But that's the thing. That's why none of them can help me. They all think I'll feel so much better once I get over the guilt about feeling responsible for Gabe's death, but it's not a feeling—it's a fact. I'm responsible for Gabe's death.

I won't negate my responsibility so that I can feel better about myself. I was driving the car that night when I was exhausted. I was the one who slammed on the brakes when the deer jumped out in front of us on the road, despite knowing that's the last thing you want to do on ice. I was the one who couldn't control the car and let it go flying into the lake.

What I need is someone to tell me how I'm supposed to live in a world where I'm responsible for my son's death. That's all. I don't have any trouble accepting I'm the reason he's gone. They're the ones that have a problem accepting that fact. I came to terms with it a long time ago. Maybe almost immediately. The first time the doctor told me.

Shane had been sitting next to my bedside twisting and twirling his hands in his lap since I woke up after being unconscious for six hours. My entire body felt like it was being pricked with needles. Blinding and shooting pain everywhere. My fingers and toes felt like frozen pieces of meat. None of that mattered, though. All I cared about was Gabe.

"Please, Shane, what's going on with Gabe? How is he?" I kept asking.

"We need to wait for the doctor." It was the same answer every time. I might've had a head injury, but I understood that wasn't good, and his refusal to look me in the eye only heightened my suspicions. It felt like days instead of hours before the doctor finally made his way into the room. He was an elderly man with kind eyes and white tufted eyebrows. Age spots dotted his nearly bald head.

He stuck his hand out to mine, and the touch of his skin sent piercing needles down my spine and made me cringe.

"That's going to happen with hypothermia," he said, noticing my reaction. "Your body is going to be sensitive to touch, and your body temperature is going to be dysregulated for quite some time. It—"

"Okay, okay," I said, interrupting him and waving him off. I didn't care about any of that. All I wanted to know was what kind of shape Gabe was in. He'd been underwater so much longer than me. "How's Gabe? Tell me everything."

He blinked twice, then spoke in a soft, even voice. "I'm sorry, Mrs. Hart, but Gabe did not survive the accident."

In that instant, it was as if a gaping sinkhole just opened up and swallowed my normal life. Gone. Just like that. Never to return.

And now I'm here.

Trapped in this purgatory of sorts with a psychologist who's about as clueless as he was when we started, but at least he's cute.

"I appreciate you saying that," I tell him, referring to his original point about me not being responsible for Gabe's death, "but I think we're going to have to disagree on that one."

I'm responsible for all this. He just doesn't know that yet.

SIX

AMBER GREER

My phone buzzed next to my head and startled me awake instantly. I pulled up Katie's FaceTime. Her face filled the screen. She gave me a tiny smile. There was color in her cheeks. That was good.

"How did you sleep, sweetie?" I asked, pulling myself upright on the couch so I could see her better. I'd meant to go back upstairs last night, but I'd fallen asleep here instead.

"Good. Grandma let me sleep with her again." The sound of her voice made me smile.

"I knew that's how the two of you would end up." She'd had her grandma wrapped around her fingers since she was born. Both my kids did, but my mom didn't mind. She loved her grandkids, and she was an amazing grandmother, even moved to Minnesota so she could be closer to us after Katie was born.

"She's making pancakes and eggs right now. Can you smell it?" She tilted her phone toward the kitchen, and I spotted my mom's back in front of the stove. She was wearing the bathrobe we got her last Christmas.

"Smells delicious," I said, but in reality, the thought of food made me nauseous.

She turned the phone back on herself. "Mom, do you think it would be okay if I stayed with Grandma for a while today before I come home?" She said it softly and carefully like she was afraid she'd hurt my feelings by asking. "It's just that . . . well, it's just not as sad over here, you know?"

"Oh honey, I know," I said, my emotions thickening my voice as I did my best not to cry and to stay strong for her. "It's really sad in the house right now, and it looks like a block party outside with all the media trucks and vans, so I understand if you want to hang out over there longer. It's a total circus here. Stay away from the craziness. Give yourself a break today."

"Are you sure? You're not mad? You're going to be okay?" Her green eyes were wide with concern and filled with compassion. How did I get such great kids?

"I am." I nodded to emphasize the point. "Let Grandma bake cookies for you and spoil you rotten all day. Try to forget about things for a while."

"I love you, Mom," she said just as Mark walked into the living room. At the sound of her voice, he grabbed the phone out of my hand.

"I love you, honey." He perked up, pulling it together for her.

"Love you too, Dad. I'm staying at Grandma's again today."

Mark shot me a glance, and I nodded back, signaling I was okay with it. "Sounds good," he said to her. "Let's chat later." He blew her a kiss and ended the call.

He handed me my phone. I reached for it slowly, studying his face to see where he was at emotionally this morning. I knew he'd slept because I'd heard the sounds of his snores all night long, but he didn't look like it. He looked worse than he did yesterday. At least he'd finally changed clothes, but he still hadn't showered.

"Detective Hawkins just texted me. He said he'd be over around ten," Mark announced. The night shift was still out in the garage, and the regular crew wasn't here yet, but they would be soon. They came at eight and waited with us all day long, for our phones to ring or contact to be made in some way. That's all we did.

Wait.

And wait.

Our kitchen had turned into a command center that looked straight out of CSI. I used to be a true-crime junkie. I wouldn't be after this.

"At least now that the police have Isaac's phone, they'll be able to see what we mean about those awful texts he was getting." I tested the waters, treading carefully. It was an upsetting topic, but at least one we agreed on.

"You mean they can see how messed up and cruel kids are these days?" he asked. The corners of his mouth instantly pulled into an angry frown.

I had hesitated telling him about the texts back when I'd discovered them because I was hoping that whoever had sent them would stop. That it would be only a temporary situation so I could spare Mark the agony that had stolen my breath and crushed my heart when I'd read them. It was one of those moments seared into my brain in a way I would never forget.

I'd suspected Isaac was having a bad day since it'd been hours since he'd left his room, and I'd learned to predict his new patterns. There'd been no movement or sounds of him playing video games, which meant he was either crying or lying on his bed staring lifelessly at the ceiling. My gut was screaming at me that he was in trouble again too. It just hit me out of nowhere, like it had before. Every time I'd had the feeling, I'd gone to him immediately and found him distraught on his bed. I'd walked into his room that day expecting it to be one of those times.

He was on his side in the fetal position, curled up tightly like he was trying to disappear inside himself and take up as little space as possible. His face was tear streaked and his shirt drenched in sweat. All the lights in his room were turned off.

His phone lay next to him. I pushed it aside so that I could sit down, and something compelled me to look at it. I swiped the screen and quickly typed in his passcode. His recent text thread opened in front of me:

It should've been you.

It was a sucker punch to my gut, knocking all the air from my lungs, followed by white-hot fury shooting through my veins. What kind of a monster would send something like that? I scrolled up. There were hundreds of them. The vilest, most awful things you could say to another human being piled on top of each other manically:

I hope you die.

I wish you would've drowned in the lake.

Why'd you steal his life?

All this time I'd thought his torment came from inside himself, but it was so much more than that. Someone had been torturing him since the day after the funeral. Who would do such a thing? And why? I just didn't understand. Debilitating nausea flooded my body, and my protein bar from breakfast lurched up my throat. I shoved it back down.

Why were kids so cruel?

They always had been—making fun of his clothes, teasing him about how long it took him to take tests, and laughing at him for being shy—but this was a new low. As if Isaac hadn't been through enough. All I did was apologize to him over and over again while I rubbed his back. I'd never felt so powerless to help him. Or so angry.

I shifted my thoughts back to the present moment. I couldn't change the past. Nothing was going to change how we'd handled things.

I threw the blanket off me and headed toward the kitchen to get coffee going before everyone started showing up. Mark followed behind me.

I turned around and placed my hand on his shoulder. I did my best to look kind. I didn't have enough energy for this if he wasn't on my side. "Look, I know we got into it again the other night, and I'm sorry, but can we just try to be friends today? I mean, if I have to battle against you on top of all this, I'm not sure how much more I can take. I just—"

He pulled away. "Will you just listen to yourself speak? Everything is about you. *I* this and *I* that. How much more *you* can take?" He glared at me. "Don't you mean how much more *I* can take?"

I slammed the coffee mug down on the counter. The resolve to get along and be friends gone that quickly. "What are you talking about? What are you going through that's just so much greater than what I'm going through?"

He pointed at me. "This." He was almost yelling. "The fact that you are so delusional you don't even know what's going on here. What I'm talking about. That that statement needs an explanation."

"I don't understand."

"Oh my God, Amber. You're driving me crazy. My son was taken eight days ago, and there's a pretty big possibility that the clothes he was wearing that night are going to show up in a park somewhere today, so that's some pretty tough shit right there. But on top of that? I also have to deal with a wife who's so terrified of that being true that she's gone off the deep end and created an entirely fictional tale about how some other grieving mother is somehow linked to our son's disappearance. So yeah, it's pretty maddening, and I'm not sure how much more I can take."

I yanked on his arm. "But those texts, Mark. Those awful texts. What if they were from her?" He couldn't just dismiss them. Maybe they were from other kids, but what if they were from her? Could she have been toying with him all along? I let my hand travel down to Mark's wrist and rest, my fingers creating a bracelet. His entire body went rigid instead of relaxing. He didn't take my hand. Any other time he would have.

"Those texts were from kids. Spoiled-brat kids with nothing better to do than torture someone else for kicks. They're sick, but those texts don't have anything to do with this." He shrugged out of my hold and headed to the fridge to get milk for the coffee. We didn't have much longer until the investigators and technicians started showing up. There were more technical people on the team than detectives, but they were monitoring everything inside and outside the house, ready to record anything in an instant. They'd done the same for Brady and Josh. There'd never been any contact.

I stood next to the counter waiting for the coffee to finish and wondering how I was going to get through this torturous day. He turned around from the refrigerator, holding the milk carton.

"Okay, for argument's sake, let's just say that you're right, Amber. Somehow, someway, Jules is involved in this. We'll go with your theory. Okay?"

I nodded at him, unsure where he was going with all this and not sure I wanted to follow.

"She's living in a group home for adults with severe mental illness. Her comings and goings are limited and strictly monitored. Where is Isaac the rest of the time? How is she keeping him alive? She has to sign in and out to go anywhere. She's not allowed to come and go as she pleases. And I double-checked yesterday because I wanted to be sure, but she's still on one-to-one peer support. Even when she does leave the house, she's not allowed to do it by herself. She has to have someone with her. So, tell me, how would she kidnap a boy and keep him somewhere?"

"I mean, she could figure out a way." I tried to sound confident, as sure of myself as I felt. "There are lots of ways, and maybe she has help."

"How? I mean really, how would she do any of this? And don't forget—she hasn't got any money. She's under conservatorship of the court, and her mom is her executor. Have you seriously thought about the logistics of all that? They're impossible."

I shook my head. I wanted to give him something to prove him wrong. A valid reason. An explanation, but I couldn't explain things the way he wanted me to. I couldn't come up with anything that made sense given everything he'd just said. He had me in a corner. A good one.

"Don't you see, Amber?" He put the milk back in the refrigerator and walked over to stand next to me at the island again. He took my hand and finally held it in his, giving it a tight squeeze. "This goes nowhere. Let it go. For the love of God, please let it go."

CASE #72946

PATIENT: JULIET (JULES) HART

The light is giving off that annoying buzz again. I try to ignore it and focus on explaining my relationship with Isaac to Dr. Stephens. "Isaac saving my life allowed him to create meaning out of all the suffering, and he needed that narrative to go on. Otherwise, there was no point. He made me feel like I owed him something for saving my life, like I couldn't waste what he'd done for me, and I couldn't take away his meaning. It would be like taking away his life too. I guess that's the best way to explain it." My stomach growls. Dr. Stephens has got to learn to time his sessions better and work in breaks. Another rumble. "Sorry." I giggle, placing my hand on my stomach. "It's been a long time since breakfast."

He doesn't take the hint and ignores my hunger pain, acting like it wasn't time for lunch fifteen minutes ago. "Do you think you owed him?"

"No, but I could understand why he felt that way. We all need to create meaning out of trauma. Saving me gave beauty and light to something so dark and tragic. If I died, then all that was left was darkness. He didn't know how to live in the dark any more than I did. He's one of those people with an easy life too. And he was a kid, so imagine how hard that was for him."

But that was only part of the reason he was so angry. I'm not going to tell him the other part. I'm not even sure why. I've never told it to Shane either. It's my biggest regret about that night, my deepest shame.

"It should've been me, you know," Isaac said from the doorway of my hospital room. His voice was thick with emotion.

I motioned for him to come closer inside. In a normal world, I would've told him to shut the door behind him so that we could speak privately, but I didn't live in a world with closed doors anymore. Or furniture that wasn't bolted to the floor. He took a few tentative steps toward me and quickly stopped. His jaw worked constantly. His fists were clenched at his sides like he might be holding himself back from coming at me. I'd never seen someone so angry.

I patted the spot at the end of the bed the same way I used to with Gabe when he'd storm into my room upset. Isaac shook his head, refusing to sit. I should've told him to be quiet, that he was wrong. That there was no reason it should've been him that died in the accident, and if I was his own mother, that's probably exactly what I would've said. But we both knew I would've been lying: I'd made the two of them switch seats in the car at the last minute that night.

I had noticed immediately when I grabbed them after the game that Isaac was already looking a bit pale from the long bus ride. He got carsick so easily. He'd thrown up twice in my car as a toddler. Once we'd only gone six blocks. I hated puke. Gabe had just buckled himself into the front passenger seat when I reached over and undid the latch, motioning behind us. "Let Isaac sit in the front on the way home. I don't want him to get carsick."

Gabe was instantly annoyed and had given me the most hostile teenage glare. "Mom, no. I'm sitting here," he'd said like a spoiled toddler.

"It's okay, Mrs. Hart. That's fine," Isaac had piped up from the back. "I'll be fine. It's really not that far. Don't worry about it."

But I didn't believe him and didn't want to risk him throwing up in my car. The last thing I wanted to do was clean up puke that night. Even though he was a teenager, I didn't trust him to make it outside the car in time. I had pushed Gabe's arm and shoved him toward the door. "Come on, switch places with him now so that we can go."

"Fine," he had huffed and rolled his eyes at me.

The two of them had quickly exchanged places. Isaac mumbled an embarrassed apology to Gabe, and we took off. Gabe forgot to buckle his seat belt when he got in the back. The impact from the crash into the lake catapulted him through the back seat window. A piece of his scalp was attached to it. The only part of him still in the car. His body was found over fifty feet from the car trapped under the ice. He'd never stood a chance.

Isaac locked eyes with me, reliving that fateful moment along with me. I'd never told anyone that was how we'd started out. That I was responsible for killing my son from the very beginning. Isaac was the only one who knew. Had he kept it a secret too?

"I should've told you no." His voice shook along with his body. "All I had to say was no, and Gabe would still be here, but I didn't. I was too big of a punk to say that. I didn't even need to move up front. I would've been fine, and I knew that. I also knew it would make Gabe mad, and I didn't want to make him mad since he'd actually been kinda nice to me at the game. Well, not nice, exactly. More like he tolerated me, you know?"

I did know. As hard as I'd tried to make Amber and myself become friends, I'd done the same with the two of them, but for some reason unbeknownst to me, Gabe had always treated Isaac like he was an annoying younger brother even though they were the same age.

"I wish you'd sit," I coaxed. He'd moved into the center of the room and was pacing it like a caged animal, running his hands up and down his arms.

He shook his head. His long hair was stringy and matted together. When was the last time he'd showered? His clothes hung on him like he'd lost weight. There were dark circles underneath his eyes, which were bloodshot. Was he on drugs? Was that what he'd done to cope? Did Amber know? Should I tell her?

I felt so bad for him that day as I watched him wrestle with his inner demons, and all I wanted to do was help him. I had no idea what that would lead to. I refuse to beat myself up for how things turned out, though. I did my best. My intentions were good. That's what counts, and that's the part Dr. Stephens needs to understand.

"I was in the state security hospital for over a month, as I'm sure you know," I inform him on the slight chance that he doesn't. I started in the maximum security section at Falcon Lake Hospital. They kept me on the same ward as the prison inmates from Shakopee. They gave me twenty-four-hour surveillance and sedation. It was days before I had a recognizable thought. That's what happens after you try to kill yourself the way that I did. Especially since the first thing I said when they peeled me out of the car with the Jaws of Life was, "I just want to die. Please, God, let me die." Statements and actions like those bring your risk to an entirely different level, so it takes a long time to get to a place where you can have visitors. "Isaac didn't just visit me that one time at Falcon Lake Hospital. He came to see me at the state security hospital too. He visited me the entire time I was there."

"That's what I've never been able to understand." His face lines with confusion. "Sneaking into your hospital room was one thing, but getting onto the locked psychiatric ward, especially as a minor, was another. How did he get on your visitor list? Did he sign himself in every time? Did anybody question him? Ask for identification?"

I laugh. "Sheesh, one question at a time." He doesn't smile or laugh. He never does. At least not when I want him to. "Getting him on my visitor list was easy. My mom put everyone on it because she was always trying to get people to visit me. Some doctor had told her in one of the family groups that social support would be huge for my recovery, so she'd latched on to that and put almost our entire family tree on the list. I just tucked him on it, slipped him right between my cousin Shelby and my uncle Ray. Nobody noticed when I added him."

"And nobody said anything about him visiting you?" He doesn't try to hide his disapproval or his disappointment.

"Maybe." I shrug. "If they did, nobody ever said anything to me about it."

It's weird. I know. It felt odd to me in the beginning, too, and I wouldn't have wanted Gabe to be able to visit some old woman in the psych ward either. But Isaac wasn't a regular fifteen-year-old, and I wasn't a regular forty-one-year-old woman. Not anymore.

"What kinds of things did the two of you talk about?" He tries to keep the judgment out of his voice, but there's no mistaking its presence.

"Nothing really at first. Like I said, he was angry. It took him a few visits to stop being so mad." I'd been more surprised to see him the second time he showed up at my door than I had been the first.

"What are you doing here? How do you keep getting in?" I asked after he startled me with a tentative knock. The truth was he was the one who snuck himself in the first time. I never had anything to do with it.

"I told them I'm your cousin Carl." He grinned and beamed, clearly proud of himself to have done his research on my family. He got lucky picking Carl and even luckier that my mom had put our entire family on there.

"Come in," I said, straightening my gown and tucking my hair behind my ears. I must've looked a mess. I hadn't showered since the weekend.

He scanned the room slowly, then took a few tentative steps inside. He shoved his hands in his baggy blue jeans and stared at his tennis shoes while he announced, "I'm not exactly sure why I'm back or what I'm doing here."

"It's okay, it's okay," I said, motioning him closer. In a weird way, it felt good to see him, like an old friend I hadn't seen in a long time. I gave him a big smile so he could see that I was still okay: that I hadn't done anything stupid again with the gift he'd given me. Being alive wasn't a gift, but I couldn't tell him that any more than I would've told my son the tooth fairy wasn't real when he was little. It would've been too mean.

Isaac shuffled farther inside the room, taking in all the plants and flowers hanging in the window. You'd swear I was battling a terminal illness, as many as were up there. The cards that accompanied the balloons and flowers were taped on the wall behind my bed. My mom had insisted. She'd spent her first Saturday visit putting up two bulletin boards and tacking them on with stuff she used for scrapbooking. Each time she came, she made sure to add any new cards.

He spotted the beat-up leather chair in the corner and took a seat, perched awkwardly on the edge of it. He tapped his hands on his knees.

"You don't have to be so scared," I said gently. I wanted to reach out and hug him, but I intuitively knew that it'd push him away, and I didn't want to do that.

He peeked out at me from underneath his long bangs. "But I am. It's so weird. I'm always scared now. I haven't stopped being scared." His vibrant green eyes that used to sparkle were hollow and dull. His face an ashen white like he was the one sick and in desperate need of a hospital bed. He brushed his hair off his face. "Do you remember what it was like right after we almost hit the deer? That feeling? Do you ever think about it?" There was an earnestness to his voice and his question like if he didn't get it out fast enough, he might lose his nerve.

"That second has played itself out a thousand times in my mind," I responded, nodding. "I've gone over every single part of that night ten thousand times. Every tiny second. Every word. Every moment. It's like a video I obsessively rewind and watch over and over again."

"Me too." He gave me a tiny half smile.

It was our beginning. The way out of the horrible place we'd found ourselves in.

I shift my gaze back on Dr. Stephens. Does he wonder where I go when I mentally travel out of here during our sessions? So far he hasn't asked. Maybe he hasn't noticed. He's sizing me up, trying to decide if he should give me a few more seconds to speak or if he should direct the narrative with a specific question. I can almost see him spinning the two options in his head. I make the decision for him.

"I had a friend who was in AA, and she used to always tell me that the way their program worked was that whenever you were really in a bad spot, that you should go find someone worse off than you and help them. Take the attention off yourself and your own problems and help somebody else solve theirs. It was kind of like that with Isaac." At least it was in the beginning. He gave me someone to mother at a time when I desperately needed someone to be a mom to. I just didn't know that then. What's that saying? Hindsight's twenty-twenty? "He needed to talk about that night with someone who didn't try to fix it, so I just listened to him a lot. It was almost like he was one of my old patients." I don't realize what I've said until after it's out of my mouth, but I can't take it back.

He doesn't flinch or pick up his pen to make any kind of note. Maybe he missed the significance? I have a feeling he's not paying attention to the right things.

"Was it hard for you to listen to him talk about what happened?" he asks next.

"At first it was, definitely it was at first. I used to get all sweaty and nauseous whenever he started talking, but it almost became this weird form of exposure therapy. The more he talked about it, the less impactful it was on me. I stopped sweating and shaking." He did too. The only reason I sat through how uncomfortable and hard it was for me was because he had it much worse. Trying to articulate his internal state was so tough for Isaac and painfully slow. "Something shifted when I was listening to him talk about that night, and searching for ways to help him change the way he thought about himself and the accident made me start processing it differently for myself too. That pretty much happened by mistake."

"That must've been really nice and helpful for both of you," he says.

"It was magical. That's what it was. Isaac was willing to talk about things that nobody else would, at least not back then. Nobody besides my psychologists and counselors wanted to talk about that night. But regular, normal people? They couldn't handle horrific, totally unfair things happening to children. And the death of a child? The horrible way we all knew Gabe must've died—terrified and alone—that nobody dared mention? Those things shook you to the core. How couldn't they?"

People live their lives under the illusion of a protective shield. I used to live the same way, but not anymore. Nobody is safe, and I remind people of that, which is why I make them uncomfortable. I remind them that we don't live in a safe world. People slowly stopped coming around after the funeral. They didn't stop sending food, though. I didn't have to cook for months. They still sent text messages asking how I was or forwarded inspirational quotes and books that they thought might help me. But nobody knew how to talk to me in person or be around me. Looking me in the eye was too much. I reminded them of the thing we all feared the most.

Except Isaac. He was the only person who wasn't uncomfortable around me. And I wasn't uncomfortable around him. We were the perfect match.

SEVEN

AMBER GREER

The house was filled with nervous tension. It'd been that way all day. All of us just listening, waiting, and watching, but trying to pretend like we weren't. Like there wasn't an almost-audible clock ticking over our heads. There was nothing to do to stay busy, and it was driving me crazy.

Mark had taken up his usual post on the couch. I'd already heard him get sick in the bathroom twice. His face still looked pale and clammy. My dad showed up about an hour ago and took over answering the house phone. It was weird to hear it ring. Nobody ever called on the house phone. We only had it for emergencies, and most of the time, I forgot it was even there. I couldn't remember the last time I'd used it before this, but it'd been ringing off the hook. That was the only real sound interrupting the excruciating wait.

"We ask that you respect the family's privacy at this time, and the Greers aren't interested in any interviews or media appearances," my dad said over and over again like he was a recorded message.

No media interviews was the one thing Mark and I agreed on in all this. We'd made the video with the police asking for the safe return of Isaac and anyone with information to come forward, but that was it. We weren't going to put our family in the spotlight. Not any more than it already was.

I paced the lower level, treading circles throughout the house. I stopped frequently in the kitchen to fill coffee mugs and make new pots. Sometimes I drained what was left in the old pot and made a new one just to have something to do with my hands. Normally, when I was super stressed and worried, I cleaned the kitchen spotless. If I still wasn't calm after that, then I set out organizing the cupboards, and if something was especially bad, I ended up tackling the refrigerator too. But I couldn't do any of that with all the people in my kitchen, which only added to my anxiety.

I stepped upstairs to put away a load of laundry, and I could tell by the way the energy had shifted in the entire house when I came downstairs that something major had happened. The thing I'd secretly been holding my breath against.

Everyone tried to busy themselves as Detective Hawkins motioned for me to follow him into the family room so he could speak with Mark and me privately. Mark picked up on the change as soon as we entered the room, and he slowly rose to his feet, never taking his eyes off Detective Hawkins. Mark walked toward us like he was dreading each step because each one took him closer to hearing whatever awful thing was about to come out of Detective Hawkins's mouth. Part of me wanted to scream at him to go sit back down on the couch. Like if he'd just sit down, Detective Hawkins wouldn't be able to tell us the news, and if he didn't tell us the news, then somehow that would make the news not true.

Mark stood next to me, and Detective Hawkins wasted no time getting down to business. "I just received a call from one of my patrol officers, and a sealed cardboard box was found at Plummer's Park twenty minutes ago. The box looks identical to the ones left in the other cases." He kept a straight face while he talked. No emotion while he plunged a knife into our guts. "The forensic team has been dispatched to the scene, and they'll be combing the entire area within a two-mile radius for any evidence or clues. I'll be leaving shortly to oversee the questioning of any potential witnesses we can find in the park. Our media-relations person will sit down with you while I'm gone to go over the statement we'll be releasing to the media. She'll work with you on creating your own. Much like we did when we gave the statement that the cell phone was found and when Isaac first went missing. You won't be alone. She'll walk you through all of it." He was talking too fast. This was too much. He needed to slow down.

Mark was just shaking his head like he didn't understand half of what Detective Hawkins had said either. "But I don't get it. I thought that all the local parks were under surveillance?"

"They were—still are."

"So, someone just waltzed in there undetected by all your officers and left a box?"

"Yes, I wish we had cameras in all the trees so we could have eyeballs on every area of the park at all times, but unfortunately, that's just not possible. We also couldn't question everyone that came into the park or even search them for that matter. All we could do was monitor any activity that looked suspicious. Whatever happened, they slipped in undetected by us or anyone else."

"But I thought they were patrolling the park." Mark repeated himself despite the explanation Detective Hawkins had just given.

It didn't seem to bother Detective Hawkins at all. He didn't skip a beat. "We're hopeful someone in the park might have seen or heard something. Maybe someone noticed something out of the ordinary."

None of his words penetrated Mark. He looked like he wanted to yell at him, and he worked hard to control his voice. "Isn't that what the police were already supposed to be doing? I thought that was the whole point of them being out there."

"I'm sorry, Mark. I know this is difficult information to hear and not the outcome we would like, but remember, ultimately, it's not what we'd hoped for, but it's what we expected." He shifted his gaze to me. "Do you have any questions? I want to be here for the two of you and to answer all your questions, but I really want to get out to Plummer's Park. I'd like to get to work as soon as possible interviewing people and canvassing the area for any potential leads. Anything I can answer before I go?"

I shook my head. He tilted his head to the side as if to say, *Are you sure?* I always had questions.

But not today. Not now.

All I wanted to do was sit down. None of this was what I wanted to hear. The buzzing wouldn't stop in my ears. I reached behind me for the banister to steady myself. This didn't mean anything. There were still other possibilities. We still had six days. Six days was a lot. A lot could happen in six days.

CASE #72946

PATIENT: JULIET (JULES) HART

Dr. Stephens slides his way through the door and back into the room, double-checking to make sure the door is secured behind him before taking a seat in his usual spot at the table. He stepped out ten minutes ago to take a phone call. He's never done that before, so it must be important. He crosses his legs, and I want to tell him that it's okay to just sit in the chair in a comfortable position like a regular person, that he doesn't have to try so hard all the time, but I hold myself back. I do a lot of holding back in here.

"That was Detective Hawkins on the phone," he says, jumping back into things immediately. It's a very abrupt transition.

"Am I supposed to know who that is?" I've assumed he wasn't working alone, but we've never actually discussed that or talked about anyone related to the case. Not even the extent of his involvement.

"Oh, I'm sorry, I guess not. You probably wouldn't know who that is, would you?" He's clearly caught off guard and a bit shaken. He must be under enormous pressure. "Detective Hawkins is the lead detective on the Isaac Greer case."

"Oh, yes." I nod with a smile teasing the corner of my lips. "That is why we're here, I suppose." It's easy to slip into therapy-land with him and forget what brought us together in the first place. He's just so much fun to play with.

"They've had a major development in the case." That's all he says, and then he stops. His long, drawn-out pauses are annoying. I know exactly what he's doing. He's testing me. Seeing how I react to the little bits of information that he gives me. Seeing whether if he leaves it ambiguous enough, I'll unintentionally reveal something.

"I hope it works out for them," I say, holding back the urge to smile. It's the last thing he expects me to say. I was supposed to ask what happened. He blinks a few times. Shifts in his seat. He keeps trying to rearrange his face, but he can't decide which expression he wants to go with, and it's really tough not to laugh.

Finally, he speaks. "Yes, yes, I hope it works out for them too." He clears his throat like he's suddenly nervous to talk to me. Am I really that intimidating? I can't be. It's so sweet that he's so nervous, though. "The thing is that it's not looking like it's going to head in that direction."

"Oh no." I fake surprise and sadness. I give it to him. I can't help it. He works so hard; he deserves it. "What happened?"

"Are you familiar with the cases of the two boys who were murdered—Brady and Josh?"

Does he think I've been living under a rock? He's not good at this part. Transitions can be tough. You only really get good at those by experience.

"Yes, I'm familiar," I say. I could say so much more, but I hold back. I'll let him think he's leading the way.

"In both of those instances, the boys' clothes they were wearing on the night they disappeared showed up at a park eight days after they were kidnapped," he explains like everyone doesn't already know every minute detail about the cases, but then I quickly remember that I live with people who have no idea what's happening right now. They don't know that we have a serial killer stalking adolescent boys. Some of them don't know what day it is. Does Dr. Stephens think I'm that sick? That far removed from what's happening in society like them? God, I hope not. He cracks his knuckles. "Well, earlier today, Isaac's clothes were found in a cardboard box at Plummer's Park just like those boys'."

He drops his news into the room and waits to see what I'll do with it. He doesn't even try to pretend like he's not watching my reaction. His eyes are locked on mine.

"What are you looking at me for?" I ask, batting my eyelashes at him. "I've been sitting here with you all day."

EIGHT

AMBER GREER

I hadn't been downstairs since Detective Hawkins left, and it had been over three hours. I'd been sitting cross legged in the center of Isaac's room unmoving for the last two. At first, I'd wanted to crawl into his bed and throw all his blankets around me. Just lie there and inhale the smell of him, since he was all over his bedding. I'd flipped up the comforter and had been about to get in his bed when I'd suddenly stopped. If I buried myself underneath his covers, then my smell might replace his. That couldn't happen. I'd quickly dropped the covers and sunk down to the floor. I'd been there ever since.

Hiding.

Nobody bothered me when I was in here, but I wasn't sure who I was hiding from more—the investigators, Mark, or myself. Maybe all of us. I just wanted to cocoon myself in Isaac. Shut myself off from the rest of the world. The rest of the world was spinning too fast again, and I couldn't keep up.

I spent so much time arguing with Isaac to clean his room and pick up his clothes, and now ironically, I was grateful he never listened. The combination of dirty socks, body odor, and leftover food that was rotting away somewhere undetected had overpowered the room since he was thirteen. But in the middle of all his teenage-boy smell, there was still the scent of him that was uniquely his. The one we all carried, as unique as our fingerprints—that was here too. I wanted to shut his door and lock every part of him inside.

I was avoiding the call to Katie and my mom, but we had to tell them about the clothes soon. They couldn't find out about them on the news or social media, and it was only a matter of time until the story broke, but I still couldn't bring myself to do it. How did you crush your child's world? That's what it would do to Katie. She'd looked up to Isaac since the moment she was born. Her eyes searched for him in the room when she was an infant, and she'd done everything fast and early just to be able to keep up with him. He adored her right back, giving her piggyback rides around the house and letting her do sleepovers in his room. I'd always felt so lucky that I got kids who liked each other.

She was going to have just as many questions about what happened as Mark. It wouldn't make any more sense to her than it did to him that somehow, even despite the surveillance, a person had snuck into one of our local parks and delivered Isaac's clothes. According to Detective Hawkins, the park bench had been clear when the officers did their sweep at 2:30 p.m. They did full sweeps of the perimeter and the picnic areas every hour. By 3:30 p.m., the box was there, and they'd sealed the area immediately. It was the exact time that Jules was with Dr. Stephens, and there was no arguing that fact because they recorded all their sessions. She couldn't have dumped Isaac's clothes in the park. It wasn't possible.

Still. It didn't mean she wasn't involved.

The Dog Snatcher didn't have my boy. He just didn't. Somehow, she was making it look like he did.

But why?

And how?

Clearly, she wasn't doing it herself. She had to have help. Mark acted like I didn't think about the problems with her being involved in something at this level, but I'd factored all those issues into it, and at the end of the day, that was one of the things I kept coming back to over and over again myself. How could she pull something like this off?

Despite Mark's accusations, I'd thought through the logistics plenty of times. They didn't make sense, but none of this made sense. Her involvement seemed impossible, but none of this was supposed to be possible. So we lived in an upside-down world now, and in this new upside-down world, anything went. You couldn't try to make sense of it like you did in the old world. None of the regular rules applied, and everything was twisted, which meant that I wasn't willing to let go of her being involved yet.

And then, suddenly, it dawned on me, and I couldn't believe I'd never thought of it before: Jules lived in a home filled with a bunch of other people who were just as messed up as she was. Every single person at Samaritan House was diagnosed with some form of severe mental illness. You couldn't even get in there without a court order.

There was no mistaking Jules was seriously mentally ill. Not anymore. That'd been up for debate at one point, but all that changed after she'd moved out of her family home. That was the first sign that anything was wrong—at least that's what most people said, but I disagreed. Every time I saw Jules—which was super rare since she quit going anywhere—she looked terrible. She wasn't coping well. Not that anyone who lost a child coped well, but I took one look at her while she was getting into her car a few weeks before she moved out, and there was no mistaking something was seriously wrong with her. She was carrying on a conversation, waving and flailing her arms around while she spoke animatedly, but there was nobody there. She was all by herself.

It would've been one thing if she'd moved out and gotten an apartment by herself, but she basically started living out of her car. It was like she left home and turned into a homeless person overnight. We didn't have homeless people in Falcon Lake, and nobody lived out of their car in the open, so everyone took notice.

Shane had to be mortified, but she didn't seem to care. You'd see her car everywhere. Slowly becoming part of the town's tapestry. There were days when all she did was drive up and down Main Street. Other days she made circles around the mall. Sometimes she parked in the ramp and sat there for days. One of her favorite spots was in the Walmart parking lot on the east side of town. She stayed there for three weeks once until the police finally had to make her move.

I heard rumors that she drove around with photo albums and all Gabe's things stacked in the car like a superhoarder, but I also heard contradictory stories that her car was empty. How she'd left with nothing and still had nothing. I didn't know which was the true version of events. There were so many rumors about her. She kept the town buzzing. Lots of people assumed she'd gotten on drugs. Heroin. Crack. Pills. It all depended on who you talked to.

Those were just rumors, if you asked me. I'd seen her on more than one occasion, and she wasn't high. She was gone, but it wasn't on drugs. I think she punished herself by staying sober so that she had to feel all of it.

She gave in to her grief, and it devoured her. She'd seemed mind-numbingly depressed before but got scary after she moved out. There was a crazy in her eyes that I'd only ever seen on TV. And she got mean. Super cruel.

Sometimes she went into these manic rants, accosting people and following them into the store. Nobody had any clue what to do about it or how to stop her. Things like that happened when you lived in the city, but they didn't happen in small rural towns on Sunday afternoons when families were rushing into the grocery store to grab something to eat so that they could be home in time for the football game after church.

She screamed at people about the unfairness of life and how she was being punished. But other times, it turned personal, and those attacks were brutal and ugly. Parents covered their children's ears and hurried them inside so they wouldn't hear the horrible insults she unleashed on people. One day she grabbed Beverly Wayne's arm on the way out of Kroger and wouldn't let go. She called her a disgusting pig, but she didn't stop there. She kept going on, screaming she was a three-chinned gossip that nobody liked and that everyone made fun of her behind her back as soon as she was gone. Beverly had gotten so upset she'd left her cart full of groceries in the parking lot.

Jules's erratic behavior hadn't stopped there. She'd taken scissors to her gorgeous red hair that flowed past the middle of her back and hacked it to pieces. She'd gotten caught going to the bathroom in the middle of the park even though there were facilities she could've used. Father Tommy had to call the police on her more than once after she became violent in the sanctuary at Saint Michael's Episcopal Church. It was one of her favorite spots. When she was quiet, they let her stay, but sometimes she got violent. She'd broken two windows with a brick. The other time she'd sliced into all the cloth Advent murals draped on the walls, and he was afraid she'd turn the knife on herself next. Shortly after that arrest, it'd seemed like she'd gotten better. She cleaned herself up. Stopped harassing people. She even showed up a few times at the coffee shop and sat outside at one of the round tables sipping her cup with an almost peaceful expression on her face. Everyone said she'd finally turned the corner.

And then she parked her car on the train tracks.

People who had lost all hope were dangerous, and she wasn't the only one. She lived in a home with other people just like her, and she'd been there long enough to make friends. Those people might help her. Those people might hurt Isaac. What if one of them was the missing link?

I turned on my heels and marched downstairs to find Detective Hawkins. Katie's package from Amazon sat untouched by the door, which meant she still wasn't back from my mom's. Mark sat aimlessly scrolling through his phone in the empty family room. I hurried into the kitchen, but Detective Hawkins wasn't there either. Only the others posted up in front of their computers and laptops. Stan gave me a nod.

"Everything okay?" he asked, noticing my frantic expression.

"I just wanted to talk to Detective Hawkins. Is he here?"

He shook his head. "Should be back in about an hour or so."

"Thanks," I said, squeezing past the table and heading to the patio door. I slid the glass wide and stepped into the backyard without bothering to grab my coat. The cold bit me, stealing my breath almost immediately. For a second, everything spun. I hadn't left the house in eight days. The prospect of any contact happening with Isaac while I was gone had kept me inside. I couldn't risk not being here if he reached out.

I shivered as I grabbed my phone from my pocket and pulled up Detective Hawkins's contact information. He'd given me his cell phone number that first night, and I hadn't used it yet, but I couldn't wait for him to get back. This was too important. He answered on the second ring.

"Detective Hawkins." His voice was a much deeper baritone over the phone.

"Hi, Detective Hawkins. It's Amber. Amber Greer," I spoke quickly like I did every time I got nervous. "I'm sure you're really busy, and I'm sorry to bother you, but I just had a few questions. I know I could've waited for you to get back, but you told me I should call whenever I wanted to, so . . ."

"No problem. Don't ever hesitate to call me. I'm here for you," he said quickly.

I let out a sigh of relief. "Can I ask how many people stay at Samaritan House with Jules?"

"There are twenty-two," he says without needing any time to think about it.

I hadn't expected there to be so many. "And all of them are mentally ill? Just like her?"

"Yes." He didn't give me more. I detected a hesitancy in his voice even over the phone.

"Have any of them committed crimes?"

"There're twenty-two people living in that house. The likelihood of one of them committing a crime in their lifetime is pretty high."

"That's not what I'm talking about, and you know it." My boldness surprised me. "Is Jules in the house with any criminals? Anyone who's been to jail?"

"You know I can't tell you who lives in that house."

"I don't want names. That's not what I'm asking." I shook my head to emphasize my point even though we were on the phone and he couldn't see me. "Is she connected to bad people? Could one of them be helping her with Isaac?"

"Anything is possible." His vagueness infuriated me. Why couldn't he be more concrete? Let me know what he was thinking? What the investigative team was doing?

"But is that what's happening? Are you looking at any of those people?" I probed, hoping he'd give me more.

"We're examining all leads." His voice sounded like my dad's when he answered the phone for the reporters and media outlets: scripted and robotic like an automated recording.

"And are there leads at Samaritan House? Other people besides Jules?" Maybe if I asked it in a different way, he'd give me a better answer.

He cleared his throat. "Amber, I understand what a difficult place you're in right now, and I'm so sorry you're going through any of this, but you're just going to have to trust me, okay?"

The silence stretched out between us until it grew uncomfortable, but I didn't know what else to say. The truth was that I didn't trust him. I wasn't sure he was doing this right, and I didn't know what to do.

NINE

AMBER GREER

"Amber, come on, please, just let me in." Mark pounded on the bathroom door, trying to keep his voice low so that everyone downstairs wouldn't overhear, but it was a little late for that after what they'd just witnessed. I pictured him on the other side of the door, leaning flat against it.

I sat on the toilet with the lid down since there was nowhere else to sit. My head was in my hands. They were still shaking. I'd finally worked up the nerve, and we'd called Katie and my mom together a few minutes ago. It went worse than I'd imagined, but not for the reasons I'd assumed it would.

"Why don't you go back to sitting on the couch? I like you better that way," I yelled at him.

"God, you're impossible, you know that? I came up here to try to help. To make things better for you even though I didn't do anything wrong."

I leapt to my feet and whipped open the door. "Didn't do anything wrong? You practically told Katie her brother was dead." I started mimicking him. "'Honey, you need to start preparing yourself for the worst.' What the hell is that?"

His chin jutted out. "It's called trying to take care of her and keep her from getting crushed."

"By telling her that her brother is going to die?"

The vein in his forehead bulged. He worked his jaw while he spoke. "Yes, because that's the truth, and despite whatever denial you've decided to bury yourself in during this, I'm sticking with the truth."

He reached out and yanked the door out of my hand, then slammed it in my face before storming off. I stumbled backward and slowly sank onto the tiled floor in front of the tub as tears spilled out of the corners of my eyes. I pulled my knees up to my chest and wrapped my arms around them. This was it. Right here. Why couples didn't survive a child's illness or death.

I didn't know how Mark and I were going to sustain this. If it was even possible. We'd been struggling for months and at each other's throats constantly about how to deal with Isaac. He favored a heavy-handed approach since things had gotten so dire and out of control, whereas I favored a lighter one. We hadn't been on the same page from the beginning. We weren't even in the same book. And now this?

I'd watched the statistics play themselves out with Jules and Shane over these past ten months. They'd been together since college and always seemed to adore each other. Not in a way that seemed fake or put on for other people, but you could see it in the way their eyes melted when they looked at each other and how their bodies softened when they were together. It was awful to see the tragedy pull them apart. They rarely looked at each other; their bodies stiffened next to each other instead of relaxing, and their smiles were forced. Even if their bodies could've hidden their demise, their eyes bore the truth, and you could hear the thousands of things unsaid between them.

I saw Shane and his girlfriend at the grocery store the other night. It was the first time I'd seen them out in public together, and I couldn't stop staring despite myself. She was a twenty-six-year-old yoga instructor named Chloe. I took one of her classes last year when she first moved to town, and everyone was raving about her. She'd had her own studio in Miami, where she made it no secret that she'd worked with celebrities. I could see why everyone was smitten with her. She had the kind of figure people liked to drink in with their eyes—a flowing perfect tan, taut strong legs, and a flat stomach while still somehow managing to have amazing curves in all the right places.

I couldn't help wondering why she'd given all that up to move to Falcon Lake and didn't trust her motives with Shane for a second. The Harts had turned into celebrities overnight, and she was seizing the moment, clearly taking advantage of the opportunity. I'd watched as her Instagram followers skyrocketed these past few months. She went from a nobody to a somebody as quick as the Harts did. Her reels with Shane got hundreds of thousands of views. She gave the whole world a sneak peek inside the greatest tragedy ever to hit our community.

Was that going to be Mark in a few months? Coupled up with some twenty-year-old who was using him for the spotlight? I didn't think he was capable of something like that, but I hadn't thought Shane was capable of it either. Grief did funny things to people.

It changed Isaac in unfathomable ways. One of the downfalls of living in a small town was that everything you went through played out publicly, so Isaac's change in behavior was on public display, just like the Harts' marriage. Isaac had never been in the spotlight before, and he hated every second of it. Suddenly kids who'd never given him the time of day, even ones that had been mean to him before, wanted to be his best friend. In the days and weeks following the accident, they were always stopping by the house, even though nobody had invited them. Isaac begged me not to let them in or make him hang out with them, but I didn't know how to tell them no. Part of me hoped it might be good for him.

"Mom, please don't make me go down there and hang out with them," he'd begged the last time they'd come by. They'd shown up at the front door five kids deep—two boys and three girls. One of the boys was the star quarterback of Falcon High. His perfectly made-up girlfriend hung from his arm like an expensive purse.

"Just go down there for a little bit. It'll be good for you," I encouraged him.

"I told you the last time they showed up that I was done sitting down there with them. I'm not doing it again." He shook his head. His jaw was set just like his dad's.

"It can't be that bad. They're just trying to be nice," I pleaded.

"No, they're not. They've never cared about me. Not even a little." He shook his head. "Those kids hate me, and I don't want to hang out with them, Mom."

"Don't be so negative. Maybe they realized how poorly they treated you before, and they're ready to behave differently."

He snorted and rolled his eyes.

"Come on, Isaac. It puts me in such an awkward position if I have to ask them to leave." That was the real reason I wanted him to go down there. I couldn't stand up to them any more than he could.

I badgered him into doing it in the same way they'd badgered themselves into the house. I'd tried telling them no when they showed up because I knew Isaac wouldn't want to see them. I'd made up some excuse about him having a headache and lying down upstairs, but the petite one that chomped gum nonstop pushed her way inside like she'd been in my house hundreds of times. The rest followed her, and once they were there, I didn't know what else to do.

I was in the kitchen cutting the vegetables to go with the roast I was making for dinner when Isaac's bloodcurdling screams ripped through the house. I dropped the knife on the cutting board and went running for him.

"GET AWAY FROM ME!" he screamed as I rushed into the living room. He stood in the corner next to the fireplace with the metal poker clenched in his right hand like a bat. His entire body shook. His eyes bulged. At first, I thought he was screaming at me, but it wasn't me. It was them. All the kids on the couch, scrambling to get their things as fast as they could. "GET OUT OF MY HOUSE!" he screamed again, even louder this time.

"We didn't even do anything," one of the girls cried, flinging a backward glance at me as they hurriedly gathered their backpacks and stuffed their phones into their pockets.

"Oh my God, he's totally losing it," someone else said underneath their breath as they made a beeline for the front door.

I followed behind them, apologizing.

"I'm so sorry," I said over and over again, but they all ignored me. Nobody turned around. Just as I shut the door behind them, the sound of glass shattering ricocheted through the entryway. I raced back into the living room. One of my expensive lamps lay in pieces on the floor. Isaac was hovering over it, the poker still in his hands. He raised his head to look at me. Angry red blotches dotted his pale face.

"I told you I didn't want to hang out with them," he said in a voice devoid of all emotion.

He'd never thrown or broken anything before in his entire life. Not even when he was a toddler and going through the terrible twos. We didn't behave that way in our house either. Mark had been as disturbed by the outburst as I was, but we didn't know what to do about it.

He withdrew even more after that and didn't want to be bothered with anyone. He spent all his time alone in his room. He barely ate. He wasn't sleeping well either. I checked on him almost every night, and his light was usually still on. I could hear him moving around in there, tapping away on his keyboard while he played games on his computer. The light from the monitor glowing underneath the door. Those were preferrable to the hours he'd spent crying in his bedroom with the door tightly shut, refusing to let anyone get near him. As horrible as those early weeks were after the accident, I was able to get through them because I kept telling myself they weren't permanent. It was just the beginning phase of the trauma, and it would change. That's what everybody else said too.

But as the weeks stretched into a month and then another month, things hadn't changed at all. Isaac had completely shut himself off from the rest of the world. We could barely get him to come out for dinner. All he did was sit in his room and play video games or lie in there in silence with the lights off for hours. I didn't know which was worse. He went days without showering. That was when we decided that we were going to have to start making him take steps back into the world again. He couldn't live in his bedroom forever. Theresa supported our decisions and helped us come up with a plan at his next session. School was the first step.

He didn't want to go. He kicked and screamed on his bed like a toddler in the throes of the worst tantrum, but we wouldn't budge. We shoved him back into his life.

Did we shove him out too quickly? Had he been right all along? It wasn't that long after his return to school that he started visiting Jules at the hospital. Had his visits followed her to Samaritan House? Despite Detective Hawkins's promises that they were exhausting every lead, I still wasn't convinced they were looking into the other residents at Samaritan House. Were they just interviewing Jules as a way to placate me?

What if Isaac had talked to other people while he was visiting her at Samaritan House like he'd done while she was in the hospital? It was certainly possible. If he wasn't afraid to talk to seriously mentally ill people in a hospital, then he probably wasn't afraid to talk to them in the real world either. What if one of them had done something to hurt him? What if she didn't have anything to do with it outside being the means of introduction? Who else was living in that group home?

I had to know, and I'd do whatever it took to find out.

CASE #72946
PATIENT: JULIET (JULES) HART

"I've noticed something . . ." Dr. Stephens lets his voice trail off in that annoying way he does, trying to get me to the edge of my seat in anticipation of the hidden insight or knowledge he has to reveal.

"What's that?" I ask, playing along to please him. Mostly because I'm starting to get bored with all this. He treats me like I'm an idiot, and I don't like being treated like an idiot.

"You don't seem very upset that Isaac's missing." He gives me his most pointed look to date. "For as close as the two of you were, it seems like you would be more worried about his whereabouts, and you don't seem the least bit concerned that they just found his clothes in a cardboard box or that he might be the next victim of a serial killer."

"What makes you think I'm not worried?" I meet his pointed stare with my own challenging one. "Because I'm not emotional? Because I'm not a big puddle of tears on the ground right now sobbing?" I stretch across the table, getting as close to him as possible. "Would you be asking me the same questions if I were a man?"

He snaps back in his chair. It's a direct hit. One he wasn't expecting. I keep going. Not giving him a chance to recover.

"Truth is, I'm worried sick about Isaac. I have been ever since I heard the news. I work really hard at not thinking about it, though, because it only makes me sad. It takes me to some dark places and, Dr. Stephens, I don't need to tell you how important it is for me to stay out of there, you know?" I bat my eyelashes at him. I'm not sure why I'm toying with him. Maybe because he doesn't think I'm smart enough to do it, and that bugs me.

"So, you are upset about Isaac?" He folds his hands on the table.

"Absolutely." I nod vigorously. "What kind of a terrible person would I be if I wasn't?"

"It just seems like you would be asking more questions about it if that were the case."

"Why?" I wrinkle my nose at him. "What kinds of questions need to be asked? We all know what happened to him."

He shrinks back. "Do we?"

Nice try, Dr. Stephens. He's going to have to work harder than that.

"We do," I say with a smile. "Same thing that happened to those other boys." I quickly erase the smile from my face. "Honestly, I just can't believe it." I shake my head. My hands twist underneath the table. "You're concerned that I'm not worried, but I think that's probably because I'm more shocked than anything else. Like, what's the likelihood of something like that happening to Isaac? The kid survives a terrible car accident where his friend dies, and then he gets kidnapped? All within the same year?" I shake my head in disbelief again. "I just feel so bad for the family. Don't you?"

"Me?" He points to himself as if there's any misunderstanding about who I'm referring to. We're the only ones in the room. "Of course I feel bad for the Greers. I feel terrible." There's no mistaking he feels slightly insulted that I might've implied he was the uncaring and disconnected one. I try not to smile.

I sit back in my chair and fold my arms across my chest. "I'm not really sure what I'm doing here. If we're both on the same page about what happened to Isaac, what is it that you think I might be able to help you with?"

He tilts his head and speaks slowly, drawing out the words for dramatic effect. "Well, we're not *entirely* sure what happened to Isaac."

"What do you mean? It's obvious, isn't it? Isaac fits the same profile as Brady and Josh: similar age, quiet and reserved, keeps to himself with just a few friends." He's studying me closely as I speak, but none of this is information you couldn't find with a decent Google search. "Then he goes missing while he's walking the dog? I mean, I hate to say it, and of course I'd never wish anything awful like that on anyone, but come on . . . it only gets worse from there. Then the phone. Now the clothes." Naked dead body discarded in a field six days later. I leave out the last part, but he's thinking it, too, just like me. All anyone's doing is hoping they can find him before then.

"Maybe it's too obvious. Too perfect." He raises his eyebrows at me, widening his eyes along with them.

"What do you mean?"

He shrugs nonchalantly and tries to act casual, but he doesn't do anything without a purpose. "Maybe someone set it up to look like the Dog Snatcher."

"Like a copycat?"

"It's possible."

"Why would anyone do that?" I have my own ideas about it, but I'm curious about his.

"There are lots of different reasons. Probably as many as there are killers, but the most obvious one is to keep the focus off themselves. There's pretty much no better way to keep the finger off yourself than pointing it at somebody else, is there?" He cocks his head to the side and raises his eyebrows at me again. I make my face a blank slate. I have years of practice. He waits a few more beats before going on. "Then, there are the copycats where all the media coverage and hype focused on the crime gives them the inspiration and the idea. Not only that—half the time, it gives them a detailed plan. Did you know there were seventy-four copycat school shootings stopped in the year following Columbine?"

"Just because it was a school shooting doesn't mean that they copied Columbine," I say with no idea why I'm defending either side.

"It does when they reference Columbine as their inspiration and their guide," he says. "But it doesn't even have to be a real-life crime for someone to mimic it. There was a guy in Georgia who learned how to dissolve a body in acid through watching *Breaking Bad*. Remember that nineties movie *Natural Born Killers*? There were at least three different couples that went on a murdering spree afterward, just like the couple in the movie. They used the same methods and everything."

This is what he's spent all his time researching? No wonder he's not any further along in figuring out what happened to Isaac.

I shake my head. "I just don't buy that sensationalizing crimes leads to people committing them. I mean, come on, no amount of media coverage about a violent crime is going to make a sane person decide to commit one. It's just not. Pretty sure people that were going to kill people were going to do it whether or not they saw it on TV or read about it online."

"There's been lots of coverage surrounding the death of the boys, and now that Isaac is missing, it's reignited all of it all over again. There's a lot of notoriety in it." The sound of people shuffling through the landing on their way to occupational therapy breaks into our conversation, and I wait until they're gone to speak.

"They must be pretty sick if they'll go to those kinds of lengths just to be famous," I say without bothering to hide my judgmental tone. I've never understood people's obsession with the limelight. People who shine from within don't need a spotlight. That's the saying stamped on the mug in my kitchen. It's always resonated with me. Still does.

"You'd be surprised. It happens all the time. Some people will do anything to get their picture in the news. To have people talk about them. Say their name." He shakes his head like he doesn't understand their motivations any more than I do.

"I guess it could be a copycat"—I shrug—"but does it really matter?" I give him a knowing look.

"Only if you're hypothesizing about the pathology of the killer."

"Is that what we're doing here? I thought we were talking about Isaac." He thinks I'm not following his steps, but I am. Every single one.

"Right. Right," he says like he's grateful for the reminder. He reaches down and grabs the report tucked inside his briefcase and pulls it out. He quickly scans the document. It's his go-to move whenever he feels the power in the room shifting away from him. "I see staff reports that you've shown tremendous progress in the last thirty days. You haven't received any disciplinary infractions or had any incidents of self-harm." He pauses, his eyes scanning the rest of the pages, and I beam. My insides and my outsides. I've worked so hard to get better. I really do deserve the recognition. "This is actually pretty impressive," he says, flipping through those case notes, and I'm wondering if it's the first time he's read them. My positive reports aren't nearly as spicy as all my other hospital records.

"I've been a good girl since I got here. I'm not going back to the hospital." Or anywhere else where my life isn't in my hands. I just want to be left alone to live my life as I please. Nobody intruding on my plans. It's been a long time since I've had any, and I don't want someone messing with them.

He scratches his chin. "What do you think helped you start getting better?"

"When you're at rock bottom, there's really no other place to go but up," I say with a laugh, but I'm only half joking. "Honestly, it was Isaac. He helped me out of my depression without even trying," I explain, hoping Dr. Stephens will understand what the others couldn't. I don't know why it's so hard for people to see that Isaac is the only one who knew what I'd been through, so we were able to connect in an unbelievably intimate way. "You don't know what being involved in a fatal accident is like unless you've been through it, and Isaac knew what it was like. During it and afterward. He got all of it."

Dr. Stephens leans over and places his hand gently on my arm. I like the way it feels. His hands are warm and soft. "I want you to know that I completely understand why you might be drawn to Isaac."

I jerk my head up. "You do?" That's the first time someone has said anything like that to me. Shane was disgusted by our relationship, and he'd let me have it when he found out.

"He's a kid, Jules. A frickin' child. What are you doing?" he screamed at me after he'd shown up unannounced and found the two of us together in my hospital room. Isaac had jumped up and ran out of the room before Shane could say a word to him.

It wasn't like I was keeping our relationship a secret. Shane just never asked. He barely even spoke to me. He didn't come to any of the family therapy groups at the hospital or Samaritan House. He didn't participate in any of my individual therapy or help with the progress goals on my treatment plan. He'd washed his hands of me and moved on with his girlfriend. I had become a big inconvenience.

But I'm not an inconvenience to Dr. Stephens. He wants to know all about me, all my secrets. I give him a timid smile. "Do you really get it?" I can't help asking him again.

Dr. Stephens reaches across the table and takes both my hands in his. "I absolutely understand why you were drawn to Isaac and why he was drawn to you." He looks deep into my eyes, and I try my best not to pull away from the intensity of his stare. It's hard giving another person a look inside your soul after you've been hurt, but I'm willing to try. He slowly pulls away and settles back into his chair. He crosses his legs again and assumes his regular therapist position. "I'm sure you already know this, but in case you've forgotten, I just want to remind you that what the two of you went through was incredibly traumatic, and people that go through traumatic events together often develop a strong bond. It's incredibly powerful."

"Maybe it was trauma bonding, or maybe it wasn't, but whatever it was—he felt it too." Our connection went beyond words, and I'd never experienced that with another person, not even my husband. I'd heard other people talk about it, but it'd never happened to me. Not until Isaac. He saw to the inside of my core in the same way that I saw him. Some days he would come and just plop himself on my bed without saying a word. He wouldn't speak the entire time he was there, and I never pushed him to say a thing. And then he'd just leave. But that was the special thing about us—we didn't need to talk. We could be together without feeling the need to fill up the space. "Things with us were okay that might not be okay with someone else. We weren't scared of the other's darkness or their intense emotions. We just got each other, or maybe it was because nothing else in the world made sense anymore. Either way, just being in each other's company was comforting."

"I'm telling you—it all makes perfect sense to me. The two of you were elevated in the community and in your families as, like, these mythical creatures that had escaped death, right? One of you represents the tragedy of every parent's greatest fear, and the other the opposite—a parent whose child was spared, the ultimate hope. And that's the thing, isn't it?" He drops his voice low. "Neither of you wanted to be alive, did you?"

TEN

AMBER GREER

I wiped the warm washcloth across my tear-streaked face and tried to pull myself together so that I could go back downstairs and face people even though I didn't want to. I was so tired of sitting in this house and doing nothing. I wished there were a way to sneak out without anyone seeing me. All I wanted was to go for a walk and to get some fresh air.

The media trucks and vans were lined up for three blocks on either side of our house. Mom said they chased her down the sidewalk every time she left and that they followed her everywhere even when she was nowhere near us—to the grocery store, at the gas station, even the doctor's office. Her house was the only other place I wanted to be. I slowly wrung out the washcloth and hung it back in its place.

I hated that Jules could be sitting somewhere right now with full knowledge of where Isaac was and what was going on with him while I was in mental torture and agony. They might even be together at this very moment. For a brief instant, the image of the two of them smiling wide at the camera with their arms wrapped around each other flashed through me—one of the pictures I'd seen on Isaac's phone the last time I'd snooped. The one I'd used after he'd initially tried to deny that they'd seen each other since the hospital. The same one I used with the supporting documentation for the restraining order to show they had a relationship.

What had she done to my boy?

I'd brought up the possibility of someone in Samaritan House working with Jules to Mark after I'd spoken about it on the phone with Detective Hawkins, and surprisingly, Mark agreed with me. He thought they should be looking into that potential connection more, too, but were they? Detective Hawkins had been gone most of the day, even though Stan said it was only going to be a few more hours when I'd asked about his whereabouts this afternoon. What had he been doing all day? Was he working on other cases he had going on while he waited on ours? The questions made me nauseous.

All this red tape and waiting were excruciating. Why couldn't the police just storm over there and search the group home? At least her room? Instead, they had to send in some specialized forensic psychologist to work with her because she wasn't mentally stable? Unstable people couldn't be trusted, and she'd already shown on more than one occasion that she could cross the line from sanity to insanity without warning. That only proved we needed to move fast.

Every second mattered, and with each one that ticked away, it felt like we were losing valuable time and opportunity to get him back. Not being able to do anything was maddening. I pulled out my phone and loaded Safari, then stared at the blank page that opened. The cursor blinked at me from the empty search bar, but I was at a loss for what to type. I'd scoured almost everything I could find on the Dog Snatcher, combed through thousands of posts on the National Center for Missing and Exploited Children, watched hours of forensic videos on YouTube, and devoured countless other research sites on anything that might remotely connect to or help Isaac. Where else could I possibly look?

I pulled up the Moore County Court website and found the court docket index, but without a name or case number, it was impossible to find out if anyone at Samaritan House had a criminal record. The only thing I knew about Samaritan House was its address, and I wasn't even supposed to know that. Nothing came up if you googled the facility. No name. No address. No contact information. I'd learned group homes were a lot like domestic violence shelters—cloaked in privacy. But I'd computed it to memory automatically when I'd seen one of the technicians writing it down last week: 256 Emory Street.

I let out a frustrated sigh.

The only thing I could do with an address was look it up on the sex offender registry. The police never said there was evidence of sexual assault on any of the boys, but you never knew what they weren't telling us. I'd plugged our address in as soon as the FBI made the official announcement that there was a serial killer stalking adolescent boys. Thankfully, there wasn't anyone on the list within two miles of us. I hadn't given it a second thought since then.

I typed in the Samaritan House address instead of mine this time. The site took forever to load, and unlike the search with my address, this one came back with two results. My heart beat faster. I clicked on the first one.

JEREMY GUNKLE: Class II Felony: Cruel and Lascivious Acts with a minor

I dropped the phone like his face would jump out of the screen and attack me. It clattered loudly on the tile. They had to have heard it downstairs, but I didn't care.

He's there. In that house with her.

I reached down and slowly picked up my phone. I forced myself to look at him even though I didn't want to. He looked like the creepy guy who used to sell tickets at the drive-in movie theater up north that we went to every summer when we visited my grandmother growing up.

"Stay away from Pete," my mother would always hiss in my ear as we got out of the car. "He'll try to peek up your skirt any chance he gets."

Sneaky Pete. That's what we called him, and Jeremy Gunkle looked just like him. Every part the pedophile. Even his name sounded like one.

Could Jules be innocent? What if she'd led Isaac right to a predator without knowing it? Was it possible Isaac had been visiting her, and Jeremy had spotted him? Where did they meet when they hung out? He'd always refused to tell me. Another one of the reasons we fought with him to put a stop to their relationship. Did they hang out in the group home together? Who else might've seen them? Been interested in Isaac? Fear balled heavy and slick in my stomach.

The investigators had to know about Jeremy. There was no way they didn't, which meant they were keeping it from us for a reason. The fact that they had to send in some specialized forensic psychologist to interview Jules and that no one else could talk to her also meant something. It had to. They couldn't just storm over there and search the group home. They had to do things a certain way and make sure everything was done by the book, but I wasn't the police or the FBI. I was just a mother, and when it all came down to it, so was Jules. What if I just went there and spoke to her mother to mother? Pleaded with her straight from the heart. Would it work? Could I get through to her? I'd never considered reaching out to her myself.

The mother that she used to be was in there somewhere, buried underneath all the fractured pain, and maybe if I could reach her in that place, she'd tell me what she'd done with my son. That's all I cared about. We could keep it a secret. No one would ever even have to know. I didn't care whether she or whoever else was punished for taking him. I didn't care if they got caught or brought to justice. All I wanted was my son back. My pulse quickened at the prospect.

I straightened up, then took a good hard look at myself in the mirror. My eyes were hollow and gaunt from days without sleep. My skin pasty and pale like I was sick. I'd never looked so weak and worn down, but none of that mattered. Not when it came to finding my son. It was time to leave the house. I rested my hands on the counter.

"You can do this," I said to myself in the mirror.

ELEVEN

AMBER GREER

My insides shook as I reached for the door of Samaritan House. It looked like a regular run-of-the-mill apartment building from the outside, with its nondescript gray siding and identical windows lining all three floors. Besides it being a little beat up, you'd never suspect that the complex housed twenty-two adults with severe mental illness. It was a specialized group home, reserved only for those who were under conservatorship by the courts or a family member. I hadn't even known places like this existed until they'd put Jules in it. Her husband had helped put her here. I'd overheard Detective Hawkins telling one of the detectives that a few days ago.

I took a deep breath and checked behind me again, making sure I wasn't being followed. It'd taken me forever to lose the news trucks. I didn't know how celebrities lived with the paparazzi following them everywhere. I couldn't stand it. I understood why Britney Spears attacked one of them with an umbrella all those years ago. Thankfully, there was nobody behind me. I'd parked the car four blocks away and walked just in case.

I turned back around and pulled on the front door. It didn't budge. It was locked tight. I scanned the entrance to see if there was a call button on either side of the glass doors listing all the different units and names, but there was only an old-fashioned intercom with one button to push. I pressed it.

"Can I help you?" a female voice called out through the speaker with only a tinge of static in the background.

"I . . . uh . . . I'm . . . ," I stammered. I hadn't thought any of this through. The adrenaline had fueled me here, but I didn't have a plan for getting inside. Only what I'd say to her once we were face to face. "I'm here to see Jules Hart." I had to think fast. There wasn't time to screw this up. "And, uh, I'm one of her old friends from college, and I thought she might be able to use an old friend right now, you know?" I tried to keep my tone light and cheerful like I was one of those people who could only have good intentions.

"I'm sorry, we don't allow visitors into the house at this time. We—"

I interrupted her. I hadn't come all this way to be told no. "I understand you have policies, and I'm so sorry that I came at an unscheduled time, but I'm literally only going to be in town for a few days, and I have to be in the cities by nine, so I won't be back this way again. Please"—I flooded my voice with desperation—"it would really mean a lot to me if you'd let me see her, and I know it would mean a lot to her too."

I waited for her response, but the intercom went dead. Just as I was going to press the button again, a woman cracked the door open and stuck her head out. She was a large-boned woman with frizzy hair who towered over me. She held the door partially open with one hand and rested her other hand on her hip. She gave me a quick once-over.

"What'd you say your name was?" she asked, peering down at me from behind the tiny wire-framed glasses perched on her nose.

"I didn't." I pointed to myself. "I'm Stella Winter," I blurted out awkwardly, giving her the name Carrie and I used to use on family trips when we were kids. Whenever we traveled, we made up fake names and told everyone we were visiting from the UK.

"I'm Ruth Ann, and I'm one of the den mothers at Samaritan House. I've been here for over twenty years, and we run a pretty tight ship around here," she explained with a serious expression. "We have a strict schedule that all the residents follow, and that includes only being allowed to see visitors during scheduled visiting hours. We can't have friends and family showing up at all hours of the day and night trying to see the residents. That's not how it works. Maybe in some houses, but not in mine."

My armpits were sweating. *Just look her in the eye. Keep looking her in the eye,* I instructed myself as I spoke. "I know, and I'm sorry. I didn't mean to disrespect the rules of the house. I just really wanted to see her. She means a lot to me, and I can't imagine she gets a lot of visitors."

Ruth Ann's face softened. "Well, even though our residents have full schedules, we make sure to include visiting hours on it because we encourage them to build and maintain social relationships. That's one of their treatment goals. It just so happens that you showed up at a time when they're in mandatory programming, but there are lots of other available hours for you to come by later if you'd like."

I swallowed, trying to think, but I couldn't gather my thoughts. "I don't know if I'll be able to do that. I wish that I could."

"Look, why don't you let me grab you the list of our visiting hours so you have it, and if you decide to stick around, then you can come back later and see her?"

"That sounds like a good idea," I said, even though there was no way I'd be back. I couldn't work up the nerve to do this a second time, and even if I did, I wasn't sure I'd get away without any media or police company.

She held up a finger. "Give me one second," she said and stepped back inside. I stuck my foot inside to keep the door from shutting behind her. The door opened to a long rectangular hallway with two doors on each side and stairs flanking each end. Ruth Ann ducked into the first door on the right. A few beats passed. I heard her rifling around. "Oh shoot," she said. "The sheets aren't on my desk. I've got to grab them from Laurie's office. Hold on."

I didn't think. I just took one glance at her office and then darted inside the apartment building, pulling the door quietly shut behind me. I hurried to the stairs at the other end and dashed up them to the second-floor landing. I had no idea where anything was, but Jules had to be here somewhere if what Ruth Ann had said about the scheduled programming was true. I would find her. I just had to be fast.

My eyes scanned the floor. It was arranged identical to downstairs. Four doors. Two on each side. How many rooms were in each apartment? Did everyone have their own room? What if Jules did? Would it be possible to stash Isaac here someplace? Had anyone looked?

My heart sped up at the thought of being in the same place as my boy. I picked the door on my right and hurried toward it just as Jules came up the stairs on the other side. She stopped midstride, halfway across the landing. Her mouth fell open. I was the last person she was expecting to see.

She was too stunned to speak, to even move. She looked like a completely different person. Her long flowing hair that she'd spent hours bragging about and just as much money making perfect was gone. It was clipped and cut short, awkwardly framing her face. And she was bigger than she'd ever been. She must've gained twenty pounds from the meds. Maybe more. Her neck swelled with double rolls.

I stepped cautiously toward her, afraid she would run if I moved too quickly. I raised my hands up in a peaceful gesture. "Please, Jules, I'm not here to cause any trouble. Just please tell me where Isaac is. I know you know where he's at, what's happening. Please tell me."

She looked around to see if anyone was watching, but we were still alone. I had to hurry. I just needed to appeal to her good, nurturing side. Mother to mother. It was in there somewhere. It had to be.

"I'm so sorry for what happened with Gabe. I am. I want you to know that." I looked at her with pleading eyes, hoping she'd see me.

Really see me. How much I loved my son. How much I knew she loved hers. "No parent should ever have to go through losing their child like you did." I clasped my hands together in front of my chest like I was praying, and part of me was. "Please don't make me lose mine. Please don't make me go through that."

"Believe me, Amber, you have no idea what it's like. Trust me. Losing a child feels just as badly as you imagine it would. No, it feels even worse. And I would never put my worst enemy through it." She looked insulted that I'd suggested she had anything to do with Isaac's disappearance.

I took a deep breath. "Please, Jules."

She raised her shoulders and shook her head slightly. "I'm sorry, Amber. I wish I could help you. I really do, but there's nothing I can do. I wish there was." She shrugged her shoulders again. "These things just happen, and there's nothing you can do about it."

I stepped closer to her, invading her space, but I didn't care. There could be cameras in this place, and I didn't want anyone to hear what I was going to say next. I dropped my voice to a whisper. "I promise you that nobody ever has to know I was here or that we had this conversation. Nobody. If you tell me where Isaac is or return him to me safely, you have my word that I will never breathe a word about it to another soul or anyone else. I—"

"What's going on upstairs?" someone yelled from below us.

I talked faster, whisper-hissing closer to her face. "Nobody ever has to know, Jules, I swear. Whatever you've done. Whatever happened. Whatever you know. It doesn't matter. I don't care. Just tell me where he is, and I'll go get him. I won't ever tell another soul, I promise. We can make up a story about what happened, and we'll tell that to the police together."

"Oh honey." Jules glanced behind me, checking to see if anyone was coming up the stairs. "Do you want me to call someone to come get you? It seems like you're having a rough time."

Her look of pity made me sick. "I'm fine. Just tell me where he is," I snapped.

She shook her head. "I wish I could help you, but I have no idea."

"Is he with Jeremy Gunkle? Can you at least tell me that? Please, Jules. Does he have Isaac?"

"Sweetie, you're really having a hard time, aren't you?" She reached out like she was going to touch me, and I jumped back. "There are lots of counselors here if you need to speak to someone. You seem a bit frazzled."

I lunged at her, getting in her face. "Where is Isaac?" I grabbed her shirt in my fist and gave her a firm jerk. "Where is he?"

"Amber, calm down." Her eyes darted around the landing. "You shouldn't be here."

"Tell. Me. Where. He. Is." I clutched her shirt in my hand and pushed her backward. My hands trembled with the urge to shake her, to grab her by the throat and slam her against the wall as hard as I could.

An elderly man popped his head out of one of the rooms, interrupting us.

"Oh my," he said, putting his hand over his mouth as soon as he saw us. He quickly darted back inside the room without saying another word. He could be calling someone. I had to hurry, but before I could say anything else, Jules jumped in.

"I'm so sorry Isaac's missing, Amber. I really am. Believe me, I know *exactly* how it feels." It wasn't what she said—it was the combination of pride and satisfaction in her eyes when she said it that put me over the edge. There was a part of her that enjoyed seeing me so upset. She was getting off on this.

That's when I lost it.

TWELVE

AMBER GREER

Detective Hawkins grabbed my arm and jerked me down the sidewalk just like I used to pull my kids out of the toy aisle when they were toddlers and throwing fits because they didn't want to leave the store. He didn't speak a word as he stomped away from Samaritan House. He pounded his way down the pavement until we reached the squad car parked alongside the street in front of the entrance. I waited for him to open the door on the passenger side, but he whipped open the back door of the car instead and pointed at the back seat.

I recoiled. "What? I—"

"Get in there," he practically growled at me in a way that left no room for arguing as a crowd of staff and residents from Samaritan House sat watching behind us from inside the building. I put my head down and slid into the back seat, instantly claustrophobic because of the wire mesh in front of me. The seat was too close to my legs. The black leather pressed against my knees. No wonder people freaked out and started kicking the windows back here.

"Can you roll the windows down, please?" I asked as he slipped into the driver's seat. He didn't say a word. It was like I hadn't even spoken. He tapped something out on his phone. It was impossible to see what he was typing or the expression on his face when I was staring at his back. "You're taking me to my car, right?"

He continued ignoring me and pulled the car away from the sidewalk. He drove slowly, making his way down Marshall Street.

"I'm parked on Ninth," I said in plenty of time for him to turn, but he drove right past the street when we reached it. Panic thrummed through me. Where were we going? Was I actually in trouble? It wasn't illegal to confront Jules like that, was it? It couldn't be. I wiped my sweaty palms on my jeans and forced myself to calm down. Leftover adrenaline pounded in my temples, making my head hurt.

Detective Hawkins drove for a few more blocks before he finally spoke. "Don't you ever do something like that again, do you hear me?"

I wanted to be sorry, but I just wasn't. I would do whatever it took to find my son.

"I'm sorry," I lied. "I won't go there again."

"What possessed you to go there in the first place?" His voice was laced with shock and disbelief like it had never actually occurred to him that I would do something like that. I'd surprised myself too. I'd never done anything like it in my entire life. Certainly never gotten physically aggressive with anyone, not even Carrie, and we'd gotten into some horrible fights growing up.

"I was just sitting upstairs in the bathroom after Mark and I had finished arguing." There was no use hiding our constant fighting. It wasn't like it was a secret. We lived in a house full of strangers who heard everything. "And I just felt compelled to confront her." I shook my head. "No, not confront her. That's not what I wanted to do. Not at first. I wanted to speak with her mother to mother, you know? I thought that if I connected with her like another mother, and she saw my face, then she wouldn't be able to say no to me. She'd confess to me on the spot." I hadn't meant to get so upset with her. I'd had no idea that was going to happen, but I'd just snapped when she looked so smug.

"Believe it or not, my team and I have discussed the possibility of having you do something just like that with Jules at some point depending on how things went with her. We talked about arranging a meeting where the two of you could sit down together, and you could connect with her over being parents."

"What?" I couldn't believe it. They'd never said anything to me about meeting or talking to Jules, which shouldn't have been surprising, since they were never direct and straightforward when it came to her or where they stood with her involvement in the case. That's why it was so frustrating and infuriating. One of the major reasons I'd just done what I did was because they didn't seem to be taking it seriously enough or have any sense of urgency about things with her.

He took a left and then pulled up alongside the curb on the next block. He turned to look back at me. The anger had left his eyes. Annoyance and irritation had taken its place. "Yes, Amber, we're always strategizing different ways that we can get information out of her, and you may have been one of our options given your connection over being moms. Nobody understands a mother like another mom."

"So, you do think she took Isaac?"

"It's unlikely, but it's not outside the realm of possibility," he admitted.

"See! I knew I was right!" I jumped in my seat excitedly, forgetting I was in such a tight space and almost hitting my head on the top of the car's ceiling, with Detective Hawkins admitting what I'd been pushing for all along. What Mark could never see. "And what about Jeremy Gunkle? Do you think he's involved? Could he be helping her?"

"Jeremy Gunkle." He laughed and smacked the dashboard. "Of course that's why you went there tonight. I should've known." He shook his head.

He'd never laughed at me before. Dismissed me or purposefully evaded answering my questions, but he'd never laughed. I didn't like it.

"Jeremy Gunkle is a class-two registered sex offender, and we know all about him since we've looked into every single sex offender in southern Minnesota during this investigation. That's how wide our scope is, so yes, Jeremy Gunkle was definitely looked into, but guess what?" He paused, building up the suspense. "He was crossed off our list of potential suspects almost immediately." Another dramatic pause so he could let his words really settle into me. "Jeremy Gunkle works second shift as a parking attendant at the Marriott in Minneapolis. He was there the entire night Isaac went missing. Clocked in and out, and he's on camera. Doesn't get any more rock solid than that." He finally looks at me in the rearview mirror. His eyes are angry and insulted. "Come on, Amber. Give us more credit than that."

"I didn't know," I mumbled, feeling like I had when I was a child after a harsh scolding.

"And as far as Jules goes? I'm not sure what gave you the impression that we weren't considering her as a potential person of interest in this case. We've had Dr. Stephens with her for three days now. Do you know how much that's draining the resources for this case? But we're shoveling it out because we think it's a good enough reason to do so. And guess what you did today?" The excitement drained from my body as quick as it'd come, due to the change of tone in his voice. "You spooked Jules. You showed her our cards. Up until this point, we've been approaching things a certain way—showing up like her allies, building her trust, making her think we respect her and understand her, never approaching her like she's a suspect. That's been the most important part. It's probably the reason we've gotten as far as we have with her, but you might've just wrecked all that."

All my angry words quickly flashed through me. The way I'd waved my fist in her face as I shouted that I knew she took Isaac and the cops did too. That it was only a matter of time before they found out everything about her. How I'd make sure she got the harshest punishment.

Detective Hawkins had arrived within seconds of me going at Jules. He'd come up the stairs right as Ruth Ann was pulling me off her. Another staff member had stepped away to call Detective Hawkins the moment I'd shown up on the doorstep asking to speak with Jules.

"You might've just jeopardized our investigation. Thrown away everything we've worked so hard for. I know you think you know what you're doing in all this, but let me set you straight—you have no idea what you're dealing with. Stop trying to do my job for me, understand?" He locked eyes with me in the rearview mirror.

"Why didn't you tell me all that before? It would've made me feel so much better to know that you were actually taking me seriously. Hell, that you were looking at her that seriously. That's all I wanted." It had seemed like he was on Mark's side. Not that there were actual sides, but there was no way to avoid feeling like that when you had opposing viewpoints.

He cracked the window at the light, and for the first time since we'd gotten inside, I could get a good breath of air in my lungs. Some of the tension released in my back, and I didn't feel like I was going to throw up anymore.

"I've been honest with you since day one that we are exploring every lead possible when it comes to Isaac's case. I shouldn't have to say anything more than that because I mean what I say, and I say what I mean. That's just the kind of guy that I am." He hadn't taken his eyes off me. "And look, I'm going to be honest with you and let you know that we don't tell you everything. Only what you need to know. And for this very reason. Parents are too emotional. They can't detach enough to think straight, and they're too close to the situation. Anything can set them off"—he paused and gave me a pointed look—"and we can't risk the investigation."

I hung my head in shame. How badly had I screwed things up? Did she really not think they were looking at her as a person of interest in

Isaac's disappearance? She had to know that's one of the main reasons they were talking to her, right? She couldn't be that delusional, could she?

"I'm sorry," I said again, except this time I was apologizing for real.

"This is all I do"—he motioned to the squad car like it was his office—"and I do it well. I'm not trying to brag, but that's the truth. They called me down to Falcon Lake because I'm one of the best at finding missing kids, so that's why I'm the one in charge and you're not. I'm just letting you know how things are done so we're clear about how things are going to be moving forward."

I nodded in agreement. At least he wasn't mad at me anymore. Did Mark know what I'd done? What was he going to say about it? "I didn't think any of it through. I just want to find him and bring him home."

"Parents lead with their hearts. They can't help it. That's how it is in every single investigation, and believe me, every single parent thinks they'll be the one to solve the case and that they'll be able to be objective without letting their emotions get involved. They all think that. I'm sure you do, too, but let me set you straight. It's impossible to do, so don't even try. You're too close to this thing. You can't see clearly when you're looking through broken pieces."

I nodded again.

"Good." He gave me a clipped nod back. "You can't do anything like that ever again, do you understand me?"

"Yes, I do." I took another deep breath. No matter what I promised, I was going to do whatever it took to find Isaac.

CASE #72946

PATIENT: JULIET (JULES) HART

"I heard Amber showed up here last night," Dr. Stephens says, not wasting any time getting started on our session. He didn't bring me any coffee this morning, and I'm bummed. Did he take it away as punishment? That's mean. You can't bring a girl a cup of coffee one day and not bring her one the next. This isn't the best way for us to start our day.

Day four. That's how long we've been at this. It feels like forty. Is it ever going to end?

"She did," I say, not freely offering up any more information than that, knowing that it will bug him, but I'm so over all this. Nobody's going to find Isaac this way.

"How'd that go?" He spares the "can you tell me more about that" and gets right down to what he wants to know. I wish he'd do more of that and skip all the unnecessary rapport building and trying to be nonjudgmental and supportive no matter what. That's not what we do in our time together anymore because we're long past pretending this is any kind of regular client-patient relationship.

"It was pretty weird seeing as she attacked me, and she's the one who has a restraining order on me." After the police left last night, Ruth Ann told me that Amber had snuck into the building when she wasn't looking. She'd seemed so shocked that Amber had been able to do it, but I'm not. It's easy to get people into the house undetected. People do it all the time. Chelsea and the woman across the hallway are always sneaking their boyfriends in on the weekends. "She totally freaked out on me. Like big-time freak-out. Came at me like she wanted to choke me and everything. For a second, I thought she was going to throw me down the stairs." I give him a big grin. "Afterward, all the clients that were around to see it kept asking me who the woman was, and when I told them, all they did was laugh and be like, 'I think you might need to get a restraining order on her.' It was so funny."

He laughs, too, just like they all did. The mood in the room instantly brightens. So does my heart. "You don't talk about the restraining order much," he says, still smiling.

I flick my hand at him and give him a coy look. "Who wants to talk about a silly thing like a restraining order?"

His eyes twinkle. Is he flirting with me? "Um, hello? Have you just met me? I thought we were better friends than that." He motions back and forth between us.

That was flirting. He is definitely flirting. "There's really not much to tell. Amber filed a restraining order against me because she didn't understand my relationship with Isaac."

He tilts his head to the side. "I think it was a little bit more than that, don't you think?"

"Whatever do you mean?" I tilt my head right back.

"Did it have something to do with the hair?"

I giggled. "You know about the hair? Is that in the report?"

"Yes to both." He smiles back. If this is the way he wants to get his information, then I'll play along because I kind of like it. Plus, we're finally getting to the good stuff. It's about time.

"The hair." I can't help but smile, taking in a deep cleansing breath and letting it out slowly. My therapist would be so proud of me. My real therapist. The one I see every Tuesday and Thursday whether I want to or not. Not Dr. Stephens. "That's something you definitely wouldn't understand."

He smiles. That smile. So cute. There's the tiniest dimple in the right cheek. I'm a sucker for dimples. Always have been.

"I don't know about you, but I tend to think I've been doing pretty good so far understanding what some of the other psychologists you've seen haven't been able to. Now, I could be wrong, and I have no problem admitting I'm wrong when I am, but"—he nods his head confidently—"I think I'm right. What do you think?"

I'm not sure he understands like he thinks he does, but he's done the best job listening and not trying to fix me. He doesn't even look at me like I'm broken. He makes me feel like I'm a real person.

"You've done a decent job," I say, smiling back at him wide.

He doesn't try to hide that he's pleased.

"Do you believe in God?" I ask next.

He balks. "I uh . . . I hadn't expected that question . . . I can't remember the last time someone asked me that. I just, I don't know," he stammers, trying to figure out how to answer something like that from a therapist's perspective.

I laugh at him playfully. "It's okay. I'm not trying to convert you to any kind of weird religion or anything. I'm not even religious myself. Never have been. I wasn't a person into any of the spiritual stuff, so there's no right or wrong answer to the question. This isn't a test. It's just easier to understand if you do."

My parents never even took me to church growing up. I guess that's why they always say that you never know how you'll react in a situation until you're in it, even if you think you do. I wouldn't have understood such a profound soul connection with someone else, especially someone so young, if it hadn't happened to me.

"There are all kinds of different love, and people always act like romantic love is the greatest love of all, like that's the one you should strive for above all the others. We're constantly bombarded with the idea that you've lost out on the best part of life if you haven't achieved great romantic love by the end of it. I always believed that fairy tale too." I let out another laugh. This one's bitter. It leaves a dirty taste in my mouth. "I thought I had that—the ultimate fairy-tale life. I'd achieved what I'd dreamed of since I was a little girl. But I was wrong." I was wrong about a lot of things. "Romantic love might actually be the cheapest version of love."

I give him a second to digest what I've said before going on. "I would never hurt Isaac. He was my heart living and breathing outside of me, but not in the same way as Gabe. Gabe was my son, so that went without saying, but Isaac and I have been together before. There is a familiarity and a comfortability in the way our spirits connect at a deep soul level that couldn't happen if we hadn't already traveled a million lifetimes together. And the reason I'm not bothered about Isaac being missing or possibly hurt somewhere is because I know that no matter where he is or what's happening to him, even if he's dead, it doesn't matter. I will see him again. Not in this lifetime, but in the next and in the next one after that. It's how it is with us. We'll find each other. We always do." Just the thought of it brings me so much peace. It's why I'm not worried. Not like everyone else.

"It sounds like you are trying to tell me that you developed strong feelings for Isaac?" He tries to reflect back what I've said, but he's missing the point.

"I'm trying to tell you that we didn't have to develop anything. The feelings and the connection were already there."

He raises his eyebrows. "I'm sorry if I'm having a hard time following all of this, but I am. The two of you had this deep soul connection?"

I nod and let my joy out. It feels good not having to hide or hold anything inside.

"The part that's difficult to wrap my brain around is why you didn't experience that connection before. You said yourself that you'd known Isaac since he was a baby. Wouldn't you have felt the connection then?"

I shrug. "I'm new to all this. I don't know how all these cosmic things work, and I don't expect you or anyone else to either. I don't think we can understand them in a linear or logical fashion like we do most things. There wasn't any connection between Isaac and me previously. But that night on the lake woke us up to each other. That's when we remembered."

The force drawing me toward him had been incredibly powerful from his very first visit in the hospital. Just this strong gravitational pull. It was almost hypnotic. I've never experienced anything like it in my life. I doubt I ever will again. You only have one soul mate.

Dr. Stephens doesn't look convinced. "But the two of you didn't start your relationship until after you met at the hospital, right? Isn't that what you told me? You said you hadn't seen him since the funeral."

"Yes, I hadn't seen him since the funeral." He's starting to get irritating. This is why I don't bother explaining how it was with us. Nobody understands. Sometimes Isaac couldn't even wrap his brain around the magnitude of it.

"But why not? If that night on the lake is what woke the two of you up together, then why wait to start spending time together until months down the line? Why wouldn't you hang out together right away?"

"Because of Gabe." Is he stupid?

"I don't understand." He might be if he still doesn't get it.

"Isaac might've been my light, but it didn't change the fact that I was grieving. I plunged into the darkness afterward, and you can't see anything when you're covered in pitch black. That's what it was like in the months following the accident." I already told him that. At our very first meeting when he asked me about Gabe. I'd explained how everything got turned off, and nothing else mattered, or it was insignificant. I was unreachable. I would've died there in that pit. Until Isaac.

"He shone the light, and it penetrated my darkness." The realization dawns on me as the words fall into the room for us to dissect that that's the reason I could never connect with Shane after the accident.

He couldn't get into my darkness. He was always outside it. From the very beginning. I was in my tailspin, and he was in his, but we were never in it together.

"Can we get back to the hair? We're going to break soon, and I don't want to forget about it. It's a really important piece." It's an abrupt shift and definitely not the smoothest transition. We must be running out of time.

"Well, first of all, it was for Isaac." I motion to his briefcase. He carries it with him every time he comes but never sets it on the table. It stays next to him, and he grabs the stuff he wants out of it as we go along. "I've read that report in there too."

He looks surprised. "You have?"

"The restraining order one? Yeah, I have. Why wouldn't I read the report, especially when it's about me?"

"I just thought . . . I don't know . . . it might be hard to get a copy . . . ," he offers weakly.

I shake my head. "It wasn't hard." Patients are always entitled to any kind of reports written about them. All you have to do is ask. "I thought it was really interesting to read what Amber thought of me. All of this is because of her, you know."

"All of what?"

I motioned back and forth between us. "You. Me. This."

"I can see how you might think that, but Amber isn't in charge of this investigation. The Falcon Lake Police Department and the FBI are the ones calling the shots." A pinched expression takes over his face. He's trying to hide his annoyance. "The hair?"

"Oh yeah, right. The hair." He's not letting that one go, is he? Are they trying to match my hair with something? "I knew Isaac would know what it meant since he's the one who told me about it in the first place. How hair symbolizes a person's soul, so giving someone your hair is like giving someone a piece of your soul. It's a beautiful symbolic gesture and one of the reasons witches use it in their spells.

Some people also offer it as a symbol of putting your protection and care around someone." I lay my hands on the table. At least this part is easy to explain to him. "It's really simple. I sent it to him because I wanted him to know that I was thinking about him and I was there for him no matter what."

"That seems nice, but didn't you also send it to him at a time when they'd asked you not to have any contact with Isaac?" He changes his voice to quote from the report. I swear he's memorized the entire thing. *"The hair felt threatening and caused us to worry about our safety."* He pauses at the end to give me a chance to respond.

I snort. This is all so ridiculous. Overblown and exaggerated by people who've probably never felt or experienced real love.

"The Greers didn't really care about the hair. They made it into a much bigger deal than what it was, like they did with everything when it came to my relationship with Isaac. The truth is that they were just really freaked out by our relationship, and they didn't want us spending any more time together. They—"

He cuts in. "Why do you think they were so bothered by it?"

"Really?" I roll my eyes at him. "Of course I know why they were bothered by our relationship. For the same reason I'd be bothered if Gabe was in a relationship with a forty-one-year-old woman." He nods satisfactorily like he's relieved I agree with him and am able to see things that way, but I've never had a problem understanding why our relationship makes people uncomfortable, especially his mother. I just had a problem with her keeping us away from each other. She didn't know the implications of her actions. "Once Amber found out how much time we were spending together and how close we were, she totally lost it and forbade us to have any contact. She took him away and isolated him inside the house. That's when she got into his head." I was gutted all over again when Isaac was suddenly jerked away from me out of the blue. Neither of us were prepared for it, and it left both of us reeling. I could tell by how his texts spiraled, and then they just stopped. "It wasn't just that we weren't allowed to see each other—she didn't allow any contact whatsoever. I wouldn't have sent the hair if I had any other way of communicating with him."

"I'm still not sure I'm following what the hair was actually for. Why that's what you chose to send him. Flowers couldn't have sufficed?" he jokes, and I appreciate it, even though it doesn't let me off the hook with his question.

"I wanted him to know that he wasn't alone. That I was still there and our bond was still solid. I had promised him at the hospital that I would be here for him in this life no matter what, and he needed to know I wasn't breaking that promise. True love is forever."

And I still mean it. My promise was as true that day as it is today.

THIRTEEN

AMBER GREER

I lay in bed staring at the ceiling. Mark had gone downstairs with Katie hours ago, but I couldn't bring myself to get up and face another day just yet. I was still upset from my confrontation with Jules and the discussion with Detective Hawkins afterward. I'd expected him to follow me home last night, but he hadn't. He must have gone down to the station instead.

What was Jules doing at this exact minute? What had she done when Detective Hawkins pulled me off her and dragged me out of the building? Had she run downstairs and found a way to call Isaac? Was it possible she was hiding him somewhere in that apartment? Was there a basement? Had anyone checked?

If I'd been able to sneak in there that easily, then other people could too. The only reason the staff member was suspicious or even knew me was because my face had been plastered all over the news. If I hadn't been positioned dead center in the middle of the story captivating the entire nation, she wouldn't have even noticed who I was or given it a second thought. She probably would've just let me inside.

What was Jules planning on doing with him? No matter how delusional she was, I still didn't think she'd hurt him. She was more likely to keep him locked up in the basement or in a closet like he was some sick pet than take away his life. She couldn't handle not having any contact with him for a few hours and lost it completely when he broke off everything. Killing him would be punishing herself, but even though she might not kill him, it didn't mean she wouldn't kidnap him and go to any lengths to keep him. She was convinced that she and Isaac were in this incredible, almost mythical relationship with each other because of what they'd been through together. It completely freaked Isaac out. He said he only talked to her because he felt sorry for her, and in the beginning, I thought it was really sweet. That was before they started spending so much time together outside the hospital. Nothing about that was normal.

She'd wormed herself into his head and tangled her messed-up logic in his thoughts. The fury rushed through me again just like it had when she was standing in front of me on the landing. She needed to leave him alone. How many times had I thought that?

Too many.

Guilt crept in like a slow fog. I'd known their relationship was creepy from the very beginning. How he went to visit her when she was at the hospital after her nearly fatal accident on the train tracks. He said he felt sorry for her and that he read her books to help pass the time and distract her from her terrible headaches. I thought it started out as innocently as he said it did, and there was no denying that it made him feel better. He smiled on the days that he went to visit her, and that smile was enough for me to shove any other misgivings I might've had about it aside. Besides, it wasn't just about her.

He started meeting other patients, too, and under normal circumstances, I would've been worried about my fifteen-year-old boy making friends at the state hospital, but our world was so far beyond anything that I'd ever considered normal that I didn't bother putting a stop to it. So he read books to Jules, and I'm sure they had conversations too. But he also played chess with Donald Higgins at the end of the hallway every Saturday morning. Donald was a veteran who had severe PTSD coupled with a nasty traumatic brain injury left over from the accident that had given him the PTSD to begin with. He'd been the only survivor out of four on an ATV that had gone over a land mine in Iraq. Isaac connected with him in a way he wasn't able to connect with anyone else, and it was because they shared the same survivor guilt.

All I cared about at the time was that Isaac was finally starting to leave his room. And yes, it was weird, but for a few minutes every day, he was out in the sun and breathing fresh air. He spent time with real people. Even if they were mentally disturbed ones, at least they were real. More and more, he interacted only with the people he played video games with, and most of them were probably forty-year-old men still living with their moms. At least he was helping people by giving them something to look forward to in their day.

That's what I told Mark. I pitched his hospital visits like messed-up volunteer work that would look good on his college applications. We never would've known about it if the school hadn't called and busted him.

"Hi, Mrs. Greer, this is Beth calling from Falcon Lake High School, and I just wanted to check in with you about Isaac's absences," the guidance counselor had said after we'd given our customary hellos and made comments about the weather.

"His absences?"

"His absences," she said again, implying that I should obviously know what she was talking about.

"I'm sorry, it's been a really busy week, and I'm not sure what you're referring to." Isaac was supposed to have been at school every day from 8:15 a.m. until 3:45 p.m. As far as I knew, he had been.

"He's been signing himself out for the last two periods most days this week. The sign-out sheet says you pick him up and that he goes home. I just want to make sure he's going home." Mark and I had had numerous discussions with the principal and guidance counselor before sending Isaac back to school. We'd stressed that they should alert us if there were any changes in his behavior or anything we needed to know about. I appreciated her doing her job and following through on what we'd agreed on.

"Yes, he comes home," I said, knowing full well he was at school for pickup every day at 3:45 like he'd been there the entire time.

"And why haven't you notified us?" There was a hint of annoyance in her voice. I couldn't blame her. I was the one who'd said there needed to be open lines of communication about everything happening with Isaac and that I wanted us to check in if anything changed or was out of the ordinary. Skipping the last two periods certainly qualified under the rules I'd established when he'd first gone back to school.

"Honestly, I was hoping that it was just going to be temporary and within a few more days, he'd be able to work it out. If it looked like it was going to become permanent, I would've told you."

She was irked. I could tell, but it didn't faze me. I was happy, which was definitely the wrong parental response to have when you found out your teenage son had been skipping school, but how could I not be? Not because of the missing school, but for the first time since the accident, Isaac had done something completely age appropriate. He'd acted like a regular teenager.

Mark wasn't nearly as pleased or excited about the idea as I was when he found out Isaac had been skipping school.

"I can't believe you lied to the school about it," he said that night after he'd gotten home from work and I'd filled him in on all the details.

I shrugged. "I don't know, I just did. The lie popped out of my mouth without me even thinking about it." I hadn't lied to cover up for him. The agreement had simply rolled off my tongue without me thinking. "Where do you think he's going?" I asked, still thrilled over it even though I was trying to pretend like I wasn't. Maybe he had a girlfriend. That would do it. His first girlfriend would definitely pull him out of the dark hole he'd buried himself in.

It never occurred to me that he'd been going anywhere sinister.

Mark was the one who concocted the plan to figure out where Isaac was going and what he was doing when he left school early. Mark liked to put all the blame and responsibility on me for how things turned out with Isaac, but he'd been plenty involved in all this too.

"Let's not tell him that we know he's skipping school," he said the next morning over breakfast. We were still trying to figure out how we'd approach him and what we'd do depending on his response afterward.

"That seems a bit dishonest," I pointed out. I wanted to throw it in his face that he'd spent the first part of our conversation last night berating me about lying to the school, but not telling Isaac about the phone call with the school and that we knew he was lying to us seemed like more of the same—lying. Once again, he was mad at me for the exact same things he was doing. How did he not see what a hypocrite he was?

Nonetheless, I agreed not to say anything to Isaac when I picked him up from school that afternoon, and I did everything to act normal, but it was hard. I couldn't stop sneaking glances at him out of the corner of my eye while I drove. Nothing about him looked any different. He dragged himself into the passenger seat and plopped himself down like he always did. After a quick mumbled hello, he pulled his hoodie over his head, popped in his AirPods, and listened to his music while staring out the window. He'd never been one to talk about things when you picked him up from school, and adolescence had pretty much stolen away any chance of that ever happening.

I was quiet and agreeable. Just like I was when Mark told me about his plan that night. About how we needed to start stalking our fifteen-year-old. It started with him sneaking into Isaac's room and turning on location services on his phone. He was always turning it off so we couldn't track him on his phone. It was one of the things we found over and over again when we checked our kids' phones. They liked disabling the feature so we couldn't find them. They'd both been grounded for it more than once.

Mark spent the next two days monitoring Isaac's activity like he was training to be a private investigator. He tracked him everywhere. And it was the most boring trail you'd ever do because Isaac didn't do anything or go anywhere except home and school every day. Not until the following Tuesday. That's when his spot on the Life360 app started moving. It moved out of the high school down to Main Street and across Fifth Avenue, where it stopped for seven minutes. Seven long minutes until he started moving again. By bus? Uber? There was no way to tell.

Mark had been in the middle of an important meeting when he'd gotten the alert about Isaac's activity, and he'd left right in the middle to see where he was going. He said he couldn't focus on anything else. Isaac arrived at the state hospital fourteen minutes later, where he stayed for an hour. He followed the same path back to school, arriving to the pickup lane at school at exactly the right time for me to scoop him up.

"I'm not going to work tomorrow afternoon. I cleared my entire schedule, so I'm free. I'm leaving at lunch, and then I'm heading to the school. I'm going to follow him there. Watch everything that he does and then I'm going to see what he's doing inside the hospital." That's what he declared that night like there was no room for disagreement, with a look of pure determination in his expression, so I didn't bother arguing. Besides, I wanted to know what Isaac was up to too.

There was only one thing Isaac could've possibly been doing at the state hospital. It only housed mentally ill patients, and we knew only one patient who was there. But a parent's denial was a powerful force, maybe one of the strongest in the universe, and neither of us could admit what might be happening.

And it was.

"I walked with him all the way in," Mark explained to me after he'd got home from their excursion. He'd given Katie some lame excuse about needing to talk to me about a private family matter upstairs and told her she was on her own for dinner.

"How did he not see you?"

"He was so wrapped up in himself that he didn't even notice me. Besides, I put on a hat and had it real low," he said like that was a good disguise, but all Isaac would've had to do was take one look around him, and he would've spotted Mark. Mark was lucky that Isaac hadn't. "I just hung back and watched. He went all the way up to the seventh floor. I didn't get on the elevator, but I watched what he pushed and where it went. I took the next one up, and sure enough, there he was in the waiting room. I watched him walk right up to the receptionist and introduce himself as someone named Carl. He said, 'I'm here to see my aunt Jules.'"

We should've kept him away from her. Stopped it right then and there, but Isaac had shown the first signs of life in months, and neither of us wanted to stop it. So we didn't say anything. We didn't tell him we knew he was skipping school, and we didn't tell him we knew where he was going and who he was seeing when he was there.

I did, however, call his guidance counselor back at the school. She was happy to hear from me.

"Oh, and I just wanted to let you know that Isaac is going to keep coming home after sixth period when he needs to. Right now, that's about all he can handle," I said.

"That's totally fine. I completely understand. We don't want to push him too hard."

"Exactly," I'd said. "Thanks for being so understanding."

The same feeling that I'd had that day after I hung up the phone washed over me as I listened to the sounds of the media vans and news trucks pulling up at the end of the street. I didn't have to look out the window to know they were all pushing, prodding, and juggling for space. It was the same competition every day—finding the perfect spot so they could snap my picture the moment I walked out the front door. It didn't matter what picture they got, though; the tagline for the article would be the same. They'd call us innocent victims. They always did in some way:

Another innocent family falls victim to the Dog Snatcher.

The latest innocent victims of the Dog Snatcher.

If this innocent family isn't safe, nobody is.

We might be victims, but we weren't innocent.

CASE #72946

PATIENT: JULIET (JULES) HART

"So, what do you think? Am I crazy, Doc?" I ask after I've finished answering his questions about Isaac's and my relationship. I gave him as much as he's going to get from me.

"Do *you* think you're crazy?" he asks, immediately grabbing the nugget from the air and holding on to it like he discovered precious gold.

"Do you?" I lobby the question back to him. I'm not letting go of this one.

"I think grief makes people do crazy things."

I'm not going to argue with him there. I've done lots of insane things. It happens almost automatically when you've got nothing to lose. There's an incredible freedom in having nothing left to lose. And it's really hard to be afraid of anything when the worst thing has already happened to you.

"Have you seen my scans?" Of course he has. I just want to see if he'll tell me the truth. Nobody likes to talk to me about what's on them. They hide all that like it's not affecting the entire way they treat me or their case conceptualization.

"The ones from the neurologist?" he asks, feigning innocence.

"Those are pretty much the only ones that I've got." I can't keep the sassiness out of my tone. My former life had no reason for a neurologist. Now I've got two, and a psychiatrist to go along with all my different therapists. Ironic how you can spend your entire profession in mental health but never know anything about it. I didn't see clients who had experienced trauma at this level or were this messed up. You couldn't pay me enough money to do the kind of work Dr. Stephens does. I worked with a very different clientele. My patients were people who were going through painful divorces, ones that had lost their jobs and were depressed, and ordinary, everyday anxiety disorders. I was in light mental health before. This is the real deal, and I'm in the thick of it with no idea how to get out.

"Did you want to talk about them?" Dr. Stephens asks after a few seconds pass and I don't say anything more.

"I wouldn't have brought them up if I didn't," I blurt without thinking. I quickly cover my mouth. "Sorry, I didn't mean to be rude."

"No worries," he says. "It's been a long day." He breathes slowly in through his nose and lets it out through his mouth, watching me like he expects me to follow suit. Normally I would, but not today. Taking deep breaths only makes me feel like I don't have enough air, and then I get scared. "I'm just interested in why you want to talk about those."

"It seems pretty important, don't you think? I mean, that's what they blame all my feelings about Isaac on." I lock eyes with his. I'm not ashamed of my feelings or my behavior.

"The hypersexuality from traumatic brain injury?" he asks, slipping into doctor mode and inserting the clinical language so he doesn't insult me and it's easier to talk about. That's sweet of him.

"That's what the doctors call it anyway, but I'm not hypersexual, and I'm not super sold on the idea that I have a traumatic brain injury either." I don't know how many times and in how many different ways that I have to tell them that my relationship with Isaac wasn't sexual. Yes, we touched. Physical contact was part of our relationship, but not like that. What we shared wasn't sexual. It was beautiful. Perfect. Pure. Transcendent.

He reaches across the table and takes my hand in his. "I just want you to know that hypersexuality following brain injury is extremely common even though it's something that we don't often go around talking about or think of as one of the consequences of those types of injuries. Damage like you have on the orbital parts of your frontal lobe almost always result in some type of sexualized feelings and an uncontrollable urge to act on those feelings." His voice softens. "You don't have to be ashamed."

I shake my head and pull my hand out from underneath his. "I'm not. There's nothing wrong with me." That's why I want to know if he's reviewed the scans. I want a second opinion.

"You didn't get knocked out during the crash?"

I shrug. "Did I hit my head in the accident? Pass out from fear? Drown? Who knows?" I shrug again.

All my hospital MRIs showed I got knocked out—either from impact or terror. Nobody knows, and I can't remember. The last thing I remember is sailing through the air. The acute and penetrating awareness of what was about to happen. The powerlessness to stop it. And then nothing.

Nothing until I woke up in the darkness feeling like I was being buried alive by the water. It was so sinking and heavy. This massive pressure pushing me down. Sluggish and slow. I made it up to the surface once, but it didn't do my brain any favors losing consciousness again when I went back in for Gabe. According to Isaac, I was gone for over a minute, so that's why he dove back in for me. He said it took forever to find me. Who knows how long I was really down there, though. Time was too warped in those moments to have any base in reality.

The doctors say the minutes spent without oxygen underwater might've damaged my brain too. It only takes three minutes without air for brain damage to occur. Four minutes until it's permanent. That's how they think of me now: permanently brain damaged.

The doctors say those minutes are responsible for the grayed-out areas on my frontal cortex. It's that damage that they blame all my disturbing behaviors on. The reason why I've rubbed myself raw and got caught with my hands down my pants at the park. It was only that one time, and I was asleep, but nobody sees it that way. Lack of impulse control is what they say, like that explains my compulsions. They give each other knowing looks when they think I'm not watching. They speak to my parents—especially my mom, since she's in charge of my conservatorship—like I'm not sitting right there in the same room with them. As if I'm a child again, except I don't feel young, and my parents have never looked so old. I don't see them as elderly or frail, but that's exactly the way they look now. All this loss and uncertainty have taken a toll on them.

Some of the other people at Samaritan House are really angry with their parents or loved ones for putting them here and controlling their every move. I could be mad at my mom, but I'm not. I get why she did the conservatorship, and she'll keep doing whatever the doctors tell her to do because she's terrified of losing me. And trust me, I get it. Losing a child is hell.

"Seriously, though, no matter what has happened or not happened to your brain, I think you're incredibly strong," Dr. Stephens says, interrupting my thoughts and bringing me back to the present moment like he always does.

I snort. "It's not being strong when you don't have any other choice. It's not like you can say, 'No thank you. I don't want to do this anymore.'"

"That's not necessarily true. The level of resiliency that you've demonstrated is astounding. You should take a moment and just really let that sink in," he says. "I've never met anyone who has escaped death twice. That's quite a feat." He beams proudly at me, but I didn't have anything to do with that. "I can't imagine how it must've felt waking up after you'd beat death a second time."

Has he not been listening to anything I've said these past four days? I frown at him. "You think I was happy when I woke up? Thankful that some divine force in the universe had determined I deserved another chance on this earth? That as it turns out, we're on a cosmic clock that we can do relatively little about?" I shake my head hard. "I was pissed that I didn't die. Living through the accident wasn't a blessing—it was a curse. And I shook my fist at and cursed God almost as much as I did when I woke in the same hospital in a similar bed ten months ago. That day I learned Gabe hadn't survived the accident."

"That's when you attacked the nurse?"

"I attacked a lot of people back then. Something broke inside me when I woke up that second time. The thing that keeps you from doing bad things. It was more than just not worrying about what other people think. I didn't care."

There was an out-of-control fury that lurked below the surface. Anything could provoke it, and once it was released, that was it. I couldn't even tell you what I did. Let alone be responsible for it.

I kept trying to kill myself from the moment I came to, pulling and ripping out my IV and all the other cords attached to me. People like me were the reason for the safety rules on the unit. Why all the furniture was bolted to the ground and you couldn't have shoelaces. I only remember those days in bits and pieces. They had to keep me heavily sedated. It was the only way to keep me from hurting myself or someone else. Even then it wasn't enough. I came unleashed. Psychosis causes superhuman strength, and I had it. It took three attendants once to detain me in the rec room when I had one of my fits. Someday I'll watch the security footage. I wonder if he has? God, I hope not. How embarrassing.

"What about the physical therapist? Do you remember any of that?"

"Again, only bits and pieces. I remember filing down to the gym for the usual session. My head was throbbing. I was overtired and exhausted from not sleeping well the night before." And I just wanted to hurt someone. It really was that simple. Just this uncontrollable urge to lash out, but I leave out that part. "Whatever built-in mechanisms that we have to keep us from acting out on our impulses was gone in me. It was the strangest sensation to not restrain myself. Not caring at all and just giving in to the dark parts of you, every dark thought, not trying to fight it or change it. Find hope. Or a reason to keep going. Because that's what you do in regular life. That's what everyone does. That's what I did. How else do you get through life? You'll probably never believe this, but I used to be so hopeful. And bubbly." I burst out laughing just thinking about it. "I won the version of Miss Congeniality in our homecoming court two years in a row. Except we didn't call it Miss Congeniality, we called it Miss Spirit, and I was everything the stupid title implies. I had an optimism for this world that was unbelievable." I shake my head. "I couldn't reach that place no matter how hard I tried now."

"That must be so hard," he says, a mirror reflecting my words. He makes it easy to keep talking.

"Before Gabe's death, I never had hopeless thoughts. It wasn't something I struggled with or even tried to fight against like some people because they were just pessimistic by nature. I'm not sure I even had one back in the days of little Miss Spirit. I didn't have any clue what true hopelessness was. I had no idea. None. Not a clue. I hate that person now. She was so innocent and immature." I pause, considering whether I should continue with what I want to say next. It doesn't take me long to decide. "Maybe in some sick way that's what the Dog Snatcher is trying to teach all of these parents—be grateful for what you have. People that have everything are never grateful for it. I know I sure wasn't. It could be his way of warning them not to waste a single day because you never know what's going to happen the next. Everything you love could be ripped from you in an instant."

Everything in the room stills. I hadn't mentioned the Dog Snatcher or my thoughts on him so specifically since we'd come into the room. We've talked about what happened to those other boys and the likelihood that Isaac shares the same fate, but neither of us had made mention of his actual name. We hadn't opened that door, and I just flung it wide open. The silence between us starts growing uncomfortable. Dr. Stephens shifts in his seat.

"It's interesting that you bring up the Dog Snatcher." He clears his throat, looking nervous and uncomfortable. Here we go. Finally. What we really came for. "It sounds like you've given some thought to his motives."

"Hasn't everybody?"

"Everybody has definitely been thinking about the case and worried about their children's safety, but . . ." He rubs his chin and narrows his eyes at me. "I'm not sure how many people have given that much thought to the why of it. It takes a certain kind of person to want to get into the mind of a serial killer. That's a scary place to go."

"Are you saying I'm special?" I place my hands on my heart and smile at him.

"I guess I am." He smiles back.

"Well, I couldn't be more flattered."

"I'd love to know more about what you think his motives are behind all of this."

I shrug. "That's pretty much it. I mean, besides that this is obviously not a crime of passion. Everything is strategically thought out, planned, and executed. He also shows great care for the boys, so the act has emotion and personal meaning attached to it. He clearly cares for the boys."

"Really? You think so?" he interrupts before I finish. "Then why kill them so violently?"

"He should kill them nicely?"

He bursts out laughing, and his face turns red instantly. He puts his hand over his mouth. "I shouldn't laugh. That's so terrible of me to laugh, but I can't help it. That's really funny."

I give him my most alluring smile. Demure. Like a cat. If he touched me, I'd probably purr.

He quickly regains his composure. Good for him. He shouldn't let me throw him off like that. He's had good clinical training. "Strangling someone to death seems pretty brutal. It's almost always a sign of excessive out-of-control rage. If he's that angry, why take it out on the kids? Take it out on the ungrateful parents."

"But everyone knows there's no better way to get to parents than through their kids. That's where you've got to hit if you want it to hurt the most." I bring my hand up to my mouth. I've said too much, but I know way more than most about hitting people where it hurts.

He locks eyes with me from across the table. Green with tiny specks of gold housed in long lashes. I could stare into his eyes forever. I gaze right back, allowing him to swim into the sea of me.

Finally, he breaks the silence and the spell. "Would you mind telling me where you were on Tuesday, December seventh, between five o'clock and six thirty p.m.?"

CASE #72946

PATIENT: JULIET (JULES) HART

Tuesday evening, December 7, between five and six thirty. That's when Isaac went missing, but I wasn't anywhere near him. I make sure Dr. Stephens knows that. He can tell everyone beneath him too.

"I was at home helping prep for dinner. It's my job for all of December." Samaritan House follows a very strict schedule that all residents are required to abide by in order to live here, including being responsible for all the chores and upkeep of the apartment building. Each month residents are assigned a job that ranges from things like taking out the trash to cleaning the bathrooms. We even clean the windows. I'd finally worked my way out of the nasty jobs and into the coveted jobs in the kitchen, so I took my job seriously because I wasn't about to lose it and go back to scrubbing toilets.

"Can someone besides yourself verify that?" Dr. Stephens's pen is in his hand and poised to write. It's the first time he's taken out paper this entire time.

"Ruth Ann . . . and . . . I'm trying to remember what other staff member was there that night. I think Corinne, but I could be wrong. I know Ruth Ann was there for sure because she always leads a group on Tuesday nights." I lean across the table and give his hand a playful tap.

"Oh, and I went to the meditation class afterward, too, just in case you were wondering. That took up most of the night."

He spreads his hands out on the table. "As you can imagine, part of the way we solve any missing persons investigation is by ruling out different options and hypothetical scenarios. I—"

"You're calling me hypothetical? I mean, I think I'm a pretty real one, don't you think? There's not much that's hypothetical about me." I tug my T-shirt down. I picked it on purpose this morning when I knew we'd be spending all day together again. It clings to my chest, and even though I'm not happy about all the weight I've gained, at least it's given me cleavage.

He's a gentleman, and he doesn't gawk down my shirt, but you can't mistake that I'm not wearing a bra. He gives me a confident smile, though. "There's nothing hypothetical about you, that's for sure."

I beam. I don't try to pretend like I'm not pleased.

He clears his throat. "So, like I was saying, part of what we do in any investigation is get rid of things on the list as quickly and easily as we can. We start with what we like to call 'low-hanging fruit.'" He gives me another grin. I appreciate the fruit reference.

I wonder which fruit he imagines me as? Have I crept into his thoughts these past few nights? His dreams? Does he think of me when he reaches his hands between his legs? I pull myself away from the images. Focus on what he's saying. I missed the first part.

". . . the more possibilities that we can cross off our list, then the more focused our list becomes. Does that make sense?"

"It makes perfect sense to me," I say, but I can't stop staring at his lips. He brushes his fingertips against them as if he feels me staring at them.

I've got to get out of this room. Quick.

He's still blabbering on.

I interrupt him. "Can you just get to whatever it is you want to ask me?" I don't say *please* like I would in the past. My heart is beating too fast, and the heat between my legs is burning the seat. It's working its way through me.

He's taken aback. "Okay . . . I just thought we were getting somewhere."

"We're not getting anywhere," I snap. I shove my hands underneath my thighs.

"Do you have any idea where Isaac is at?"

Finally. There it is. The question everyone cares about. The only one he's really here to ask. All the others have only been precursors leading up to this.

I shake my head. "I have no idea."

FOURTEEN

AMBER GREER

I hurried down the sidewalk, doing my best to keep up with Mark. He was marching to the police station the same way he marched his way through amusement parks. Like he was on an important mission and everybody else better fall in line or get left behind.

FALCON LAKE POLICE DEPARTMENT was written in bold black letters above the entrance doors, and he pulled open the one on the right and held it for me. In all my years in Falcon Lake, I'd never been inside the police department. I'd never had a reason to. I didn't know what the reason was now, and it had my heart in my throat. Detective Hawkins called thirty minutes ago and asked if we could come down to the station, which is super weird because we'd had all our meetings and discussions at our house. We'd never come down here for anything, especially not at eight in the morning, but he's been acting strange ever since I went to Samaritan House. He didn't even come by the house yesterday.

The room was arranged like the DMV waiting room with brown plastic chairs attached to the floor with metal legs. A mousy woman with a huge necklace hanging down her chest sat in a reception desk at the front of the room behind a plexiglass divide. There wasn't anyone else in the room. We made a beeline toward her.

"We're here to speak with Detective Hawkins," Mark said at the same time I said, "We're the Greers."

She gave us each a quick once-over. "I know who you are. Detective Hawkins is expecting you." She pressed a button next to her and motioned to the metal door on her right. "Head down the hall. He's in the second room on the left."

"Thank you," I said. Mark didn't bother thanking her. He was already through the door and heading down the narrow hallway. Brown metal doors lined each side. He still hadn't said a word to me since we got the phone call.

Detective Hawkins was already in the room when we got there, and he rose from his position at the head of the table to meet us after Mark barged in without knocking. I met Detective Hawkins's eyes awkwardly, trying to read if there was any residual anger from me confronting Jules. He only glanced at me briefly before turning his gaze to Mark, then quickly pointing to the chairs around the beat-up conference table. "Please have a seat."

His change in demeanor was obvious. Everything about him had become a bit more formal. His shirt was unbuttoned and his tie loosened when he worked in our kitchen, but he was buttoned up tight today. I didn't know if that meant anything or if it was just because he was at the office. I tried not to read too much into it, but it was hard.

I sat on one side of the table, and Mark sat on the other. The room smelled like old smoke despite the air freshener plugged into the wall. It felt strange not having Mark beside me, so I quickly got up and switched seats so we could be next to each other. I grabbed his hand and gripped it underneath the table. No matter how mad I was at him and how much we were fighting, I needed someone to hold on to right now.

"Hope you got some sleep last night," Detective Hawkins said, and my anxiety went down a notch since that was how he greeted us each day.

"We got a little." I gave our standard greeting right back. The truth was I'd ended up sleeping on the couch again, and Mark had slept with Katie in her room. Katie was the only one who'd gotten any actual sleep. Sleep was still impossible for me.

"That's good," Detective Hawkins said, nodding. He laid his hands on the table. "I wanted to bring you down this morning so that we could talk about a few things and get you brought up to speed since I got so busy I never made it to your house yesterday. I hope that's okay."

"Of course," Mark said eagerly as I nodded my agreement.

"Great." He looked pleased with our cooperation. "Let's get right down to business, then, shall we?" He didn't wait for us to answer. Our presence said it all. "There are some details about the Dog Snatcher case that we release to the general public just like we do any other crime, but there is always information that we keep to ourselves about an investigation. We only release information that's going to help the investigation. We never release the stuff that might harm the investigation or interfere with it in any way. Do you follow?"

We both nodded.

"Good. That's important. I just don't want either of you to feel like we've kept anything hidden from you when we talk about the case today, because we're going to be talking about things we haven't released to the public before. Stuff we haven't talked with you about either." He shifted his glance back and forth between us.

I dug my fingernails into Mark's hand. His entire body was rigid next to mine. My heart thudded in my chest.

"Everyone is aware of how the victims' clothes are folded in a box and how they're delivered, but the piece we've never released to the public is that the clothes from each boy were laundered with the same detergent. And not just Brady and Josh. I'm talking about all the other boys that have been linked to the Dog Snatcher. All five. Their clothes were also washed with the same detergent. It was one of the primary reasons we felt confident in saying that we were dealing with a serial killer." He was silent for a few seconds before continuing. "We got the results back from the analysis on Isaac's clothes last night, and his clothes weren't laundered with the same detergent as all the other boys'."

"I knew it!" I squealed.

Mark jerked his hand out of mine and turned to me with a look of pure disgust in his eyes. "Are you serious right now? Like you actually care that much about being right? I can't believe you." He looked like there was a bad taste in his mouth that he wanted to spit out.

I grabbed his arm. "Oh my God, no. It's not about that at all. It has nothing to do with being right. I'm excited because it means Isaac might still have a chance. We could save him."

He didn't look convinced. Just angry and disgusted with me.

"Mark, listen to me. Please, just hear me out. We know how things end with the Dog Snatcher. You keep acting like I don't understand that, but I do. I always have. If the Dog Snatcher took Isaac, his chances of being found alive aren't good, but if someone else has him, then they're a different person with a totally different personality and makeup. We don't know if they're capable of murder. Maybe they just want attention. Or help? Who knows? But there's a much greater chance of finding him alive if he's with someone else." I turned to Detective Hawkins. "Right? I mean, I know there aren't any guarantees, and he's still at a huge risk, but there's got to be some truth to that, right?"

He gave Mark a reluctant nod. "Yes, I don't want to give you false hope where there is none or even pretend that I have any idea how this will end, but this piece of information does change things. All I can tell you is what I've told you since the very beginning, and that's that I will do everything within my power to bring your son home to you alive. That still stands."

"But his odds are better if it's not him, right?" I wouldn't let it go. I couldn't. I'd hold on to anything hinting at hope.

"Slightly."

I smacked the table. "I'll take it."

Detective Hawkins looked back and forth between us, making sure we'd settled our dispute and weren't going to launch into another one before he continued. "Things aren't as cut and dried as we'd previously imagined, so we're going to be looking in some different directions. Right now we have multiple working theories, and of course we're going to continue pursuing all leads and information regarding the possibility that Isaac was taken by the Dog Snatcher. However, we are also going to be examining other possible copycat scenarios. We—"

"So, you'll be really narrowing in on Jules then?" I interrupted. Finally. They should've been there this entire time.

He nodded slowly and spoke even slower like he was annoyed with how many times he'd had to reassure me of the same thing. "Yes, we are going to continue our examination of Jules and how she might be connected to Isaac's disappearance. But"—he drew out the word and then sped up—"we're also going to look at alternative options that we might not have looked at or taken as seriously before this. We—"

"Alternative options?" This time Mark was the one to interrupt him. "What do you mean you're going to look at alternative options?" An angry edge still lined his tone.

"We've been looking at the threatening and bullying text messages that Isaac received as two separate and unconnected issues. That might not be the reality. It's possible the two of them are more connected than we previously thought. We're going to dig deeper into those messages with his peers at school and see what happens. We didn't push too hard last time, but maybe if we exerted some pressure this time around, one of those kids might fold. It's possible this could be a prank gone wrong."

"A prank?" Mark guffawed. "What kind of kids would do something so sick and twisted?"

"The same kind that would send hateful messages to him," I said.

Detective Hawkins nodded at me in agreement. "Teenagers are some of the most vicious groups of people on the planet, and if they cross the line into delusional thinking, which lots of them do . . ." He let out a whistle and shook his head. "Watch out."

Mark and I looked at each other, trying to read what the other was thinking, but I couldn't tell what was going through his head. All I saw was the same nervous energy and tension that had been there all morning. We quickly looked away from each other and back to Detective Hawkins.

"Did either of you follow the Slenderman case?" he asked next, taking me by surprise with the question.

I pointed to Mark. "I did, but he didn't."

"Got it." He shifts his attention to Mark. "Two teenage girls were obsessed with the fictional character Slenderman to the point where they planned a slumber party and tried to murder one of their other friends in order to please him. Both of the girls had convinced themselves that he was real and that they'd win his favor if they did it. Crazy stuff. Both of them were only twelve, and they stabbed that poor girl nineteen times. She barely survived."

"I do remember hearing something about that. It's awful, but I'm not sure what it's got to do with Isaac," Mark said.

Detective Hawkins nodded. "That's the thing with kids these days. All of that mess with Slenderman started online. It started as an online photography challenge. Can you believe that? Then, there was this entire online community that just grew and grew. It became like this huge urban myth. There was—still is—tons of fan fiction about Slenderman. All these kids and adults formed a community, and it was very real to them. Throw in a little mental illness and you've got yourself a very scary situation, which is exactly what it grew into."

"You think something similar like that happened to Isaac?" Mark looked skeptical. I couldn't blame him. It sounded far-fetched to me too.

Detective Hawkins shook his head. "Not exactly. I'm using it to illustrate how things can grow in that online world and eventually bleed over into the real world. We already know that kids were sending him some pretty awful messages, and you said yourself that he'd always been one of the kids they teased. Maybe there was more going on than we knew. That's why we're going to take a look at Isaac's online activity."

"But I thought it was going to be weeks before you got the recovered information back on his phone?" I asked.

"I'm not talking about his phone. We'll be taking a deep dive into where he was hanging out online. What he was doing, who he was talking to. Those kinds of things." He shifted in his seat and sat up straighter. "Since I've got you here, either of you have an idea about any of that?"

I turned my attention to Mark. This was definitely his area of expertise and not mine. He was as into video games as Isaac. The two of them used to play together even though they had opposite tastes in games.

"Isaac isn't a big social media guy, so you're not going to find any of that stuff. Don't bother looking at any of the sports games either. He doesn't even have a profile. He didn't like any of them no matter how hard I tried to get him hooked." His eyes briefly misted at the memory. It was the biggest joke between them. Mark was obsessed with all things Madden, but Isaac wouldn't have anything to do with it in the same way that Mark couldn't stand Isaac's first-person shooter games. "He played all the first-person shooter games. He played *Call of Duty* and *Valorant* a lot, but his favorite game was *Dracho*."

"Is that another first-person shooter? I've never had too much time for them myself, so I don't know anything about them."

"No, it's more like a role-playing game where you build your own worlds. Kind of like an older kids' version of *Minecraft*. Lots of adults play it too," Mark explained.

"Got it." He appeared satisfied. "A few of my officers and myself are going to head out to the school in about an hour and start interviewing students. I just wanted to meet with the two of you first to give you a heads-up. I didn't want you to get wind that our officers were sniffing around at the school again and wonder what was going on. Also, I can't stress how important it is that you keep this information to yourself about the laundry detergent. We don't want that piece getting out in the public."

"Sure." We nodded in agreement.

He put his hands on the table again like he was getting ready to stand when he suddenly asked, "Oh yeah, I do have another question for you, though. Didn't you say that Katie has eczema?" He directed his question at me.

I eyed him like he'd lost his mind. There was no reason for him to ask me if Katie had eczema because he already knew she did. We talked about it all the time because his mom had it too. Katie's was related to specific foods and other sensitivities, but any form of stress was almost always sure to result in an angry outburst on her skin. This was the most stressful thing she'd ever had to endure in her short life, and most of her body was covered in scaly, itchy patches. Sometimes she scratched so hard she drew blood. He had noticed almost right away, and on the second day of the investigation, he'd shown up at the house with his family's homemade lotion recipe of aloe, lavender, and oatmeal mixed with another secret ingredient he refused to disclose.

"I did," I said slowly.

"That's what I thought," he said like he wasn't sure he remembered things correctly, but there was no way he'd forgotten about her eczema. He'd asked her about it two days ago. "I also thought I remembered you saying that you used special laundry detergent because of her skin sensitivities. Am I remembering that correctly?"

"You are," Mark replied, answering for me before I had a chance to respond.

"Would you mind if we got a sample of the detergent?" Detective Hawkins asked, keeping his attention on me even though Mark was the one to answer the question.

"Why would you do that?" I asked.

"We just want to be able to rule things out and narrow the focus of our search," he said like it wasn't a big deal.

Mark gave me a look like I was totally missing something.

And then it dawned on me.

"You can't think—"

Mark pinched my thigh to stop me and jumped in before I could finish my sentence. "Definitely. Not a problem," he said quickly. "We'll get you a sample. We can run home now, and I'll bring it back to you." He jumped up from his chair and pulled me up with him. I gripped his hand to steady myself.

Detective Hawkins smiled. "I wish it worked that way. That sure would make my life a lot easier, but the department has specific procedures and policies that have to be followed for all evidence collection. I was thinking I'd just have one of my officers who's at the house collect it since they're already there. I just need you to sign off on the paperwork that gives us permission to do that." He handed me a form from the stack of papers sitting in front of him.

I took the paper from him and tried to read what it said, but I couldn't think straight, and my hands were shaking. So were my knees. I was still reeling from the news. I tried to focus and read what it said, but the letters and numbers swerved in front of my eyes. It was probably just standard legal jargon anyway. I grabbed a pen from the cupholder in the center of the table. Mark put his hand on top of mine on the table and stopped me from writing anything.

"We'll take this with us and look it over," he said, snatching the paper from my hands.

I looked at him in alarm. What was he doing?

Detective Hawkins pursed his lips and squinted his eyes at me. "It shouldn't take you more than a second to read through. It's very standard language for whenever we collect evidence. You know how we have to be so careful with liability these days." Even I recognized the used-car salesman in his voice.

"We'll look it over." Mark's jaw was set. You weren't going to move him anywhere when he had that look in his eyes. Detective Hawkins might as well give up. "Is there anything else we can do for you?"

"I think that's it for now. Just get that signed and back to me so we can move things forward. I wouldn't want there to be any holdup in the case. Like I said. All I'm trying to do is get your baby boy back home to you alive."

"I—"

Mark jumped in again, not letting me talk. "Thanks so much. We appreciate that. Let's go, Amber."

CASE #72946

PATIENT: JULIET (JULES) HART

I got here before Dr. Stephens. Ready and in my seat. He walks in empty handed. No coffee again. He never should've set up that expectation at our first morning meeting. If he was my student, I'd flag him for it in supervision.

He holds his jacket over his arm, an iPad tucked underneath the other one, which is holding his briefcase. He steps back, clearly taken off guard. "How . . . where?" He looks behind him to see if there are any staff members sitting outside the door like they're supposed to be since nobody's allowed in these rooms alone, but the lobby is empty. "I don't understand. How did you get in the room?"

"Hank brought me down early and let me in. He has a key to all the rooms," I say with a beaming smile. Hank's the overnight staff, or babysitter, as I like to think of him. He shows up at eleven and stays until eight. He has a thing for redheads, so I made sure to make friends with him immediately. It didn't take long to learn that the key to surviving institutions was making friends with the staff. But not just any staff member. Just the ones who could help you with things if you needed it, and Hank would do just about anything for a carton of cigarettes.

Dr. Stephens sweeps his eyes into the hallway and across the way into the other offices, but they're empty, too, except for Corinne sitting at the main desk in the reception area. He knows I'm not supposed to be in the room by myself, and he can't decide if he wants to call me out on it or not. He might be the cutest when he's conflicted.

I give him another smile. He's flustered. I've never seen him flustered. Not even yesterday when I turned up the heat. This is good. I need him off balance.

"Sit," I say, pointing to the chair across from me at the table. The one he always sits in every time we meet. The table is the one piece of furniture that they threw into this room as a last-minute effort to try to get it not to look so institutional, but that's a lost cause. There's no mistaking the harsh fluorescent lighting and the peeling paint on the concrete walls.

He sets his things down next to the chair and takes his time sinking into it. He loosens his tie. He must've come from court or an important appointment. Sometimes I forget he has other clients. A life away from here. I wonder if he's married. He doesn't wear a ring, but lots of shrinks don't, so that doesn't mean anything. He probably is. Does he talk to his partner over dinner about me? Ask them for advice on how to deal with the complexities of my case? Or does he leave his working life at the office like a good little boy? Tucked away behind these dirty walls and aluminum doors.

Every therapist always promises their clients that they won't talk about them outside therapy, and we sign confidentiality agreements outlining just that, but nobody abides by those rules. Not any therapist I know anyway. There's no way to listen to other people's lives and not process those experiences somewhere else. Sure, we have supervision all the way through school, and there's always somebody there to talk to on the job, but you watch what you say when the person you're seeing for therapy has the power to kick you out of the program or fire you.

You have to find places where you can talk about your thoughts and feelings without consequences or being judged.

Where does Dr. Stephens go, and what does he say about me? What does he think when nobody's listening and his thoughts travel unchecked? I spent all last night obsessing about him. He even crept into my dreams, just like Isaac used to do all those months ago before everything got so screwed up. But it's different with Dr. Stephens. Everything's going to be different with him. I'll make sure of it.

"Look, I'm sorry for how snappy I got with you at the end of our time yesterday." I fill my words and my eyes with deep apology and regret, hoping he can feel how sorry I am. "It must've been confusing for me to be so nice to you one minute, then suddenly flip the script and get so short."

He waves me off with his hand. "Don't worry about it. It was nothing."

"Nothing? It certainly wasn't nothing. There was a whole lot of something between us." He felt it too. I know he did. I'm glad he's so quick to forgive my moodiness, though. I reach across the table and brush my fingers across his hands. Electricity surges through me. Instant heat. He pulls away, but only because he feels it, too, quickly folding his hands on his lap underneath the table. He probably doesn't trust himself either.

"I think before we go any further today, we should talk about what's going on here." He pushes his chair a few inches back from the table, trying to create as much distance between us as possible. That's going to be hard. No amount of space is going to stop the pull that's beginning. I've been here before. I know how these things go.

"What do you mean what's going on?" I instinctively reach for my hair to twirl it around my fingers, but the long strands are gone. I have phantom hair like other people have phantom limbs. I rub my hand awkwardly against my face instead, hoping I don't look too silly. I'm still learning how to be sexy with short hair.

"It's inevitable that transference is going to happen at some point in therapy. There's no reason to be ashamed of what you're feeling. Developing feelings for your therapist is extremely common." I've never seen him look so earnest and sincere.

I burst out laughing. "Transference?" I point between him and me. The illicit fantasy. "You think this is transference?"

"Yes." He nods agreeably, his voice clinical and detached. "Whatever strong feelings you're experiencing toward me are completely normal. People transfer romantic feelings toward their therapists all the time. It's an extremely common reaction. It's natural to develop strong feelings toward people that make us feel good about ourselves, that really listen to us and see us. It's—"

"I know what transference is," I snap, interrupting him before he gets any further. "That's not what this is. I'm not projecting my desire for intimacy and closeness onto you or trying to get you to fill some unmet need of mine." I shake my head, disgusted with his outdated and oppressive Freudian garbage.

"Hey, hey, hey." He raises his hands up like he's sorry he's offended me, and he should be. "I'm not saying that you are. All I'm saying is that if that were to ever happen or even be the smallest part of whatever emotional attachment is going on between us, I want you to know it would be totally normal, especially since we're talking about really deep topics centered around love and intimacy." He smiles wide. "And I mean, Freud did say that the entire point of therapy was to experience and interpret transference, so I don't think you should just immediately cast it off as a bad thing. I'm free to explore anything that comes up in our time together."

"There's nothing to explore." I wouldn't have said the same thing ten minutes ago, but I can't stomach the idea of him after all that.

He places his hands on the table and folds them in front of him. He cocks his head to the side and gives me a playful smile, which seems completely inappropriate given our conversation, but what do I know? He's the expert.

"I'm going to set a few things straight for you just in case there are any fantasies about me being the perfect partner starting to stir around in that head of yours." He puts up two fingers. "I'm not even forty and I've been divorced twice." He nods at his fingers, making sure I don't miss the point. "I'm a terrible husband and an even worse boyfriend. I get offended super easily, and I don't like to talk about my feelings. I know, ironic, right?" He laughs at himself, and I can tell he's being honest. He's like a dentist with bad teeth. "I never remember to take out the trash. I don't cook. I give horrible back rubs and massages. Oh, and I'm a total slob," he adds.

"I'm glad we got that straight," I say, returning his laughter. He doesn't know that the right person can change everything. That's okay. He doesn't need to.

"Has anything like this happened to you before?" he asks next, even though we still haven't established what *this* is, but I'm not going to argue with him about the transference issue. I'm just going to let that one pass because if we spend too much time on it, I might end up really upset, and I don't want to get angry. Nothing good comes out of me getting angry.

"What do you mean? Like with my clients?" Does he really think he's the only one whose clients develop feelings for him?

"Sure. That works. Anything ever happen there?"

"I've had it happen with clients before." I had clients promise to leave their wives for me. He's not as special as he thinks he is.

"What about with Isaac? Did you develop transference there?"

His question catches me off guard, and I stumble backward mentally. It takes me a second to recover and find my voice. It's too late to change my face. He's already seen what his words did to me. "I mean . . . um, Isaac was never my client. It wasn't like that between us, so I'm going to have to say no on that one." It's a terrible answer. He knows it too.

"Do you think it's possible that you projected your maternal longings and desires onto Isaac?"

"Is it possible?" I reflect his question back at him. "Of course it's possible. Anything's possible."

"But is that what happened?" He's not letting me off the hook that easily. Not after we've come this far.

"No, but that's what Amber thought was going on too. She thought I was going to step in and try to be this weird second mother to him. Like I thought I could do it better than her or something." I shudder at the idea of being Isaac's mom. In the beginning, maybe, but that's not where things progressed or where they were ever meant to stay. There was a soul recognition and connection between us, so the normal rules and pretenses didn't apply to us. Neither did the labels. But I explained that to Dr. Stephens yesterday, and he still isn't listening. He doesn't get it. Is it possible today will be different? Doubtful.

Yesterday was fun. This isn't fun anymore.

FIFTEEN

AMBER GREER

"What's wrong with you?" I snapped as Mark hurried us down the police station corridor. He was walking faster than he was on the way in.

"Be quiet," he whispered earnestly, keeping his voice low and his head down. "Don't say anything until we're outside. Everyone's listening to us."

"What are you talking about?" I looked around the waiting room. The station was as empty as it was when we got here. "Why are you acting like this?"

He whipped around and shot me a hateful stare like I'd committed a horrible crime by not lowering my voice. His nostrils flared in and out with each fast breath. "Nothing until we're outside. Do you understand me?" He turned back on his heels, and I stood there for a second, dumbfounded by his behavior, before following him into the sunshine. He was practically running down the sidewalk to our car. I hurried to catch up and grabbed his arm, pulling him back.

"Stop. Just stop for a second and talk to me, okay? I don't even know why you're so angry. What's going on? You were the one that said you were going to go home and get the detergent." I tried to get him to look at me, but he wouldn't. He was too busy darting his eyes everywhere.

"I'm not saying anything until we're in the car. They could be following us. Watching us." He sounded like a paranoid speed freak. Looked like one too.

"Give me the keys. I'm driving," I said, holding out my hand. I wasn't letting him drive. Not when he was acting so erratically. He tossed them to me without argument, and we slid inside the car.

"I only said that about going home to get the detergent so that we could get out of there," he blurted out as soon as he shut the door behind himself and we were tucked inside. "That's all I was trying to do. I was never going to give them anything from our house. Definitely not without seeking legal advice."

"Why are you being so paranoid?" I asked, putting the car in drive and heading down the street, putting the ominous station behind us. Hopefully, he'd return to normal again the farther away we got from it. I glanced over at him in the passenger seat. His eyes were still manic and wild.

"Do you really not get it?" he asked, twisting his body in the seat to face me.

"What are you talking about, Mark? No, I don't get it. I don't understand why you're suddenly so upset and acting so weird." I almost didn't see the car slowing down in front of me and quickly slammed on the brakes, narrowly avoiding hitting them. Maybe I shouldn't be driving either. "All they're trying to do is rule out other possibilities." It was what I had been wanting them to do all along, but I didn't throw that in his face. Not now. It wasn't a good time.

He smacked his hand on the dashboard. "They're not trying to rule us out, Amber. Don't you see that? They think we had something to do with it!"

"With Isaac's disappearance?" I asked like there was any other crime we could possibly be involved in.

"Yes!" he snapped. He stomped his legs on the floor of the car like a toddler. "That's what I've been trying to say. That's why I was trying to get us out of there as fast as possible without giving them any more information." He looked behind us, making sure nobody was following us. "And what were you thinking? You almost signed a legal document without consulting with an attorney?"

"I . . . I mean . . ." I couldn't form cohesive thoughts. What was happening? How did the investigation make this sudden turn? Where were we going with this questioning? "I just didn't think anything of it when he asked me to do it. I guess . . ."

"Don't you ever do something like that again, do you hear me?" He shook his finger at me. He had never spoken to me like this before. I was so shocked by it that all I could do was nod my consent and keep quiet. "From now on, you need to think about every conversation you have with people, especially with the police, okay? Every word that comes out of your mouth. You have to think about it. Every word from here on out, Amber. I mean it. You need to watch yourself. Stay cognizant. Do you understand?"

"No." I shook my head, feeling lost and disoriented. "I don't understand. The only people who need to worry about what they're saying and how they're coming across to the police are the ones who have something to hide. We don't have anything to hide, so we don't have anything to worry about." I slowed to a stop as we reached the light in front of McDonald's and turned to look at him. He was gnawing at his fingernails. He hadn't done that since college. He used to chew them down to nubs every semester during finals week. My stomach rolled. "Unless there's something you know about Isaac's disappearance that you're not telling me? Do you know something, Mark?"

Nobody innocent hid from the police. They didn't have to get their story straight or think about the words that were coming out of their mouth. That's the freedom that came when you lived from a place of truth and honesty.

"Mark?" I asked again.

Still nothing.

The light turned green, and he motioned for me to go through the intersection. The question hung in the air unanswered while I waited for him to say something. The car honked behind me, forcing me to move forward.

My hands were clammy on the steering wheel. The silence grew louder with each block. What did he know that he wasn't telling me? Is that why he'd been acting so weird? I thought it was just because Isaac was missing. Was there more to it than that? My mind ran wild, searching for possible scenarios to explain any of this, but nothing made sense.

Mark looked ill. Like at any minute he might ask me to pull over the car so he could throw up on the side of the road. His hair was matted with sweat, and he anxiously rubbed his hands up and down his thighs. You could almost see the wheels spinning in his head. This wasn't good.

It wasn't long before we were almost to our neighborhood. Only a few blocks away.

Mark rubbed his legs harder. "Okay, okay, I've just got to get inside the house. That's all. I can pull it together long enough for that. I can," he muttered underneath his breath. He was practically clawing at himself.

I put my hand on top of his, forcing his hands to be still. "Mark, what's going on?"

"You don't want to know." He shook his head back and forth without looking at me. His forehead was pinched tight like he was battling with his thoughts. "You don't want to know."

Alarm bells went off inside me. My gut clenched, and my heart beat faster.

I should've whipped the car over to the side of the road and parked so that we could talk about whatever was going on. I should've demanded that he tell me exactly what happened and what he was hiding from me.

But I didn't.

I couldn't.

Instead, I exhaled slowly and tried to quell the anxiety rushing through me. I brushed the hair off Mark's face and tucked it behind his ears with shaking hands. "Just keep your head down when we get out of the car, and don't let them take your picture, okay?"

CASE #72946

PATIENT: JULIET (JULES) HART

"I can tell this conversation is making you uncomfortable. Would you like to talk about something else?" Dr. Stephens asks. It's been five minutes since I curled myself up into a ball on this chair and settled into silence. I'm done talking about transference. That's not what happened with Isaac, and it's definitely not what's going on with us.

"I feel like we might be running out of things to talk about." There are still four days left until Isaac's body shows up in a field somewhere or disappears forever. What does he plan on doing? Coming and sitting with me in these sessions every day until then? Is that what they've really hired him to do? Be my fancy overpriced babysitter until the clock runs out of time? I can't imagine what he costs in comparison to what they pay my babysitters at Samaritan House.

"Oh, I think we've got plenty of things to talk about," he says. "At least enough for today."

I raise my eyebrows at him. He's done another quick power play I wasn't expecting. Every time I underestimate him, he surprises me. Can't wait to see where this one goes. I willingly take his bait.

"We do?" I bat my eyelashes at him, but not the seductive ones this time. The innocent ones. Those might work better. Maybe he likes his women helpless.

"Sure do." He gives me a playful nod. "The police paid a visit to Shane last night."

"They did?" My response is much more subdued than he was probably expecting, but I figured it was only a matter of time before they talked to Shane. I'm surprised it took them as long as it did to get to him.

"Yes. The lead detective went. Detective Hawkins. Have you met him?" There's a slight twinkle in his eyes. He knows that I haven't. He knows everything about me. Well, at least he thinks he does. He doesn't know the half of it.

"No, I've never met him," I respond, taking the bait. I'll play his game if it means making him feel better about getting played by mine.

"Yes, he's the lead guy in all of this, and I have to tell you, he's really amazing. He's got an impeccable track record too. I've only gotten to work with him one other time in my career. Matter of fact, it was another missing persons case back when I worked in Wilmington. That was a doozy there, boy. Much harder to crack than this, but you don't want to get bogged down in all those details, do you?" He gives me a wicked grin. He's enjoying this. Whatever he's setting up. Having the ball back in his court. He most certainly doesn't like having it in mine. "Anyway, all that to say, Detective Hawkins went and paid a visit to your husband, Shane, last night."

"And? Did they have a lovely time?" I try not to let my feelings show.

"You know, they did. He had some interesting things to say."

I bet he did. Twenty-one years of marriage brings all kinds of history and drama to the table. All the garbage. So many stories.

"I was surprised to learn that you weren't living at home before the train accident. You hadn't lived at home in over three months. Shane said he didn't even know where you stayed sometimes and that you often slept on the streets for weeks at a time." He stops, giving his words a chance to sink in, but I'm not surprised by any of his news.

"It'd been a couple of months since I lived at home. I thought everyone knew that." My homelessness had been the talk of the town.

"Why'd you leave home?" he asks like I was a teenage runaway.

I shrug. "I just couldn't be there."

He cocks his head to the side and gives me his most tell-me-more-about-that look. The one they teach every therapist in graduate school. See, that's what I like about him—he's still young enough to wear that face. "How come?"

"It was just too hard." I suck in my breath, bracing myself for the impact of the memories.

Walking back into my house after being released from the hospital the first time felt like I was walking into someone else's home. Three years ago, we took a trip to California and spent a day at Universal Studios. The entire set from *Desperate Housewives* was there, and we went through it. That's exactly how I felt the day I came home: like I was walking down Wisteria Lane. Nothing would ever come close to the disorientation and shock I felt learning Gabe had drowned in the accident, but going back home after I was discharged from the hospital was as close of a second that you could get. I don't have words to put to it for Dr. Stephens, but I have to try.

"It all felt fake," I explain, doing my best to translate the experience into language. "Like none of it had ever been real, and it all seemed so trivial. A huge lie. Like when you find out Santa Claus isn't real when you're a kid? Something magical inside you dies that day, and no matter how hard you wish for or try to get it back, that magic is gone and all the light it carried with it. That's what it was like when I walked through the front door of my house but times a thousand. Nothing felt real."

"Is that when you started to dissociate?"

My jaw tightens. My cheeks flush with anger, but I do my best not to show how irritated I am. "I appreciate your assessment and diagnosis, but I don't disassociate."

"That's not what your charts say."

"My charts say a lot of things about me that aren't true."

"Well, would you like to set the record straight? I keep giving you an opportunity to tell your side of the story. Shed some light on areas where we might not be seeing things correctly." He folds his hands in front of him on the table and waits for me to speak.

"I wish that I could disassociate." I can't stress the word *wish* enough. "I'd give anything to disconnect from the pain, but I can't. That's the problem. All those people who detach from themselves and watch their own life like it's a movie playing out in front of their eyes? I wish I was one of them." I slow down the last sentence so he doesn't miss how serious I am. "You don't understand what it's like for me. I'm acutely aware of everything all the time. It's unrelenting and unending. There's no break. Not even in sleep. Because you know what happens when I sleep?" I stand, unable to sit any longer. I have to move. "I see Gabe's face trapped underneath the ice every single time I close my eyes. And I've gone without sleep for so long that I'm not sure if I'm awake or I'm dreaming, but every time I close my eyes, it's there. That same image. Him. Face up. Hands plastered against the ice. His mouth contorted into a horrific scream I can't hear while his hands slam against thick ice that won't break. It's awful."

"It sounds awful. They should give you something to sleep."

Of course his first response is to offer me drugs. That's what they all do. And I gladly take the different colored pills they give me. I'll try anything to knock me out, but nothing works. All their pills do is keep me teetering between the edge of half-awake and half-asleep. But at least it's something.

"They do, but I'm telling you, nothing works."

"None of the grief groups are helpful either?"

My new job is therapy, and my days are spent in all the various kinds. Group. Family. Individual. Art. Vocational.

"I'm not a fan," I say, which sounds funny coming from a former therapist.

He raises his eyebrows. "How come?"

"I'm different."

"Can you tell more about that?"

"I'm responsible for my son's death."

"Mrs. Hart, we've been through this. You're not responsible for Gabe's death."

"It doesn't make me feel better to hear you say that, you know, so I wish you'd just quit saying it." I let out a frustrated sigh. It's been a long five days of meeting with him. As much as I've enjoyed our little sessions and the bit of excitement they dash into my life, I'm ready for this to be over.

"How have things been with Shane since you've been here?" he asks, circling back. "I checked the notes, and it looks like he hasn't visited. You've been here almost seven weeks. Where are things at with the two of you?"

"Things are strained," I say. Every day that I'm in here and Chloe's in my house with him makes things feel more and more broken and less and less strained.

"I'm sorry to hear that." He gives the standard response. Another one. He's full of them today.

"I'm sure you've heard more than that," I say sarcastically. If he's talked to Shane or anyone else in this town about our marriage, then I'm positive nobody forgot to mention Shane's affair. Although that's not what he calls it. He says they're friends, that they share a deep connection I don't understand. He's the one who doesn't understand. I know all about deep connections.

"What do you mean?" Dr. Stephens feigns innocence like he doesn't catch my veiled reference, but I don't believe him for one second. Everyone knows about Shane's affair. Chloé posts pictures and videos of them all over social media. She's more attached to our family name than I am in the online world.

"He's moved on to a newer and fresher model," I say. Part of me hates that he's such a cliché.

"Do you know when their relationship started?" he asks.

What he really wants to know is if they were having an affair before all this went down. It's easy to assume that since they got together so quickly after Gabe's death, but they'd never met each other until after the accident. That much I'm sure of.

"I can tell you exactly when it started. Shane joined a running group three months after Gabe died, and that was the beginning." I let out a laugh. Not sure if it's bitter. "Of the end."

I was downstairs curled up in the chair next to the fireplace, which was normally one of the coziest spots in the house, except it wasn't when the fireplace was cold, dark, and unlit. The entire space was black because I refused to let anyone turn on the lights. It'd been that way for days. I kept the shades drawn at all times too. I didn't know if it was day or night, but it really didn't matter anymore because my life was over. I couldn't live without Gabe. I didn't even want to try.

Shane came downstairs that night and found me sitting there motionless and lifeless like he'd done so many times in the last three months. I hadn't moved from the position since he went upstairs over two hours ago. "I joined the Falcon Lake Leggers. I'm going to meet everyone for my first run tomorrow morning at six."

"What?" I wasn't sure if I heard him right. Shane loved sports, but only if he was watching them on ESPN. He'd played soccer in high school, but a knee injury had put a stop to all that during his junior year. He still played with Gabe in the backyard, but Gabe had out skilled him years ago, and he was definitely never a runner. He didn't even like to go on long walks.

"I need to do something." That was all he said after his announcement. He fixed himself a snack in the kitchen and headed back upstairs.

I hadn't given it a second thought because he'd come downstairs and said some pretty bizarre things over the past few months. He'd made the guest bedroom into his man cave, and he'd disappear there for hours. Every now and then, he'd suddenly rush downstairs with an important life-changing announcement. So far, he'd said he wanted to sell everything we had and travel the country in an RV and remodel the second level, and the latest had been that he thought he should quit his job and go back to school to become a lawyer even though he loved his job as an investment banker. Thankfully, that only lasted a few days because he was the only one able to work.

I hadn't seen a patient since Gabe died. I never would again. The thought of some washed-up housewife sitting on my couch and crying about how stressed she was or whining because she didn't know which uppity private school her child would get into made me want to vomit. It wasn't just that their problems seemed insignificant. It was more than that. I couldn't find it in me to offer them any kind of hope or peace. Everything felt bleak. You couldn't have a therapist who spent every waking minute wanting to die. I'd spent years developing relationships with my clients and building my caseload. Some of my clients had been with me since the very beginning, and they were almost like family. At one time, I'd cared deeply about them, but I didn't even have the energy to return phone calls or answer emails. I ghosted every single one.

And the most messed-up thing about it?

I didn't even feel bad. My ability to care was gone, and I wasn't sure I was ever going to get it back. So I barely noticed when Shane followed through on his running proclamation and got up the next morning at five so that he could be downtown by six to meet everyone. The following morning, he was up and at it again.

That's when he slowly started coming back to life.

The first thing I noticed was that he was lighter. He didn't do everything like he was moving through sludge with concrete slabs strapped to his back. The lighter he became, the heavier I felt. It was the strangest thing. Like I absorbed all his pain, too, or it multiplied mine, I don't know. But I didn't like it.

"Are you like the last one in the pack?" I asked in the middle of week two when he was scrounging through the closet trying to find a windbreaker to keep the rain off him. It was a mean thing to say, and I knew it.

"You know what?" he said without looking up, his head buried in his search. "I'm surprisingly not." He let out a small laugh.

Everything in the bedroom stilled. The air froze. So did we. Him buried in the closet. Me on the bed. Nobody laughed in the house anymore. It was an unspoken rule that we didn't laugh, and he'd just made a sound into our bubble of grief. He'd pricked a needle into it, and now what were we supposed to do with it? The moment felt like it stretched forever until he finally said, "You know what? I don't care if I get wet. I'm just going to go."

He'd taken a step. One I couldn't take. That was the day our paths officially diverged. They were already looking like they were heading in different directions, but he stepped into a new emotional space without me.

The space only grew inside him, and the more it grew, the more I shrank even further back. Eventually, he started referring to his running group as his running family, and their activities grew beyond morning runs. Sprawling into weekend activities. These long outdoor adventures—kayaking, hiking, and boating. Suddenly, Shane was this huge outdoor enthusiast that he'd never been before.

"I'm going to grab some more water and make some popcorn. Do you want any?" he asked late one Saturday night while we sat in front of the TV watching a movie together, although I had no idea what was going on in it because I couldn't pay attention. I was only going through the motions, and I was barely doing that. I couldn't believe he was still up. He'd spent all day rock climbing at Taylors Falls, and I'd expected him to be exhausted when he came home and go to bed early, but he wasn't showing any signs of slowing down.

"No thanks," I said, and he hurried off into the kitchen. He'd probably make enough for both of us even though I'd said I didn't want any.

His phone flashed with alerts on the coffee table next to me. I picked it up. Not because I was being nosy or expected there to be anything. I was just bored. Looking for a distraction. He was getting blown up with texts from someone named Chloe.

I had SO much fun today!!!

Baby, it's only been a few hours but I miss you already.

When can I see you again?

Each text was filled with annoying emojis. Heart faces and googly eyes. I scrolled up. There were hundreds of texts between them. I scrolled all the way up to the beginning. She was the one who had invited him to join the running group. They'd bumped into each other at the grocery store.

Hey hon. So sorry you're going through all this. Here's all the running info. PLEASE don't be afraid to reach out.

He hadn't been. I read through their exchanges like I was reading a short story. Flirty texts and cute selfies mixed in with all the planning for their adventures. There wasn't anything racy yet—no nudes or penis pics, but it was only a matter of time. I set the phone back on the coffee table and tried to figure out how I felt about what I'd just discovered.

Shane walked back into the living room a few minutes later. "Should I put on extra butter?"

"Whatever you feel like. It doesn't matter to me," I said. I grabbed his phone off the table and handed it over my shoulder to him. "You forgot your phone, and someone has been blowing it up."

I didn't say a word about what I'd seen. I could've. Easily. There was a chance if I'd spoken up that night and let him know I knew something was going on—that he was falling for Chloe—I would've been able to stop it. I could've easily saved my marriage. There was plenty of time. They hadn't crossed any egregious lines. Nothing you couldn't forgive or come back from. Not yet anyway. But I didn't. I kept quiet. I let him continue.

I watched the way his eyes lit up when he was on the phone with her and how his lips made a half smile like he had to hold himself back from full-on grinning whenever they talked. I could tell when she'd embarrassed him with one of her texts by the way the red crept up the back of his neck while he read it, and the way he'd type and retype his texts back, trying to compose the perfect one. I watched my husband fall in love with another woman right in front of me, and I did nothing.

"That's when I knew I was dead inside," I say after I finish filling Dr. Stephens in on all of it.

"What do you mean?"

"How do you know your husband is going to have an affair and do nothing to stop it? Not even try to intervene?" I hadn't done anything. Not once.

"It doesn't mean you couldn't stop it now."

I shake my head. "I couldn't step back into my life right now even if I wanted to. Once you reach a certain place in the breakdown of a marriage, you cross over the point of no return. We crossed that point a long time ago."

He looks sad like he's feeling sorry for me, and I don't like it. I don't want his pity, but he doesn't feel bad enough to stop his line of questioning. "Detective Hawkins says that Shane doesn't trust you to come home yet. How do you feel about that?"

I roll my eyes. "He just doesn't want me there because he's moving Chloe in. It's definitely in his best interest to keep me locked up." The scariest part is how easy it's been for him to do just that.

He testified at my conservatorship hearing and gave a stellar performance. I wish I would've recorded it. He convinced the judge with his tears and over-the-top concerned expressions that he only wanted what was best for me, for me to be safe. He shared early grief moments with her that felt like huge betrayals—how I'd wet the bed because I was too depressed to move and stopped responding to my name being called. I still can't believe he shared those things with the rest of the world and twisted them into something terrible. He also made it sound like there were signs of my instability before this, but that's not true. There wasn't a single sign of anything. I was fine. Perfectly healthy. Perfectly sane.

"Have you guys talked about a divorce?" Dr. Stephens asks next.

"We don't talk much anymore. It's weird . . ." I can't explain it to him, but my love for Shane died with Gabe, and I wasn't sure it'd ever come back. We'd grown into a threesome. The two of us no longer made sense. "Everyone always says that their lives revolve around their children, but ours really did. Gabe was the center of our world in every way. People talk about how there's all this pressure on only children, but what they don't realize is that there's an awful lot of pressure on their parents too. It's like you only have one shot to get things right, you know? And we'd both felt that. It was our only opportunity for all things kid related. I might've been a tiger mom, but there was no question Shane was a tiger dad." The memory shoves its way into my consciousness. A blue shirt with white lettering calling Shane just that. Gabe picked it out for him last Christmas because he thought it was hilarious. Shane loved it, and Gabe loved making his dad happy. His smile was as bright as the Christmas tree lights sparkling behind him in the picture. I shake my head like I need to physically dislodge the memory so I don't start crying, and continue where I left off.

"I never realized until Gabe was gone how much all of our conversations centered around him. What he was doing and how he was feeling. What he'd said that day. Who he was hanging out with. His grades. Our concerns. We were always planning. Plans for the summer. Winter. Camp. College. Oh my God, college." I shake my head, remembering how stressful it'd been to think about college. Back when we thought the hardest thing we were going to have to deal with was an empty nest. That's nothing. I don't even have a nest anymore.

"Do you ever wonder what Gabe would say if he could see you right now?"

Dr. Stephens totally blindsides me with his question, and my mind stumbles backward. So do my words. That was a nasty trick. Get me going. Spilling. Talking as fast as I can and then quickly slam one in. It worked. He caught me by surprise, and it shows.

He asked the one question I don't let myself think about. We're not going there, though. It doesn't matter what Gabe would say about what I'm doing. He's gone, and he's never coming back.

SIXTEEN

AMBER GREER

I slowly slid out from underneath Katie's arm just like I used to do when she was a baby and she'd finally fallen asleep after a long battle of crying it out. I held my breath in the same way I had then, like even the sound of it had the power to wake her. Normally, I hated the carpeted floors in our master bedroom. They were the only ones we hadn't replaced with wood in the entire house, but I was grateful for them tonight because they muffled the sound of my footsteps as I hurried across our bedroom to follow Mark downstairs. He'd gotten out of bed just a few seconds ago after he thought we were both asleep.

All I'd done since we got back from the police station this morning was stare at him in amazed wonder. We told each other everything. We weren't supposed to have secrets. Nothing about his physical appearance had changed. He still filled out the same lanky build and had all the same features, but he'd turned into a different person right in front of my eyes. This man who I thought I knew better than anyone else in this world. Whose sentences I could end. Whose jokes I could tell. Whose next moves I could almost predict. But he looked like a stranger to me. I studied him like someone I was meeting for the first time.

Unlike my obsessive focus on him, he'd barely given me a second glance once we got home. He disappeared into the guest bedroom and stayed there until all but the night shift officers had gone home for the evening. There were always two people here throughout the night since it wasn't like kidnappers would only issue their demands during working hours, but they gave us our privacy and hung out in the garage.

Mark's paranoia was palpable, and it'd worked its way into me. It was taking over the house too. It felt like all the officers were infected with it, looking at me differently when they said their goodbyes, but that was probably just in my head. I'd spent most of the day cleaning and scrubbing all the bathrooms since I didn't know what else to do with myself.

Mark had followed the same routine to get himself to sleep every night since Isaac had gone missing. He was a creature of habit even in his grief and pain. The moment he poured himself a glass of water instead of his usual bourbon at six, I knew something was up. He wouldn't veer from his routine without a reason, and the whole point of his booze-and-pill cocktail was to put himself to sleep. That only meant one thing—he didn't plan on sleeping tonight.

Dinner only confirmed my suspicions that something was going on. He couldn't sit still, and he was never one to fidget. He kept jiggling his legs underneath the table and knocking things around with his arms like he'd forgotten how to use them. Finally, he gave up trying to sit with us. He got up and paced around the dining room instead, muttering to himself underneath his breath.

"What's wrong with Dad?" Katie had asked, eyeing him over her plate at the dinner table.

Tonight's dinner wasn't anything like our usual dinners. We sat around the table with our reheated hot dish. Our freezer was packed full of them. Besides answering the phone all day long, my dad's other job was to take care of the never-ending food chain being delivered. We had enough frozen casseroles to last us through the winter. Despite the fact that we'd all skipped lunch, none of us were eating. We picked at the food, moving it around the plate without actually ever bringing it to our lips. Mark had just stared at his until he'd finally pushed it away. He hadn't even picked up his silverware.

"It's been a rough day." That's what I'd told Katie. Thankfully, she hadn't asked for more details, and she was still sleeping peacefully as I tiptoed out the door, straining for any sound of Mark. As I made my way down the stairs as carefully as I'd walked across the bedroom floors, I heard noises coming from the kitchen. I put my hand over my mouth and tried not to giggle. That was what I got for being so suspicious and paranoid. He was probably just making himself a sandwich because he couldn't sleep, and he hadn't touched his plate at dinner, so he had to be starving. Still. I kept quiet just in case and crept into the kitchen, admonishing myself the entire time for overreacting and being so suspicious.

The kitchen was empty except for the command center set up on the table. Everything else was in its place. There was no sign of Mark. I heard rustling in the laundry room.

I plastered myself against the wall and slid down to the doorway leading into the laundry room. I needed to stop being so silly. This was Mark. He wasn't doing anything he shouldn't be.

Except that he was.

He was bent over the laundry tub, pouring our laundry detergent down the drain. Our seventy-five-dollar bottle of specialized detergent that I had to order in advance and make sure I bought enough to last us for months. The only kind that didn't bother Katie's skin. I listened to the *glug glug glug* as the liquid poured out. There was a lot of it since I'd only just ordered it, and it felt like it took forever before it was empty. He pulled out a garbage bag and tossed the empty jug inside. I couldn't bring myself to do anything except watch as he reached underneath the sink and pulled out a bottle of Clorox. My eyes were glued to him as he poured bleach down the sink just like he'd done with the detergent.

I took one last look at him as he sat hunched over the tub, then started inching my way back through the house, being just as careful to be quiet the second time. My heart pounded as I tiptoed my way upstairs and into our bedroom. I hurried across the room and quickly slid underneath Katie's arm the same way I'd gotten out. I pulled the covers up to my chin and tried to still my racing heart. My pulse thrummed in my temples.

Why didn't I say anything to him? What was I doing? What was I thinking? I should just get up and go back down there. Confront him. Ask him what he was doing. Make him tell me what he knew. Demand an explanation for why he was getting rid of the detergent. But I couldn't bring myself to move or do anything except wait.

I was wide awake, and every second dragged until I finally heard him on the stairs. I quickly flipped over to my side and pretended like I was asleep. My mind screamed at me to do one thing—the right thing—but the rest of me wouldn't cooperate. I just lay there motionless and mute.

He made a stop at the bathroom before crawling underneath the covers on the other side of Katie. I told myself to turn around. To just roll over and ask him. It was that simple. Whatever it was. It couldn't be that bad. There had to be a reasonable explanation because Mark would never hurt Isaac. Never. He was the least violent man I'd ever met. That's what drew me to him in the first place. I'd watched my mom fight her way out of domestic abuse with my stepdad, and I vowed never to make the same mistake. I put every man I dated, including Mark—especially Mark—through all types of different tests to see if I could get a rise out of them. See if I got him upset enough, whether he'd hit me. Immature, sick stuff on my part, but that was before I grew up and worked through all that.

But if he hadn't done anything, then why was he worried about the detergent? That only left one other explanation—Isaac—which didn't make any more sense than Mark.

And that's when I heard it. The muffled sounds of him crying. Short jerky sobs that he tried to suppress so he wouldn't wake me or Katie, but he still shook the bed. Ones I'd only heard him make twice in our whole life together. Once when he got the call that his father had passed away, and the other time when Katie couldn't be resuscitated at birth and we thought we'd lost her. Everything felt like it was spinning. I gripped the side of the bed to steady myself.

What had Mark done?

SEVENTEEN

AMBER GREER

I didn't sleep at all last night. Not one minute. My eyes were burning, and my thoughts were still heavy and cloudy despite the three cups of coffee I'd already drunk. I'd never felt so worn down from sleep deprivation and worry. I hadn't stopped staring at Mark since coming downstairs.

I listened to him cry himself to sleep last night. It took forty-five minutes. Every time I thought he was finished, that he'd let out his last sob and pulled himself back together, they would start all over again.

He felt even more like a stranger in my house moving through the kitchen. In and out of the bathroom. He'd struggled with IBS for years, and in recent ones, it'd worked its way into full-blown colitis. His colitis was synonymous with Katie's eczema: both triggered by stress.

As if on cue, she interrupted my thoughts. "Is it okay if Paloma comes over today?"

"Are you sure you want to see her?" I asked, then quickly realized what a stupid question it was. She and Paloma had been best friends since first grade. They were practically inseparable. Theirs was the kind of friendship I'd always wanted but never had growing up. They went through a brief stint in sixth grade where middle school girl drama almost split them up, but they'd come out of it stronger than they were before.

"I do, Mom," Katie said hesitantly. It was how she spoke these days. There was an uncertainty to everything she said. A timidity to her voice and her posture because of all the uncertainty swirling around her. I put my arm around her shoulder and pulled her close to me. She wrapped her arms around my waist and squeezed tight. I breathed in the scent of her lavender-mint shampoo. We held on for a second before loosening our hold but not completely letting go of each other.

"I really miss her, and I haven't seen her in almost two weeks. I haven't seen anyone," she said.

Eleven days without any real contact with her friends was an awfully long time in the world of a thirteen-year-old girl, and I gave her another squeeze. "Has she talked to her mom? Is Cindy okay with her coming over here?"

It'd been so interesting watching who showed up at our door during all this. I had been shocked by the number of people who'd never given me the time of day who made their way to my front porch. They were always insulted when I didn't let them inside, as if I would want perfect strangers with me at my most intimate and vulnerable moments. Then there were those who showed up in full makeup with outfits that looked brand new so they'd look good for the cameras. Sally Higgins dropped off flowers in heels and a short miniskirt like she'd just come from the club. The reporters had flocked to her, and she'd soaked up every last bit of attention they'd lavished on her.

Besides all the investigators and technicians working the case, it was only my parents and my best friend who'd been inside yet. The individuals handling the case had become like new fixtures in our house, but I'd been acutely aware of their presence ever since I came downstairs. Everyone gave me weird hellos and shifty eye contact like I'd stumbled in on them talking about me, and one of my favorite technicians, Stan, wasn't even pretending like he wasn't studying my and Katie's interaction as it played out in front of him.

Katie nodded. "Her mom said she's fine with it. She even said she could stay overnight. Would that be okay?"

"You want to have a sleepover, Katie? Now?"

"It's not like it's just anyone, Mom. It's Paloma. She's practically family." She shrugged. "Besides, I thought it might be nice to try sleeping in my own bed tonight, and she can sleep with me. It would give you and Dad a break."

Had she heard Mark crying last night too? Had she been lying there pretending to sleep just like me while she listened? She could've been. It was totally possible. For a second, nothing felt real. Like I was standing outside myself watching. It was incredibly disorienting, and I forced myself to say something to Katie. "If it will make you feel better to have her here, then go ahead."

She kissed me on the cheek. "Thanks, Mom. I'm going to go tell her upstairs."

She bounced off, and for just that split second, things felt normal again. I was back inside my body. And then Detective Hawkins stepped through the front door, reminding me how far from normal things were. I couldn't take this roller coaster much longer. How did people live through this?

"Morning, everybody," Detective Hawkins called out to no one and everyone at the same time as he wiped his boots on the mat in front of the door. He was in the same collared shirt he'd worn last night, which meant he probably hadn't slept, either, except he looked much better than I did. I hadn't looked in a mirror this morning, but I knew I looked terrible. I hadn't even bothered to brush my teeth. Detective Hawkins caught my eye. "Did you sleep okay?"

"I slept all right," I lied. There was no point in telling the truth.

"How about you, Mark?" he called out to him in the living room.

Mark gave him the thumbs-up sign, lying right along with me. He'd only slept for a few hours before waking up and getting out of bed again. I hadn't followed him downstairs that time. I almost wished I hadn't the first time.

Detective Hawkins had barely stepped through the entryway when his phone buzzed. His eyes lit up when he saw the name. He quickly brought the phone up to his ear.

"Marilyn?" He nodded in quick successive jerks, immediately focused and at attention. He motioned to everyone that he was stepping outside, then abruptly turned and headed out, shutting the door tightly behind him.

Marilyn was his big boss. The one from Washington. She rarely called. Only when it was really important. My heart sped up, and my mouth went instantly dry. I couldn't swallow. I felt Mark's eyes on me from across the room, but I couldn't bring myself to return his stare.

I paced the kitchen, nervously waiting for Detective Hawkins to finish and let us know what was going on. Usually when I got this worked up, someone would crack a joke or tell me a story to distract me, but there was an icy temperature in the room. A level of uncomfortableness that had never been there before despite how awkward it had been when they first set up camp in my kitchen. Whatever weirdness was going on with Detective Hawkins, it'd trickled down to them.

The minutes dragged. Would Detective Hawkins let us stay or banish us to another side of the house? That's what he'd done the first day. He said my emotions were too big of a distraction in the kitchen. When he finally opened the door and I saw the look on his face, all the blood drained from my body. I brought both hands to my mouth. The floor rose up to meet me.

This couldn't be happening.

Run.

I wanted to whip open the door and take off sprinting as fast as I could through the neighborhood. If he couldn't say the words, then they couldn't be true. It never happened.

But I was frozen to my spot. Numb. Nothing would move even if I wanted it to. I flung a terrified glance in Mark's direction. His eyes matched my terror.

Please, God.

Detective Hawkins motioned to Mark. "Why don't you come join us in the kitchen? We need to have a team meeting in the kitchen."

Mark hurried to stand next to me. He leaned against the counter for support, and I leaned against him for the same.

"Okay, everyone, listen up," Detective Hawkins called out, sliding his phone into the back pocket of his pants.

Everything stopped and stilled in the middle of what they were doing like it was a game of tag and someone had just yelled *freeze.* For a second, Detective Hawkins's eyes met ours, and he gave us a brief nod, our official signal that it was okay to stay.

"We've had an interesting development in the case," he said as if we didn't already know something big was happening. He'd never called everyone to a halt and together in a big group like this. At least not when we were there. His eyes scanned the room, making a point to briefly connect with everyone before he continued speaking. "Billy and his mother just left the station after speaking with one of our officers about the case. Turns out, Billy was never grabbed by the Dog Snatcher." I gasped out loud, but nobody else made a sound. They were seasoned professionals in this business of twists and turns. Mark's entire body stiffened next to mine. Mine flooded with relief. "Billy made it all up. None of it happened. He was never grabbed. There was never a bald man with a cute dog. He created all the details."

"Was his mom in on it?" someone asked from the back. It was the guy who brought the doughnuts every morning and always made sure the door latched behind him whenever he left the house.

Detective Hawkins shook his head. "According to Billy's mom, she wasn't in on it and had no idea what was going on or that he wasn't telling the truth. She swore up and down that she never knew he was lying, and if she'd even had the slightest inkling that he was, she never would've brought him in to give his statement. She kept apologizing over and over again. Officer Logan took her statement, and he said she seemed credible."

"What happened then? Did someone talk to Billy? What'd he say?" A woman on the other side of the room rapid-fired the next round of questions at him. It was like being in a room full of reporters.

"I'll be going down to the station immediately to speak with them both, so I'll have a much better idea afterward, and you can all expect a more complete briefing from me then, but according to Officer Logan, Billy explained that his mom had been really mad at him lately and they'd been fighting a lot. He said that she always seemed disappointed in him, so he wanted to do something that would make her proud of him again. Apparently, his parents recently divorced, and she'd also been very sad lately. He kept saying, 'I just wanted to make my mom happy again.'"

Poor kid. It made perfect sense. What better way to get your strong boss mom to notice you than to get away from a serial killer using the skills she taught you? And then go on to provide clues in an investigation that would help save other innocent kids? His plan had worked beautifully. Everyone fell in love with him over what he'd done.

"Any reason for him to be lying about it?" This time the question came from the corner of the room.

Detective Hawkins shook his head.

"What do you think made him come forward now?" My voice joined the mix.

"Ms. Pierce, Billy's mom, found him crying in the garage last night and couldn't get him to stop. She was scared because he kept saying that he'd done something really bad and was afraid she'd be mad at him if he told her. It took some convincing, but eventually, he confessed to what he'd done. He told Ms. Pierce that he never meant for it to get this far. He said the same thing to Officer Logan. Said that he liked being famous, and he got caught up in it."

The media had followed him around like a puppy after the story went viral. People had sent flowers and gifts to their home from all over the world. Someone had opened a college account in his name, and it had been fully funded within a week. He wouldn't have to worry about paying for college or much else for a while. What would he do with all that money? It couldn't have been his intention all along, could it? Twelve days ago, I never would've considered someone doing something so horrible, but it hasn't taken long for me to grow cold and hardened toward humanity and the awful things people can do.

We didn't know anything about the killer. Not a single detail. We didn't even know their gender. Billy's descriptions were one of the reasons we'd never considered Jules as the killer. She could pass for a lot of things, but there was no way she could pass for an overweight and bald white man, which left only one alternative—she was playing a copycat. But anything was possible now. Maybe she'd put her car on the tracks because she was a killer and couldn't live with herself anymore. Maybe it had had nothing to do with Gabe.

Except her being an actual serial killer was a stretch. It always had been, even without Billy's bogus confession. Not that I was an expert, but I'd done nothing but listen to all the conversations happening around me for the past eleven days, and I'd done my research. Female serial killers were sadistic. They weren't former heads of the PTA. And besides, they almost always followed patterns. None of the other families had reported a grown woman grooming their son like she'd done with Isaac.

The killer could be anyone.

I was more confused than I'd ever been with this latest development, and I turned to the one person who'd always been the one to help me make sense of the world when I felt like it was falling apart. But Mark wasn't beside me anymore. He'd slid down the counter and stood at the end, leaning against it with his head in his hands. His back was to me. I couldn't see his face, but it didn't matter anyway because I'd lost the ability to read what he was thinking.

He knew more than he was letting on. He always had. Last night I'd watched him pour potential evidence down the drain. He wasn't who I thought he was, and something about that sent chills down my spine. I didn't have any answers. Only questions leading to more questions, but I did know one thing: I didn't know my husband at all.

CASE #72946

PATIENT: JULIET (JULES) HART

Dr. Stephens just stepped away for a phone call, and he was so nervous after he saw the number on his screen that he almost forgot to shut the door behind him. I can't help but wonder if it has something to do with the case. Do they have a new lead on Isaac?

I've heard nothing from him since we FaceTimed while he was walking Duke over three weeks ago. Right before Amber ripped him away from me. I'd been afraid of her doing something like that for weeks since all Isaac said was how much she was on him about hanging out with me, and I could see how it was impacting him. He'd already started to pull away from me because of it, and that, coupled with this huge school project, was cutting into our already limited alone time. It'd been hard on me, and things had been strained between us, but it felt like old times that night.

5:55 p.m. had been our special time to talk ever since my stay at Falcon Lake Hospital. My dinnertime on the unit coincided with the time Amber made him walk Duke every night, so it was perfect. She had him on a very structured schedule, and she was diligent about making him follow it even though he was a teenager. She and I definitely had different parenting styles. I was a much more laid-back parent.

Isaac was so excited that night. I loved nothing better than when he was happy, and it'd been a while since I'd seen him smile. It'd been a while since I'd seen him period. He'd been in such a depressed funk again, and he could be so difficult when he was in those moods. That was the hard part of being involved with someone so young. It required continual adjustments in my expectations and my patience. But when he was happy? Those moments were golden. They erased every single other bad day.

"Hi, honey," I said the moment his face filled the screen. Well, it wasn't exactly his face. More like his forehead and the top of his eyebrows. He was terrible about putting his entire face on the screen.

"What's the point of FaceTiming if you're not going to look at each other? Why wouldn't we just have a regular call then?" I'd asked him so many times over the past months.

And every time I asked, his response was always the same. He'd laugh without saying anything, and I'd beam. Because he was finally laughing again. So was I. It'd taken over a month, and his first real outburst of laughter had given birth to mine. It was just one of the many ways we helped each other.

I could hear the smile in his voice that night, and I would've made him show me his face if I'd had any idea it'd be the last time I'd see him, but I didn't. Instead, I talked to his forehead and the night sky as it bounced around, making me dizzy if I stared at it too long.

"You excited for tomorrow?" I asked after he finished telling me about the squirrel Duke had just chased up the tree.

"Absolutely," he said, and I could hear the eagerness in his voice. I was so proud of him. He'd been working so hard. "I've been counting down the days."

He'd been really overwhelmed when he was first given the assignment in his CAD course, and I could understand why. Creating a 3D-printed design of the entire school was an intense project. His partner wasn't really pulling his own weight, so he'd asked for my help, and

I'd jumped at the opportunity since he'd been ditching me to work on the project. The first thing I did was create a calendar with him so we could keep everything straight. There were lots of moving parts, and it was difficult to juggle, but it gave me something to do besides therapy, so I really didn't mind at all. And besides, it gave me more opportunities to spend time with him again, which was all I cared about anyway.

The door opens behind me and yanks me from the memory.

"Sorry, that took much longer than I thought it would," Dr. Stephens says as he hurries around the table and grabs his chair. His face is flushed. He's unbuttoned his collar. He'd never done that.

"Everything okay?" I ask. I can't help myself. I'm a natural caretaker even when I don't want to be.

"I just wasn't expecting that this morning, that's all." He wipes his forehead with the back of his sleeve and slowly takes his seat.

"What happened?" Normally, he's dying for me to ask him questions about what he knows, but he's not doing that. Something's different. Something's off.

A few beats pass, and my question hangs unanswered. He's still trying to decide whether he wants to share the information with me. I can tell by the way he's gazing off to the side of my face and he has his brow wrinkled.

"Was that Detective Hawkins?" I ask, trying to help him along.

"Yes." He nods. "Yes, it was."

I don't give him any other time to think and quickly pounce. "Do you want to talk about it?" I surprise myself with how well I still sound like a therapist. I haven't lost the voice. I guess it's like they say—once a therapist, always a therapist.

He clears his throat. He always clears his throat when he's nervous. It's a telltale sign that someone is nervous or lying, the oldest one in the book.

"That was Detective Hawkins," he explains like we haven't already established that, "and he was calling to tell me that our investigation has basically been flipped upside down overnight." His voice grows more confident as he speaks, like he's finally made up his mind that it's okay to tell me. "Billy's mom came down to the police station with Billy this morning, and he told police that he made up his entire story about the Dog Snatcher."

"What? Are you serious?"

He nods. His eyes are still wide with disbelief too. "Yeah, I am. Apparently, he made it all up. He wanted attention from his mom and, I assume, probably all the attention he'd get from the media too."

"Well, if that was the reason, then it definitely worked because it made him a hero," I say, but I don't need to tell him that. The whole world knew Billy. I'm shocked by the news too. I never thought a kid would lie like that for so long, especially to the police. But even though I'm shocked, it doesn't really bother me. Not like it seems to bother him. "You look like this is really disturbing news to you."

"I'm sorry." He shakes his head like that will help clear it. "That was just the last thing I was expecting this morning, and it threw me off." He shakes his head again. "This pretty much changes everything."

"Does it?" I'm not sure I agree. "How so?"

"We've developed an entire profile on him based on the information we received from Billy. None of that's true, so we're back at square one, which means we have no insight into his patterns. No idea who he might be." He snorts. "He might even be a she."

"Now wouldn't that be something," I respond with a smile even though we both know how unlikely that is. Female serial killers are extremely rare, and the ones that exist have very different motives than their male counterparts. Females almost always kill for profit or revenge, and they kill those closest to them. He knows this as well as I do since he's taken the same psychopathology courses as me. Of course, there are always exceptions.

Every theory has exceptions.

EIGHTEEN

AMBER GREER

Mark grabbed me by the arm and whispered in my ear, "Come with me." He said it like I had a choice, but his fingernails dug into me. I quickly followed him up the stairs and into our bedroom. He shut the door behind us, putting his finger up to his lips. He motioned for me to follow him into the bathroom. Once inside, he turned on the shower and both of the faucets in the sinks and left them running full blast.

Last night, this morning even, I would've thought he was being paranoid, but there was no mistaking there'd been a shift in the way the investigative team was treating us. The silence was the most obvious change. It'd been almost nonstop constant chatter for the last eleven days. They were never quiet. But today? Ever since we'd come downstairs, that was all there'd been except for when Detective Hawkins pulled everyone together to tell us about Billy. Nobody took phone calls inside the house anymore. They all stepped outside to take their calls, and none of the usual meetings were happening around us either.

I still hadn't told Mark that I'd seen what he'd done last night. We'd been circling around each other all day. Me watching him. Trying to reconcile the man I married with the one who would . . . what? What exactly had he been doing last night? Covering up evidence? Being extra cautious? I still didn't know, and I was too afraid to ask.

"You have to keep your voice down even with this." He motioned to the water rushing out of every faucet. It was going to create an astronomical bill. Normally, that would've bothered me. Today I couldn't care less.

He was scaring me, and I didn't want to be scared of my husband. I shouldn't be scared of my husband. There's no fear in a love relationship—that's what the therapist had said in our marital counseling before the wedding. But there was fear everywhere. It was so thick I could taste it in my mouth when I breathed.

Who was this man in front of me?

"They think we have something to do with this," he blurted out.

"With what? Isaac's disappearance?" I asked because there was no way they could think we were killers. That was ridiculous. Almost as absurd as thinking we played any role in whatever was happening now. Except I was the only one who could say that. I wasn't sure about Mark.

"Yes." He nodded vigorously. "We're not on the same team anymore."

"So, we're hiding our son somewhere and making it look like he was kidnapped? Why would we possibly do anything like that?" I wasn't in denial about them being suspicious toward us. He was definitely right about that, but Detective Hawkins couldn't actually think we'd fake Isaac's kidnapping, could he? He'd been in our house for almost two weeks. He had to know us better than that.

"Same reason as Billy," Mark said matter-of-factly.

"Attention? We faked our son's kidnapping to get attention?" I scoffed. That might be a motive for some people, but it couldn't be further removed from my personality. Isaac and I were alike in lots of ways, but our main similarity was how we preferred to be alone or with just a few people. "Why would I put myself in the center of attention when I absolutely hate being there? Don't they know that not everybody on the planet is obsessed with people liking them and being on camera? I post on social media like three times a year. Seriously. I've never even gone live," I shrieked, even though I was supposed to be quiet. "And then what? After we got our attention, what exactly were we going to do then?" He motioned for me to keep my voice down, but I shook my head. My anger growing stronger the more I talked. "It's a stupid theory. There's no way they can actually think that because what happens after fourteen days? We're the ones to kill him? Or we somehow keep him hidden forever? I mean, come on, there's just no way we did this. It's too ridiculous."

"Or they think we helped Isaac set things up to look like he'd been kidnapped. There's that too." He didn't say it mean and angry like me. As if he were appalled at the idea and there was no way it could be true. He said it like there was some truth to it, like he was suggesting it as a real possibility.

"Why would we do that? And for what?" He refused to make eye contact. He shifted back and forth on his feet. "Mark, why would we do that? What are you talking about?" All my fears rushed up to meet me, leaving me weak and dizzy.

"I'm not saying we did. It's—"

"There's no *we* in this. I have no idea what's going on or what you're hinting at." I couldn't take it anymore. "Mark, what's going on? I don't know anything other than my child went to walk the dog and never came home. It looked just like the Dog Snatcher took him, but I've said all along that that wasn't the case. And you?" I leapt off the counter and pressed my face in front of his. "You're the one that has made me feel like a fool this entire time. You're the one who's gone on and on about it being the Dog Snatcher. How there couldn't be any other possibility even though I could name three, and now you've suddenly done a complete one-eighty. Had a total change of heart. What the hell is going on?"

"I don't know what's going on. I don't. I—"

"Bullshit."

He shook his head. "I'm telling you the truth. All I've done this entire time is try to figure out what happened to Isaac."

"Bullshit." I said it again. "I saw what you did last night," I blurted. There—it was finally out.

His eyes grew wide. He opened his mouth, then shut it. He did that twice.

I nodded and crossed my arms on my chest. "I saw you—"

He shoved his hand over my mouth. "Be quiet," he hissed in my face. "I know what you saw me do."

I slapped his hand off my mouth. "Tell me what's going on."

He took a few shuddering breaths like he was trying to breathe deep but struggling to get the air into his lungs. His entire body tensed. "Up until yesterday morning at the police station, Amber, I swear I thought the Dog Snatcher had him. Since day one. I really did. That wasn't a lie. And I was sick about it. Truly sick about it. For so many reasons. So many reasons." He kept repeating himself as his face crumpled like he was going to cry again. The same way he'd cried himself to sleep last night beside me while I pretended to sleep. "I just couldn't stop thinking about all the horrible things they might be doing to him. The torture and pain he must be going through and that I was responsible for it. That I was being punished. I've really just been thinking I was being punished. Taking my kid away from me in the most horrific way."

"Mark, what are you talking about?" My stomach rolled in on itself. "What were you being punished for?"

He rubbed his face with both hands as he struggled to gain control of his emotions and his voice. He'd never looked so wrecked. Even the night Isaac had gone missing. "I've been worried sick about Isaac since the accident and how he's changed. I've hated not being able to get him to talk to me or let me inside his head. He used to tell me everything." Sadness warbled his voice. It was true. Even adolescence hadn't changed that. Mark was still Isaac's best friend. "I couldn't stand the thought of him suffering alone, you know? I just couldn't."

I nodded. I knew exactly how awful it felt. There was no greater torture for a parent than being unable to stop your child's suffering. I'd sat outside Isaac's bedroom door plenty of times listening to him cry and being completely powerless to do anything to help him. It was excruciating.

Tears glistened in Mark's eyes. "So I downloaded *Dracho* and started playing it. It's a role-playing game where you can create worlds that—"

"Mark"—I put my hand on his arm—"you don't have to explain the game to me. I know all about *Dracho*." I'd held out on letting Isaac play video games for as long as I could. Not because I bought the arguments about them making him violent, but I hated the way they allowed kids to cut themselves off from the real world. The social isolation they allowed them to create. Who wouldn't want to live in a video game world in comparison to the real one? That's why they were so dangerous. And I wasn't wrong. We'd battled with Isaac about them since the first time we let him on *Roblox*.

"Right. Right," Mark said like he was reminding himself who he was talking to and remembering that most of Isaac's and my fights centered around trying to get him off his video game and into real life. "Anyway, I just thought if I could reach out to him in that world, then I might have a better chance of connecting with him. I just wanted him to have a friend, you know?" He shrugged at me as he searched my eyes for understanding. "It didn't take long to find him, but it did take a while for us to become friends. Eventually, he let me onto his server, and that's when we really started talking." He exhaled slowly. "You don't know much about video games, so it's hard to explain, but he'd created his own world on the server, and he was doing some pretty awful things on there."

"What do you mean? What kind of awful things?"

"He owned the server, so he created the world and controlled everything that happened there. He was the one who had the power to let you in or kick you out. Basically, you started out in the world with nothing. No food. No water. No shelter. No friends. You earned those things based on accumulating points. The only way to earn points was to . . . it was to . . ." His voiced cracked, and he stalled for a second. "Go to the school and kill students. He'd created a world on the server where you only got access to certain things based on who you killed at the school. The more popular the student, the more points awarded. The more torturous the death, the more points. Bonus points if the kid was a jock. There—"

I held my hand up to stop him. "I'm not sure I'm following you. So, Isaac created a fake city in a video game world where they got points for shooting the cool kids?"

He nodded.

"But it was all just a video game?"

He nodded again.

"Okay, okay." I thought while I spoke. "That's an awful game. Like a really awful game, and I'm horrified that Isaac would do such a thing, but it's understandable that he has some strong feelings after the way he's been treated." I didn't need to remind Mark about the texts. He'd seen them too. Or the fact that most of the kids at school hadn't ever been all that nice to him. "Maybe it was his way of blowing off steam."

He frantically shook his head. "It was way more than that. He and the players started doing things in the real world, Amber. Not shooting up schools, obviously, because that would've been all over the news, but they started being able to earn points in the game for things they'd done in real life too. They'd come back to the game and talk about what they'd done. At first, it was small. Only a handful of people. But it grew. It got bigger and bigger. Their pranks got riskier and riskier. They created lists of kids who had hurt them and started doing horrible things to them, like shitting in their lockers. Flattening their tires in the parking lot.

206

Spray-painting their cars. One of them even started a fire in someone's backyard. It was like this underground world of rejected kids who took it upon themselves to punish the people that were hurting them."

I rubbed my face with my hands, trying to make sense of what he was telling me, but I couldn't make the pieces fit. "But I don't know how Isaac would've been involved in any of that. He never even left the house unless it was to walk the dog or visit Jules. For a while, he wasn't even going to school."

"Yeah, but that was the thing. None of his followers knew that. They all thought he had. Isaac made up all these stories of the things he did to fight back against his tormentors. Most of what the others did were ideas he'd given them that he either told them he'd done himself or he made up. They practically worshipped him. He was the lord of their world."

"Are you sure?" I couldn't wrap my brain around any of this. None of it fit.

"Yes, I was right there in the middle of it all. It was like some sick and twisted version of the Hunger Games. I made up stories the same way he did. The same way they all did. I told myself that maybe everyone was just making it up. But then people started posting pictures about what they'd done, and that's when it got really scary." He looked stricken.

This was too much. What was happening? Isaac had never been violent. And then I quickly remembered all the times in the last three months that he had. Maybe I didn't know Isaac any more than I knew Mark.

"There was this dark shift that happened right around that time. They moved from talking about things they'd do to people's stuff and started discussing what they'd do to their bodies. All these disturbed fantasies of torturing them before killing them. It was awful, and I never said a word to anyone. Not even you." Guilt contorts his every feature. "I wanted to tell you, but I was too afraid you'd get all confrontational with him about it and push him even further way, and I just didn't want to do that to him. I'm sorry." He hung his head. "It wasn't the right thing to do, but I thought if he trusted me as his friend, then I could talk him out of it. As long as I was in his inner circle, then I would know what he was doing, and I swear, Jules, the moment it looked like he was going to actually hurt another person, I would've stepped in and done something. But then he was just gone."

He stopped. There was no denying he was reliving the moment it finally sank in that Isaac wasn't coming home that night. I felt it in my guts too. He'd been the one to call the police department and say the words that changed our world forever: *I need to report a missing boy.*

His Adam's apple moved up and down as he wrestled to speak. "I thought the Dog Snatcher took him. I really did." His voice cracked. Tears flowed down his cheeks. "And a part of me? This small secret part of me . . . was glad. I know that's so awful. You can't say something like that about your child. But I just kept thinking what if that was the universe's way of keeping him from hurting other people?" He put his hands over his mouth like he wanted to shove the truth back inside.

But he couldn't. The truth was out. There was no taking it back. It settled like a cold stone in my gut.

"Has anyone . . . has anyone . . ." My voice lowered automatically, but I was still having a hard time saying it. I cleared my throat and tried again. "Has anyone hurt anyone or done anything else yet?"

"Not that I know of, but I'm so nervous someone will that I don't even know what to do. I've been obsessively logging on to the game every day to monitor the activity, and so far, there's been nothing. I've also been checking to see if Isaac's logged on, too, obviously."

"Has he?"

"Don't you think I'd tell you if I heard from him?"

"You didn't tell me this," I snapped without thinking. I wanted to be mad at him. I really did, but I couldn't be too angry with him. After all, he wasn't the only one with secrets about Isaac.

NINETEEN

AMBER GREER

I sat staring at Isaac's blank computer screen like I'd done so many times since Mark's confession yesterday, but I still couldn't bring myself to look. Seeing it would make it a reality I couldn't take back, and part of me wanted to stay in denial that Isaac would ever be part of something so awful.

Mark and I had so many arguments over this thing in the past few years. It'd been one big argument since the moment we got it. Even buying it at the store had turned into a stupid fight. Technology and screen time were two of Mark's and my biggest disagreements. We never argued about things when our kids were young, but it wasn't due to any admirable qualities of our own. We simply agreed on most things when it came to parenting and child-rearing practices—breastfeeding versus bottle-feeding, managing the toddler years, having the kids on a schedule and trying to keep their lives structured. Bedtimes. Homework. Discipline. All that stuff. We agreed on it all. We were lucky that way.

But all that changed the older the kids got and the more complex their issues and problems became. That's when we had our first real divide. Mark was much more laid back and relaxed when it came to limiting their screen time, which of course he was since I was on him about it almost as much as I was the kids. He couldn't say there was anything wrong with the amount of time they spent on their phones and devices when I was always snapping at him to get off his.

I knew Isaac's password but rarely logged on. The world of online computer gaming made no sense to me, and I had zero interest in it. That was all Mark's domain. He understood and liked it way more than I did. I'd always figured if there was something concerning about Isaac's behavior, Mark would tell me. That'd been our agreement, even though we'd never committed to it out loud. We didn't need to. It went without saying that Mark would let me know if there was anything to be concerned about with Isaac's behavior online. I couldn't help but feel betrayed that he'd broken our agreement.

Guilt immediately flooded me. I was such a hypocrite. I didn't tell Mark when Isaac took too much of his medication last month in the same way he hadn't told me about the video game stuff. He was going to feel just as betrayed as me when I told him, and I had to tell him. We'd paused our discussion in the bathroom so that we wouldn't be gone for too long and make the police grow even more suspicious of us than they already were. But our conversation was far from over, and this was going to be the first thing I told him when we resumed it.

I just hoped he would understand that the only reason I hadn't said anything was because I hadn't wanted to make a big deal out of something that wasn't. I wanted to give Isaac the benefit of the doubt. Mark probably did the same thing I'd done when he found out about Isaac's violent world: told himself it wasn't a big deal given the circumstances. Kids, especially ones in the throes of puberty and trauma, were going to have all kinds of intense and out-of-the-ordinary reactions. At least that's what I told myself. That Isaac's behavior was a reaction to everything he'd been through.

Right before Isaac quit therapy, Theresa suggested a psychiatric evaluation for him to see if medication might help with his depression. I'd been thinking the same thing for a long time, so I gladly took her referral and made an appointment with Dr. Fritz the following week. Dr. Fritz was one of the few child psychiatrists in the area, and he didn't have an opening in his schedule for three months, but he moved things around once he found out who Isaac was. I'd never used Isaac's notoriety before, but I didn't feel bad about it since it was for a good cause. Not like I would if I took any of the money the news agencies offered for our stories.

Dr. Fritz prescribed Celexa, and Isaac started on a small dose. I was concerned about all the potential side effects, especially increased suicidality in teenagers, so we spoke about them at great length. Causing the condition you're trying to treat seems counterintuitive to me, but Dr. Fritz assured me Isaac would be fine as long as we started at a very small dose, titrated him up slowly, and monitored him closely along the way.

Within two weeks, he'd taken a handful of them. I had no idea he'd done it and would've never found out if I hadn't, coincidentally, taken him to the doctor for his annual physical a few days later. His pediatrician, Dr. Knoll, looked up at me after she listened to Isaac's heart. She'd gone through the same routine she'd been doing since Isaac was four. Listening to his chest while he took a deep breath, then listening to his back in the same way. It felt strange to sit in with Isaac on his physical since he'd been going alone for the past few years, but he'd insisted on it.

Her brow furrowed. "I'm detecting a slight arrhythmia in Isaac's heartbeat." She took a few steps back from him like the separation might help her get a better handle on things. She rubbed her chin. "His blood pressure is also elevated. Have you been feeling okay, Isaac? Any dizziness? Lightheadedness?"

"A little bit," he said.

"You have?" I asked, piping up from my position on the chair in the corner. So far, I'd kept my mouth shut.

He nodded.

He'd never told me that he wasn't feeling well. I'd heard him get up and go to the bathroom around one o'clock last night, but I hadn't thought anything of it. He was frequently up in the middle of the night, and most of the time he used the restroom in the hallway at some point during it. "Were you sick last night?"

"I didn't feel the best . . . I . . ." His words trailed off, and he was too embarrassed to continue.

"Go ahead, son. I'm a doctor," Dr. Knoll encouraged.

"I had diarrhea last night," he said, and his face instantly flushed bright red. He rarely blushed, but telling a doctor you had diarrhea was enough to mortify any teenager.

"Was it bad?"

Isaac nodded.

"Did you drink a lot of fluids afterward to rehydrate?"

"Not really."

Dr. Knoll nodded. "That might explain what's happening." She turned to look at me. "It could be that Isaac is extremely dehydrated after his bout with diarrhea. That might be responsible for what I'm seeing, but I'm just going to draw some blood and do an EKG just to be sure."

Dr. Knoll stepped outside to get what she needed for the test and the blood draw. Isaac turned to look at me. His face was pale. His eyes dilated. His voice shook as he spoke. "Mom, I have to tell you something."

"Honey, what is it?" I got up, recognizing immediately that something was wrong and rushing to stand next to his exam bed.

His eyes filled with tears. "Don't be mad. Please don't be mad at me, but I took some pills." He blurted it out fast like if he talked too slow, he might not tell on himself.

"You took pills? What kind of pills?" My head spun with the news, trying to make sense of it.

"My antidepressants," he whispered like someone might hear him and he'd get in trouble.

"How many did you take?" This was exactly what I was afraid of. The pills making him worse instead of better, but I tried to keep my face calm and my voice low. I didn't want him to think I was angry with him. This wasn't his fault.

He shrugged, but he looked worried. "I don't know."

"What do you mean you don't know how many pills you took? You have to know how many you took." My voice rose. I needed to rein myself back in. Getting scared was only going to push him away and ensure he never told me anything in the future.

"Does it matter?" He raised his eyebrows at me.

"Yes, it matters. You could've died," I snapped. As soon as I said it, I realized what I'd said. What he'd potentially done. That's when the waves of dread and fear filled my insides.

"Do you think I'm going to be okay?" he asked in a somber whisper.

That question was the reason I'd kept quiet about what he'd done and hadn't told Mark about the incident. I hadn't told anyone. Isaac was worried about being okay, and if he was worried about being okay, then that meant he'd changed his mind about being alive. That's what mattered. That was the most important thing. He had sounded so scared and terrified that day. Like when they used to send kids to prison on *Dr. Phil* and scare them straight. That's the kind of scared he was, and if taking the pills had done that to him, it might've been worth it.

It was the first time I'd kept something the kids had done from Mark. We shared everything when it came to them. Always had. They were our most important priority and the thing we loved the most in the world, so neither of us wanted to be left out of what was happening with them.

It wasn't like I hadn't thought about telling Mark. I had. I just didn't want to hurt him or create any more unnecessary pain. I told myself I was protecting him, but truthfully, I was protecting myself too. And Isaac. He didn't want to talk about it afterward either. He seemed more embarrassed by it than anything.

"It was stupid, Mom, I'm fine," he said on the ride home from Dr. Knoll's office when I tried to bring it up again. It wasn't like I hadn't tried to talk to him about it or watch him like a hawk afterward.

But I stopped worrying about it because things changed afterward. There was the first genuine turnaround in his behavior. For the last month, Mark and I had grown increasingly troubled by all the time he'd been spending with Jules, and we'd been harping on him to stop spending so much time with her. It'd been nothing but a battle because he didn't want us telling him what to do, but suddenly, from out of the blue, he stopped hanging out with Jules and cut off their communication without us having to have another heated discussion with him about it. He wouldn't tell me why he'd done it, only that he'd blamed it all on me. He told her that I refused to let him have any contact with her even though that wasn't true, but I didn't care what he told her as long as it was over. I was so proud of him. He couldn't move forward when he was bound by her toxicity and messed-up thinking. He'd even invited a friend over after school. Just that one time, but it was a start. I'd walked in on them in his bedroom and been so stunned to find him in there not alone that it'd stopped me in my tracks.

"Mom! What are you doing?" he screeched when I opened the door without knocking. I knocked on both my kids' doors before entering, but I hadn't heard him come home.

"I'm sorry. I didn't hear you come home from school." I stood there dumbfounded, with the laundry basket perched on my hip bone and staring at the kid sitting cross legged on the floor. The room smelled funny. Like they'd been vaping nicotine or pot. I couldn't tell. He had long stringy hair that hung in his face and shifty eyes that glanced up at me when I talked. The boy had terrible acne. The angry red kind.

"Get out of here!" Isaac snapped at me before I had a chance to introduce myself to his friend. I'd quickly set his clothes on the bed and hurried out of his room so I wouldn't embarrass him any more than I already had.

Isaac had been irritated and annoyed when I'd questioned him about his new friend after he left. This time I'd knocked on his door and been invited inside.

"You wanted me to have friends, right, Mom?" he asked with an angry scowl. "That was the whole point of me not hanging out with Jules so much, remember? So that I could spend time with kids my own age. Isn't that what you said?"

"Yes, I . . . it's just that . . ." Heat burned my cheeks. How could I be so nervous with my own child? When had it gotten this difficult?

"It's just that what?" He rose from his desk and puffed his chest out as he walked over to where I stood in the doorway. He towered over me. "You want me to have certain kinds of friends—is that it?"

I snapped my mouth closed and hurried away. I never said anything. Just left it alone because he was right. I wanted him to hang out with other people besides Jules. There was nothing normal about their relationship. I could justify it when she was in the hospital, but all that changed when she got out. We'd been threatening to put an end to their relationship for weeks, so all I'd focused on was being happy that it was finally over. I'd never given his new friend a second thought.

Maybe the boy that day had been one of his online friends from *Dracho*. What if the game had already crossed over into his real life, and Mark hadn't known it? Was there any chance Isaac wasn't making things up? Thoughts of the game brought me back to the computer sitting in front of me.

The police had been in his room the night he'd gone missing, and they'd searched through his stuff, but they'd left his computer alone. There was no reason to do anything with it at the time. Not when they were so focused on the Dog Snatcher being responsible for his disappearance.

I took a deep breath and slowly jiggled his mouse to wake the system up. It wasn't like I didn't believe Mark about the game. I just wanted to see for myself. The computer came to life slowly since nobody had touched it in eleven days. I entered Isaac's passcode and watched as his desktop loaded. His background was a picture of one of his favorite video game characters in a battle stance holding a gun. He just kept leaping and flashing across the screen. I had no idea you could animate your desktop wallpaper, and it quickly started giving me a headache. There was nothing on his desktop except the Google Chrome icon and the recycle bin. That was strange, but maybe he was one of those people who hated icons and folders cluttering up their screen.

I clicked on the start menu to pull up his list of programs and software, but there was barely anything listed except the basics that came with the computer system and Microsoft Office. He used to write all his school projects and reports with it in middle school before he switched to Google Docs. I opened those document files and folders, but there wasn't anything in them except old homework. I pulled up the list of recent downloads, but *Dracho* was missing. All his other games were gone too. The hardware and software needed to run the computer were on the drive, but none of his games were. His computer search and download history were missing too. All his programs. Files. Games. Applications. They were all gone. Everything had disappeared from his computer like he'd disappeared from the street.

The room pulsed and throbbed around me. The fear surged through me, leaving me weak, and I was glad I was sitting down. I pulled my phone out and texted Mark:

Come up to Isaac's room. It's important.

TWENTY

AMBER GREER

There weren't butterflies in my stomach—there were birds, and they twisted my insides as Mark's footsteps thundered up the stairs and into Isaac's room. He was by my side at the desk immediately. "What's going on? What did you find?"

"There's nothing here." I pointed at the computer.

"What do you mean there's nothing there?"

"Exactly what it sounds like. Everything is gone. All his games. His history. Files. They're all gone. Unless they're hidden somewhere in some kind of secret folder that I can't find, but they're not here." I just kept pointing at the screen.

"That's impossible." He shook his head, bewildered. "Move over." He motioned for me to get out of the chair, and I gladly jumped out of it so he could slide into my spot. I stood behind him, watching over his shoulder as he grabbed the mouse and started searching. His hands flew over the keyboard, and his mouse clicked on all the things I'd already clicked on: files, folders, servers. All of it. He kept doing it over and over again. Just like I'd done. Checking and rechecking. After a few more minutes, he sank into the chair, and his shoulders drooped with defeat. He frowned. "There's nothing there."

"I know—that's what I've been trying to tell you," I said, feeling his defeat as much as he did. I'd been secretly hoping Isaac had just tucked his stuff away somewhere that I couldn't find it and that Mark would be able to locate it since he was more computer savvy than me.

Mark put his elbows on the table and rested his chin on his hands. "I can't believe he did that."

"He deleted everything from the last three weeks on his phone, too, remember . . ." I let my words trail off. I didn't know how to complete the sentence, or maybe I didn't want to. Mark didn't either. We sat in silence, staring at the empty screen.

He finally broke the silence—his voice was barely above a whisper, but I heard every word as he spoke my greatest fear out loud: "He has something to do with this."

"Is that why you dumped out the detergent?"

He gave the most reluctant nod. I waited for him to say more, but he didn't.

"I just don't understand what's happening right now." My voice was as low as his without even trying. I was suddenly acutely aware of the police presence downstairs. Could they hear us upstairs? Were they listening? If you let police inside your house, were they allowed to put up cameras or other listening devices? Had they suspected us all along? My head swirled. I needed to sit down. I walked over to Isaac's bed and took a seat on the end of it. "I don't understand," I repeated myself, trying to stop my thoughts from spinning.

"I meant what I said earlier about being convinced it was the Dog Snatcher. But as soon as Detective Hawkins said that about the laundry detergent, everything shifted in me. Like I knew immediately Isaac had something to do with it, and I don't even know what any of that means, but I just felt like getting rid of it was protecting him. And all I want to do is protect him. I'm sorry, it's probably wrong. I'm sure it's wrong, but I can't help it."

"But he hasn't actually done anything wrong, has he? Adults do crap like this all the time. Remember that runaway bride all those years ago? Or that other woman in Washington? Everyone thought they'd disappeared and something awful had happened to them, but it wasn't like once they came home, they were arrested or anything. If there are no charges for adults, then I'm pretty sure it's got to be okay for kids, wouldn't you think?" My brain scrambled to make sense of things.

"I have no clue." He lifted his hands up. "I have no idea what to do. I've never been so lost in my life . . ."

I hadn't been either. I took a few steps back, leaning against Isaac's bed for support. I still hadn't made it. Mark twirled around in the chair so he was facing me, and the magnitude of everything we were up against washed over me, leaving me drained. I felt like I could sleep for days, but that was the biggest lie. If I lay down on this bed and even tried, my eyelids would stay open like they'd been stapled that way. Tears wet my cheeks as I searched Mark's eyes for some form of moral compass in all this.

"Can I just be honest with you?" he asked after a few more minutes had passed. He didn't wait for the obvious yes. "I hope he just ran away, and that's all this is. I really do, because at least then he's alive and still has a chance. I just want him to be happy."

Isaac was fifteen, and fifteen-year-olds ran away from home all the time, especially when they hated their lives, which there was no mistaking Isaac did. "But why go through all the trouble to make it look like he got kidnapped? Why not just take off and run away?"

"I totally get where you're coming from, and I've thought about that, too, but he had to know that if he didn't come home, we'd set out to look for him, and maybe for some reason, he thought making it look like the Dog Snatcher took him would give him more of a head start?"

Or maybe he'd wanted to be dead in fourteen days, too, and he didn't want people to think he'd taken his own life. Maybe he was trying to spare us. As soon as the thought popped into my head, I shoved it down, burying it deep.

"Where would he go?" I asked. The thought of him out there on his own when he couldn't even keep his room clean was frightening, but it was frightening in a silly, childish way in comparison to all the other potential horrors we'd been imagining. Out on the streets somewhere meant that he was alive. That was all that mattered to me. And if he was alive, maybe once he'd gotten some time away, some perspective, he'd come back home. At least reach out. He couldn't run away from us forever, could he? That wasn't possible. He loved us. He adored Katie.

"He's not going to get very far without money," Mark said, practical to a default.

"Are you sure about that?" I asked.

"That he doesn't have any money?"

I nodded.

"He only gets money from us, and he hasn't asked for any, so there's that. Plus, there haven't been any unusual withdrawals from any of his or our accounts." He said it with such confidence and conviction, but who knew what Isaac had been up to. If he was behind his own disappearance, then this wasn't impulsive. It was thought out and planned.

"Jules might have given him money," I pointed out. She was always my go-to, even now; I couldn't help it. "She doesn't have access to her funds because of the conservatorship, but we don't know how that financial arrangement works. I'm sure she gets a certain amount of money every month, like an allowance or something. They can't give her nothing. Maybe she gave it to Isaac. If anyone is helping him, it's got to be her."

"Totally," he agreed, nodding and rubbing his hands on his sweatpants. His palms always got sweaty when he was nervous.

Being on the same page felt wonderful. It hadn't felt like this between us in three years. Not since Isaac hit puberty. I'd forgotten what it felt like, but it only took a minute, and I immediately remembered how much I loved it. How much I loved him. Still. Even after all these years and buried underneath all the harsh feelings and resentments, there was an unshakable love between us. I took a moment to appreciate it before continuing.

"Maybe he's going to call us soon, you know? Like he'll reach out when he gets wherever he's going or after he's settled and things calm down. And then we can just let everyone know he's all right." What if this didn't have to end in another tragedy? Tears filled my eyes at the prospect.

"The way I figure, everyone will be so happy when he shows up that they'll all just be grateful he's alive and okay." He said like it was a sure thing, and I so desperately wanted to believe that's how this would play itself out. He did too. His hope was written all over him.

Faking your own kidnapping was a pretty brutal thing to put your loved ones through, but Isaac might not have felt like he had any other choice. Teenagers couldn't see beyond the moment they were in and had no idea that the only thing constant about life was that it changed. Isaac didn't know things would've changed eventually and all this would've passed. There was so much life ahead of him, but he didn't know that, and it was heartbreaking.

"This is so hard," I said because I didn't know what else to say.

"I know," he said. His eyes were filled with tears too. Something about acknowledging the pain and how hard it was made it feel like for the first time in all this, we were in it together instead of on separate islands. "Here's the next question." Mark dropped his voice low again.

"What's that?"

"Do we tell the police?" He pointed below us.

That wasn't the next question. Not yet. There was one more thing we needed to discuss before we did anything else.

"There's something that I haven't told you that you need to know." This was it. There was never going to be a good time. I just had to tell him.

His head snapped up. Instant mood shift. "God, Amber. I'm not sure if I can handle anything else today. I really don't."

"I don't know if it's related. It might be or it might not be, but we're spilling all of our secrets today, so it's only fair that I tell you mine." He gripped the chair. His body stiffened in preparation for news I wasn't sure either of us could handle on top of what we'd already been through, but our newfound togetherness propelled me forward. "Do you remember when Isaac had those irregularities that showed up on one of his EKGs?" He nodded. Of course he remembered. He'd been terrified there was something wrong with Isaac's heart. His best friend had died from an undiagnosed heart condition during a track meet their senior year of high school, so he was especially sensitive to it. "The reason his heart was acting funny was because two days before we went to the pediatrician, he overdosed on his Celexa medication. He got horribly ill. He had violent diarrhea and had a terrible headache coupled with chest pains. He just thought the chest pains were anxiety until we went to the doctor."

"When you say overdosed, what do you mean?"

"He took too many of his pills."

"Why did he take too many pills?"

"Why do you think, Mark?" Why was he making me spell it out for him? This was hard enough as it was without having to give him a play-by-play account.

"There are lots of reasons he could've taken too many pills."

I raised my eyebrows at him. "Name one."

"He could've taken too much because he was trying to get high. I would've done something like that when I was a teenager if I was trying to get messed up. Maybe that's all that it is." He looked relieved, but I wasn't sure him trying to get high was all that much better. Either way, he was still trying to kill himself. One was just faster. "Why didn't you tell me?"

"For the same reason you didn't tell me: I didn't want to worry you any more if I didn't need to. There was already so much going on, and things were already so hard." And like him, I leave out the real reason. The one we probably didn't even admit to ourselves—I didn't want it to be true. I wanted to pretend like it never happened. That was the truth. But there was no more pretending. This was happening. All of it.

TWENTY-ONE

AMBER GREER

Day fourteen.

Everything had shifted in the last twenty-four hours. Nothing was the same. You felt it in the house, from the thickness in the air to the way nobody made full eye contact with anyone else anymore. The house was so quiet. It had thrummed with a baseline level of activity for thirteen days. All that was gone.

We were all waiting, just like we'd been the night Isaac had gone missing. Each minute had crawled, and I'd wanted to jump out of my skin. The more hours that passed, the more it had taken away the possibility that something bad hadn't happened to him. Up until eleven o'clock that night, there had still been hope that despite what it looked like, Isaac could come walking through the door at any minute. Duke got away from him all the time. He got away from all of us. Unlike those other boys, there were plenty of instances over the last decade where the two of them left together and came home separately. Duke was an escape artist. It was his favorite game to play, and he took off any chance that he got. So we'd waited and hoped. Just like we were doing now.

All the days since then had been leading up to this. If the Dog Snatcher had Isaac, any moment his body would show up in a field somewhere. There was still a small chance that he did. I'd never doubted that possibility. Even if Isaac was up to something, it could've been a horrific coincidence. Coincidences happened all the time. And even though it was unlikely, the killer could've switched detergent.

But it was starting to look like that wasn't the case. Just like the night Isaac had gone missing and every hour that had ticked away increased the likelihood of a horrible outcome, this time it was the opposite. Every hour that passed without any sign of him decreased the likelihood that the Dog Snatcher had him. Not that there weren't other horrific possibilities—stuff we'd thought of and things we'd missed—but at least it increased the chances that he was alive. As long as he might be alive, there was hope.

There was also no denying that Isaac might've staged this. Would he have been able to pull this off by himself? My thoughts circled back to Jules like they always did. Were the two of them in on it together? Nobody had said anything to us about her for a few days. We hadn't even gotten a debriefing from Detective Hawkins last night. That was a first. Were they still talking to her? Or were they too focused on us?

It's been almost forty-eight hours since Mark and I decided not to tell anyone about Isaac's erased computer or what was on it. At least not yet. We'd decided to wait.

"Let's just give ourselves some more time to think about it," he'd said after Katie came looking for us in Isaac's room after we'd been gone for so long. "It's an important decision with a lot at stake, and I don't think we need to rush into anything."

But we weren't giving ourselves more time to think about it. We were giving Isaac time to get away and waiting for today to see what happened. Day fourteen. At least by the end of the day, we'd have one big question answered. Until then all we could do was wait in fear and second-guess everything we'd done.

"Mom, it's your turn." Katie's voice interrupted my thoughts, pulling me into the present moment and back to our Monopoly game. She insisted on playing it earlier this morning to help pass the time and keep herself distracted. It was certainly working because it was after noon and we were still at it. Even though Paloma had come over, Katie had never been away from school or her friends for this long in her entire life. It was unnatural and felt abnormal being trapped inside like this. As if our lives were paused while we lived in a gigantic bubble.

No matter what happened, she was going to have to go back to her life soon. She couldn't exist like this forever. None of us could. The TV played CNN in the background behind us, an endless recounting of our tragedy that we couldn't bring ourselves to turn off.

"I see you bought two more hotels on Park Place and Illinois Avenue," I said, eyeing the board dotted with our red hotels and green houses. The big pile of cash in the center. She'd tried talking Mark into playing with us, and he'd joined in the beginning, but he'd never had an attention span for board games even when things were good, and he hadn't lasted past the first hour. We'd auctioned off his properties.

"I sure did," she said with a tiny grin and pointed at my dwindling stacks of cash laid out in front of me. "You're going to have to cross your fingers and hope you land on Free Parking when you come around that corner, or you're screwed."

I started to laugh, then stopped just as quickly. Laughter today felt wrong. I grabbed the dice for my next turn when suddenly Robin Meade stopped midsentence and cut into her usual programming. "Folks, I have breaking news. We have confirmation of a live shooter situation at Falcon Lake High School in Falcon Lake, Minnesota. It's happening right now."

I froze. My insides heaved.

"Oh my God, Mom," Katie said, jumping up and racing to the family room. Mark was already standing in the front of the TV. I hurried to join them.

Robin Meade was in the studio. Her hand was on her earpiece, trying to hear from whichever reporter was talking in her ear. "This is unbelievable, folks. The same high school that missing fifteen-year-old Isaac Greer attended is now in an active shooter situation."

We watched in stunned horror as the scene we'd witnessed so many times in the past played out in front of us on the screen. But this time it was our school. Our people. Our friends. People we'd known since kindergarten. Students fled through the doors in single-file lines with their hands on their heads as the SWAT team led them out. Some of them walked. Others raced. The same chaos. The helicopters livestreamed air shots.

"There's no word as to whether or not there are any casualties. All we know is there were sounds of shots fired and the sound of an explosion by the gym." Robin kept her hand pressed to the microphone in her ear. "I'm getting reports that the explosion was in the boys' locker room. There are two injuries. We don't know the extent of those injuries and whether those injured are students or teachers. Sam Mercer is on the scene now, and we're going to go live there in a second. Sam?"

I turned slowly and caught Mark's eyes. He was already staring at me. We didn't need to speak. Suddenly, the living room flooded with all the technicians and investigators clamoring around the TV. Detective Hawkins was missing. He hadn't come back since lunch. Did he know this was happening? Where was he?

"Mom? Dad? I can't get a hold of anyone." Katie burst into tears as she stared at her phone, willing a notification and holding it toward us like we could make something happen. We wrapped her in a huge bear hug between us. "What if Paloma's hurt? What if it's—"

"Shhh, shhh," Mark interrupted her. "It's okay. Don't let your mind go there. We don't know anything yet. They haven't said anything."

"Why won't God just leave us alone?" she wailed. "Seriously, what did we do?" She buried her face in Mark's sweatshirt.

Mark and I eyed each other over the top of her head. We had the same questions. There were no answers. Suddenly, the sound of Paloma's ringtone played. Katie shoved us off her.

"Oh my God! It's her!" she squealed, jumping up and down while she waved her phone around in the air.

"Answer it!" Mark and I said on top of each other.

She let out a laugh and accepted the call. "Oh my God, Paloma, are you okay?" Bits and pieces of Paloma's excited voice came out. We couldn't make out what she was saying because she was talking so fast, but the look of pure relief and joy on Katie's face told us she was okay. Katie pulled the phone away from her and turned to us. *I'm going upstairs,* she mouthed. Mark and I gave her matching thumbs-ups.

His stomach had to be as twisted and sick as mine. As if on cue, he excused himself to go to the bathroom. The news played the same clips over and over again while we waited for new information to come in. Nothing had changed by the time Mark came out of the bathroom.

Most of the investigative team were still standing at attention, circled around the screen. A few of them had gone back into the kitchen and pulled it up on their monitors to continue watching it from there.

The cameras cut to the school again as more students in a single-file line flocked out of the building with their hands on top of their heads while they tried not to run. They were flanked by an officer on each side dressed in full tactical gear. It was an all-too-familiar sight, but I'd never recognized the faces. This time I did as Jessica Lowry was hurried along by Billie Rae, and the next scene panned over to Louisa Copeland with her head buried in her hands.

It was so hard to watch, but I couldn't pull myself away. Neither could Mark. He gripped my hand.

When the coverage cut to the reporter, Sam had a student with him. I recognized the student from Isaac's basketball team. Nathan Bradford. He was one of the starting five. One of Gabe's closest friends. He'd poured orange juice on the crotch of Isaac's PE shorts in fourth grade. I dug my nails into Mark's hand. I could barely breathe as Nathan started speaking.

"We were on our way in to practice when all of a sudden we just heard this loud explosion. Not like a firecracker. More like a car. You know that sound it makes when it backfires? That's what it was like. Just POW"—he makes the loud sound—"and then wham: Charlie goes flying backward. Just crashes into the lockers behind him. We just started running; everyone was screaming."

"What happened to Charlie?"

"I don't know, man. I just seen his head smash against that locker and blood went flying everywhere. Somebody grabbed him, I think. But man, I don't know. I actually don't know." His eyes were wild. His breathing ragged and hurried.

Sam put his arm around his shoulders and held the microphone with the other, trying to calm him down because he looked like he was on the verge of hyperventilating. "It's okay. It's okay. You've been through something awful."

"I just ran. I just ran." His entire body shook.

"Did you see anything? Anyone? We heard reports that there were multiple shots fired."

"He definitely had a gun. I heard it."

"Do you know how many shots he fired?"

"I don't." Nathan's face crumpled like he was upset he couldn't give him any more information.

"Can you tell us anything about the shooter?"

He shook his head. "I didn't see him, but lots of other people said they did."

"And what did they say?" Sam quickly turned to look at the camera. "Remember, everyone, none of this is confirmed. We're here with Nathan Bradford at Falcon Lake High School, where there has been an explosion outside of the gym, and we have reports of multiple shots fired. I'm going to go back to Nathan." He shifts his gaze back to Nathan. The camera follows. "Can you tell us anything else about the shooter?"

"Like I said, I didn't see him, and he was wearing a ski mask, but other people did. They recognized him." He dropped his voice low. "They said it's Isaac Greer."

CASE #72946

PATIENT: JULIET (JULES) HART

"You can get that, you know," I say, pointing underneath the table at Dr. Stephens's pants. His phone has been vibrating in his pocket for the past ten minutes. I hate when people do that. He either needs to turn it off or take care of it.

"I'm so sorry. I hate that our time is being interrupted like this, but maybe I should look," he says, giving me an apologetic shrug.

"Might be a good idea. Seems like it's important if they're trying that hard to get a hold of you." I do my best not to look annoyed.

He reaches underneath the table and pulls his phone out of his pocket. His hair falls forward as he scrolls through the messages on the screen. His face goes pale. Whatever information he's learning about, it's not what he expected. I hope it's not bad news about Isaac, but I wouldn't be surprised if it was. After all, it's day fourteen.

"It never gets easier, you know?" Dr. Stephens says with emotions thickening his throat like I'm supposed to know what he's talking about, but I'm clueless. "I was part of the team at Sandy Hook Elementary School. Did you know that?"

I don't know anything about him. Nothing other than what his profile says on LinkedIn, and that's all very brief. There's nothing personal.

Not even his marital status. "The elementary school where all those kids were shot years ago? Is that what you're talking about?"

He nods. "I was part of the federal team that went there afterward. There were so many of us that volunteered to help. I've never seen such a devastated community. The psychologists that worked with the victims and their families? Those people from the National Center for Child Traumatic Stress? They actually moved to Newton and lived there for nine months." He tucks his phone back in his pants. "Anyway, I thought we'd see huge changes afterward, but nothing's changed. It's still happening. It just happened again." He wasn't doing a very good job communicating. Guess he hadn't been lying about not being able to talk about his feelings.

"What happened? What are you talking about?" I'm not like him. I can get to the point.

"There was a shooting at a high school close to here. It's still early, so they have no idea how many people are hurt or injured. Just that one is critical and others have been shot."

"That's awful. I'm so sorry," I say to him because something like that automatically deserves an apology. There's only one high school near here. It has to be Falcon High.

"I'm actually going to have to cut our time short today so that I can get over there and help stabilize the scene. I'm the closest person to it." He reluctantly pushes back his chair. "You might be right, you know? This community is under some kind of a curse. I'm not superstitious or any kind of a religious man, but bad things just keep happening to you people. Horribly tragic things."

"They say it happens in threes." I shrug. I hadn't meant to sound so flippant and uncaring, but thankfully, he doesn't notice because I'm as concerned about the situation as he is.

He stands and puts his hand out to shake mine like we're in a formal business meeting, or maybe he just wants to touch me, and it's the only appropriate way that he can. I feel so bad for him. I wish I could help. I extend my hand and take his in mine, grateful I used lotion this morning so my fingers are nice and soft. I rub the top of his hand. That electric charge again. I know he feels it too. There's no mistaking the chemistry between us.

"I have to go," he says, reluctantly pulling away from me and heading for the door.

"It's okay," I call out after him as he leaves. "I have things I have to do too."

TWENTY-TWO

AMBER GREER

I scooted down the embankment, doing my best to keep my footing on the icy rocks and not go crashing down. Mark put his hand on my back to steady me. I grabbed the pine tree in front of me to stop myself and catch my breath. Mark followed behind me. Just like he'd followed me out of the basement window so the police wouldn't know we'd left.

"You okay?" he asked, hunched over and breathing hard. His entire body shivered since he was only in a T-shirt and it was a few degrees below freezing. Neither of us had brought coats. There wasn't time for that. There wasn't time for anything except finding Isaac.

I nodded as I scanned behind us to make sure we hadn't been followed. The harsh winter sun blinded me. My teeth chattered uncontrollably, and my chest burned from a combination of the cold and the run. We'd snuck out of the house without anyone noticing, but they had to know we were gone by now. Katie was going to be furious when she realized we'd left her alone in the middle of all that. I shoved the thoughts aside.

"That way," I said, pointing to the deer path leading to the side of the lake where Gabe had drowned. We'd just hopped the railing at Paradise Point.

Mark nodded and hurried forward, bracing himself against the wind. We'd barely spoken since crawling out of the basement window. We'd watched in stunned horror as Falcon Lake High School was swept and searched from top to bottom with no sign of Isaac. And there was no denying it was him. Every student reported the same thing—Isaac Greer tried to gun down the basketball team on their way to practice. And now he'd gone missing again, just like before.

But I knew where to find him. My instincts told me he'd be here in the same way they'd told me the Dog Snatcher didn't have him. I couldn't think any further than that. All I wanted to do was find him. That was the only thought that went through my head. It was still the one driving me forward. If only I could find him, then I could save him. From himself. From what he'd done. From whatever he was planning to do next.

That's why I'd excused myself to go to the bathroom and slowly crept down to the basement when no one was looking. I'd been wrestling with the window when Mark had reached over from behind me and tugged it open.

"Let me help you with that," he whispered, giving me a knowing nod. He didn't say anything else. Neither did I. Just squeezed through the small window and tumbled into the backyard.

The cold was an instant shock to my system. I grabbed Mark's hands and pulled him through the window next. We ducked down and slunk slowly across our backyard. My feet had never been louder as they crunched against the frozen grass and snow. We reached the end of our backyard and the fence separating our property from the neighbors'. I hadn't climbed a fence for years, but that didn't stop me. Nothing could. I hurled myself over it after Mark and we hurried through our neighbors' backyards, throwing ourselves over fences like two fugitives. We were over four blocks away before we felt safe enough to work our way onto the street. We took off at a dead sprint, partially to get here fast and the other part to stay warm. We wouldn't stop until we reached Gabe's memorial at Paradise Point.

We still hadn't stopped, but our pace slowed as we wove our way along the deer path skirting the trees and brush surrounding the lake. Mark slipped on a patch of ice in front of me and barely caught himself. I reached down and gave him a hand up. The wind howled at our backs and bit into me. I forced myself not to think about the cold and pushed forward. We rounded the edge of the shoreline, and suddenly, there he was.

There was no mistaking it was him. His yellow puffer jacket was a dead giveaway even so far away. He stood shaking and shivering, but he wasn't alone. Somebody else stood with him. Their back was facing me, but I didn't need them to turn around to know it was Jules. The sight of her made me sick. A relationship with a child was about as low as you could go. I didn't care what they'd been through.

I heard Mark's sharp intake of breath next to me, but I wasn't surprised. Somehow, I'd known this was exactly what we'd find when we left the house. All I wanted to do was stop whatever was supposed to happen next. Jules was waving her arms and motioning, very animated about whatever she was saying to him. Isaac had his head down.

We crept quietly toward them, trying to get as close to them as we could before they noticed us. If they saw us now, there was still a chance they could take off and run up the hill to the road. We were still too far away to catch them if they did, but it didn't take long for us to get close enough to corner them. The lake was behind them with no way for them to go on their right and the only way back up the embankment and on to the road was through us.

We stepped around the pine trees and into the open. Our movement startled them both.

Jules whipped around. "Get out of here!"

I wanted to pummel her and tell her to get away from my son. How was she even here? How long had she been with him? Did she help him plan the shooting? What kind of a monster would do something like that? I forced myself to stay calm and focus on what was the most important.

"Isaac . . . Isaac . . . ," I called out to him with the same voice I used to caution him with when he was a toddler and he'd climbed too high on one of the slides at the park and I was terrified he'd fall. It was the voice that said, *Be careful.* My voice that said, *Come down.* I was too far away to see if my words had fazed him the way that they used to back in the day.

"Go away!" he yelled back just like Jules had.

"Isaac, please, we love you," Mark cried as we inched forward. Both of us had our hands raised in submission like we were the ones surrendering to arrest.

We never took our eyes off them as we moved. A few feet and then a few more. They kept looking back and forth at each other and scanning the perimeter for a way out. Did she have a car? Was it parked close by?

I took another step forward. I could see Isaac clearly now. His teeth were chattering nonstop like mine, even though he was in a jacket. His face was gaunt like he hadn't eaten. Wherever he'd been, they hadn't fed him well. I fought the urge to rush him and pull him into my arms.

"I'm warning you, Mom, get back," he said as if he'd read my mind. His hiking backpack was strapped to his shoulders. His jeans were covered in mud and snow. Pine needles stuck to his tennis shoes. Blood splattered the front of his yellow jacket. Horror flushed through me, leaving me dizzy and weak.

"Isaac, please, we just want to talk to you. We love you," Mark said pleadingly as he stood next to me.

"Stop talking! Don't say that! Get away from me!" he screamed and raised his hand in the air. That's when I saw it. The gun. Clenched in my son's hand.

All this time, I'd held on to the hope that my suspicions weren't true. That he wasn't the one shooting at the school. That my baby hadn't hurt innocent people. Even when I'd seen him next to the water with Jules by his side, I'd hoped. Hoped maybe he'd been a part of the plan but hadn't been the one to carry it out. Maybe he hadn't been the one to pull the trigger. That it was one of the people from *Dracho*. Somehow the kids had gotten it wrong at the high school.

God, I wanted it not to be true.

But it was, and there he stood.

My son with a gun in his hand. A gun that he'd used to strike down his classmates.

"We're not going anywhere," I said, holding my ground even though I was shaking and terror clawed at my chest. How did he get a gun? How did he even know how to use it? We weren't like other Midwest families. We weren't gun people. How did this happen? I'd been watching him so carefully. My head spun so fast with questions; there was no time for answers.

"Go away, Amber," Jules's voice cut in. "I've got this."

I whirled around to face her. Who did she think she was? She'd destroyed him. "You've got this? You stay the hell away from my son." I lunged for her, and Mark yanked me back.

"Knock it off," he ordered without looking at me. He focused his attention on Isaac. He didn't care about Jules. He never had. "You're going to be okay, Isaac. Everything's going to be okay," he said in his most soothing voice. His breath came in thick wispy puffs like smoke.

"Okay?" Isaac laughed. "You think things are going to be okay? I just shot up my school, Dad. We're way past that, and besides, it doesn't even matter because you know why?" His voice cracked. He wore a tortured expression. "I can't remember the last time that I was okay. Did you know that? Like, I'm not joking. I'm being serious. I can't remember. It's like nothing that happened before we went into this stupid lake ever happened." He motioned behind him with his other hand. "All of it's gone. That life. Whoever that boy was. Gone. All of it. All of him.

And it's never coming back. I'm never coming back, and it's because I'm not supposed to be here."

"I know this is hard, Isaac, I do. But you can get through it," Mark encouraged him, and I nodded in agreement even though I saw no way out of this tragedy, either, but we'd find one. We had to. It couldn't end like this. It just couldn't.

"Stop saying that!" he said, baring his teeth like an angry dog. "Please just stop saying that, Dad. You can't outrun the universe. You just can't. I should've died in the lake that night. It should've been me. Everybody knows that."

"Isaac, please stop," I cried. "How many times have we been through this? You don't have to feel guilty that Gabe died and you lived. I feel awful about his death, too, I do, but you have to find a way to move past it. You can't—"

"Oh my God, Mom! You drive me insane, you know that? Please stop pretending. I can't stand the pretending." He scrunched up his face like he was going to break down sobbing, but he pulled it back together quickly. His anger returned, twisting his face into someone I didn't recognize. "You don't understand. Nothing feels right inside me anymore. Nothing! Do you get that?" he yelled at me. "There's no getting away from the feeling that you're not supposed to be here."

"Isaac." I forced myself to keep my hands at my sides when all I wanted to do was reach for him. "You can't keep blaming yourself. You just can't. It was random."

"But that's the thing, Mom, it wasn't." His voice cracked again, and for just a split second, he sounded like he did when he was a little boy—sweet, innocent, scared. He didn't know what he was doing or how he was feeling. He was totally lost. My little boy was lost, and I didn't know how to bring him home.

I shook my head. "I don't know what you have to do, but you've got to quit thinking that way. You've got to take those kinds of thoughts and not let them have any space in your head."

"Tell her it's true." He ignored what I'd said and turned his attention back to Jules. "Tell her I'm not supposed to be here."

"I can tell her?" She looked surprised, and I hated that they had secrets.

He nodded, giving her his permission.

"On the night that I picked up the boys, Gabe got into the passenger seat in the car, and Isaac got into the back. But Isaac looked carsick, and I was afraid he'd puke in the car, so I made the two of them switch seats," she explained, shifting her gaze back and forth between Mark and me as she spoke. We waited for her to say more, but she didn't.

"Still . . . so what? I mean, does it really make that big of a difference?" Mark asked. He looked as confused as I felt.

"It does when Gabe forgot to put his seat belt on when he got back there. Gabe was thrown from the car when we crashed. He was dragged fifty feet underneath the ice. He never stood a chance." Tears filled her eyes, and her lower lip quivered. "Our seat belts saved our lives, and originally Gabe was wearing his seat belt. I was the one who clicked it off for him to get in the back seat."

"So, you're responsible for Gabe's death then?" I flung at her. It was an awful thing to say, and it came out without thinking, but if we were going with their logic, then it was her actions that had set the chain of events in motion.

"But don't you see, Mom?" Isaac asked desperately. "Gabe wasn't supposed to die. He never was. There was this split second where I knew I wasn't supposed to be switching seats with him. I didn't even want to sit up front. I didn't feel sick. I really didn't. It was supposed to be me. It was always supposed to be me."

"Then be mad at her. Or be mad at someone else. Just, please, let's go home," Mark begged as if that was a possibility. Where did we go from here? What would happen to Isaac when we left? It was probably only a few more minutes before the police showed up too. What would they do when they saw he was armed? Panic gripped me. We had to hurry.

"It's not safe anywhere. That's what I'm trying to tell you." Isaac shook his head. "This thing—death—it's attached itself to me, and it's not getting off. Not until I give it what it wants. What it's always wanted." He raised the gun and pointed it underneath his chin.

Everything stilled.

I was too afraid to breathe. To move. To speak.

Mark found his voice first. "Isaac, you don't have to do this," he said cautiously with each word measured, slow, and deliberate.

"I just want it to be over. I just want it to end, Dad," he cried. "I can't go on like this. I just can't."

"It can be over, Isaac, it can. You just need help. We have to get you some help." Mark took a tentative step toward him. "That's all, buddy. Just some help."

Isaac shook his head in quick spastic jerks. "I'm not supposed to be on the planet. I'm just not. Everything in my life is a lie. All of it. There's no meaning. No reason. It's all wrong. All of it and there's no fixing it. Nothing will ever make this better." His face twisted with grief. The tears he'd been wrestling with worked their way down his cheeks.

"No, baby. No, honey, don't say those things," Jules interrupted, cooing *baby* and *honey* in a sickeningly sweet voice like you'd say to a lover. "We're both miracles. Remember? You taught me that. That's why our lives were spared. We have a purpose and a plan. It's why we're still here. You know that. We've talked about it so many times."

He kept forcibly shaking his head while she talked. "Nononono. There's no reason. None. You were right. You were always right. I should've listened to you from the very beginning."

"You know the reasons we're alive and together, baby. Nobody else has to understand as long as we do. As long as we have each other. That's all that matters. You don't have to do this. Everything's going to be okay." She opened her arms and motioned for him to fall into them like she was a mother bird who would cover him with her wings. "We can figure things out. We can make this work. I love you."

But instead of stepping into her, he stepped away from her, onto the edge of the barely frozen lake. The thin ice cracked underneath the pressure of his weight. His feet slipped into the icy water. He winced as the water slogged over his shoes.

"You're a forty-one-year-old woman. I'm fifteen." He said it like he was disgusted with himself. "Did you really think we were going to run off and be together?"

She opened her mouth and closed it. Twice. Her eyes grew wide. Had she been thinking that this whole time? Patiently biding her time and waiting for him to contact her, thinking that they'd run off into the sunset and start a new life together? I watched how his words affected her and realized that's exactly what she thought. She reached behind her like she needed something to steady herself, but there was nothing there. For a split second, I almost felt sorry for her, until she spoke.

"But you've always known that, and it's never mattered," she cried. "The normal rules of society don't apply to us. Age means nothing when you're talking about real love. You can't help who you love. You just can't." She listed off her rationalizations like they were a mental list she went through and kept track of. She probably had to just so that she could sleep at night.

"None of that's true." He stubbornly shook his head.

"What about everything you said to me? How you felt? I know you weren't lying to me. You couldn't have been. Your feelings were real. You felt it too. I know you did. You said you did. You're just confused, honey."

"I was lying." A strange smile curled into his face. His eyes went dark. He motioned to me. "My mom's right, you know. You're a crazy bitch."

She recoiled like he'd slapped her. She brought her hand up to her face like she was searching for the mark. "Baby, don't say that. You always say hurtful things when you're mad. I understand how upset you are, but you don't have to be so mean."

"You don't understand anything. You're so lost you have no idea what's going on." He let out a laugh, but there was no life behind it. It was empty and cold just like the expression taking over his face. "You actually think bringing a baby into this sick world is a good idea? I hope my sperm turns to poison inside you." He spit out the words like venom, then quickly flipped the gun around and pointed it at her.

Jules stumbled backward, stunned. Before she had a chance to say or do anything, Mark jumped in front of her and spread his arms out wide, stretching himself across her body. "Son, don't. Enough. This has to end."

"Move out of the way, Dad," Isaac begged in a strangled voice as he tried to keep the gun steady.

Mark shook his head. "You're not going to hurt anyone else today, do you hear me? Nobody else gets hurt." He took a step away from Jules and a step closer to Isaac. "I want you to put the gun down. Just put the gun down. Give it to me, son." Isaac looked at him like he didn't recognize him and turned the gun back on himself. He pointed it at his chest.

My entire body thrummed with the need to move, but I forced myself to be still. Jules cried quietly behind Mark, covering her face in her hands while her shoulders shook with sobs.

"You're not going to do that, either, do you hear me? You can't do that to yourself. You know why?" Mark still hadn't taken his eyes off Isaac. "Who is going to eat at Bare Burgers with me and throw bottle rockets over the Lion's Gate at all the jet boners if you're gone?"

I snapped my head to the side, giving Mark a bewildered stare. What was he talking about? None of that statement made sense, but for some reason, it registered with Isaac. His eyes widened, and his face went slack.

"What? I don't . . . wait . . . that was you?" he asked in disbelief. Mark nodded, and it suddenly dawned on me that they were talking about *Dracho*. "You're Loserstreet41?"

"I am," Mark confessed.

"Like the whole time? Since the start of the server?" Isaac asked like he couldn't believe it. His eyes filled with tears.

"Yes, the whole time, and I'm going to continue being here for you the whole time, Isaac, do you understand me? No matter what you've done. I mean that. I'm not going anywhere. Ever." He took another step closer to Isaac. And then another. "I love you, and nothing will ever change that. Nothing. Do you hear me?"

"But Dad . . . I just . . . I just . . ." He burst into tears. His entire body shook. We all knew what he'd done. The emergency sirens in the background told us it was only minutes before what he'd done caught up with him. My heart sped up.

"It doesn't matter what you've done. You're still my son and I love you." Mark reached out his arm and held out his hand, open palmed, to Isaac. "Now, please, son, just give me the gun."

Tears streamed down Isaac's face. Snot dripped from his nose. The sirens wailed in the background, getting closer and closer. Isaac took one last look around before he took a tentative step forward and slowly placed the gun in Mark's hand.

And just like that—it was finally over.

THREE MONTHS LATER

AMBER GREER

I sat in the back seat of the car staring at the back of both Mark's and Isaac's heads as we logged the last few miles to Bridges Academy. Bridges was so far north it was practically Canada, but it was the only acute psychiatric facility that would take Isaac while he awaited his upcoming trial. We had no idea if it was going to be days or months until it was through, and after that, he'd be looking at prison. Lots of it. Maybe forever. They were charging him as an adult for murder since two of the boys he'd shot didn't make it. He'd injured four others, including the science teacher, and he faced felony charges on those too. The familiar panic squeezed my chest, and I forced myself to breathe. To get back into the minute. Anything else was too much.

I was surprised Isaac had allowed me to come along for the ride since he hadn't let me visit him the entire time he'd been in jail. Only Mark. He said I made him too soft, and he couldn't be weak in jail. I'd only gotten to see him during his hospital stays. Even though Isaac was on suicide watch, he'd ended up at the Hennepin County hospital twice. Once after he drank the cleaning solution they used on the cafeteria tables and the other after he'd hanged himself with a drawstring he stole from another inmate's sweatpants. Each time I kept it together in front of him, but I lost it in the waiting room afterward. Mark held on to me while I sobbed, rubbing my back and whispering that it was going to be okay, that we would get through it even though there was absolutely nothing suggesting we would. Gratitude flooded me at how loving and supportive he'd been to me through all this.

As if he felt me thinking about him, he looked up and caught my eyes in the rearview mirror. His eyes lit up, and a smile pulled at the corners of his mouth. I blushed and smiled back. In a strange way, I'd fallen in love with him all over again. We'd traveled to the darkest places of humanity together and held each other's hand through it all. Nobody understood what we'd gone through—what we were still going through—and it'd bonded us together like never before.

It wasn't lost on either of us that Katie's spot was empty in the car. She'd refused to come just like she refused to talk to Isaac, even though he kept trying to connect with her. She didn't want anything to do with him. She wouldn't even write him a letter or send him a card while he was in jail, no matter how many he sent her.

"He's a murderer, Mom." That's what she said every time she heard his name or overheard someone talking about him.

And he was. My son was a murderer.

Turned out, Allen, the new friend he'd brought home earlier last month, was someone he'd met on *Dracho*, just like I'd initially feared. He lived across town in an old beat-up and run-down Victorian with his grandmother. His parents had abandoned him with her when he was a toddler. She was in no position to take care of Allen since she was in the throes of dementia, but Allen offered up her basement as the perfect place to stash Isaac and carry out their plans. Isaac wasn't the only one who went to his school and targeted classmates just like he'd done in their game. Three other boys had done the same thing. Allen was one of them.

The media referred to the two of them as the classic psycho-path-and-depressive dyad, just like the Columbine shooters. Allen had been in and out of juvenile detention centers since he was eleven for things ranging from truancy to arson. He'd been waiting for a submissive partner, and Isaac was the perfect depressed and suicidal teenager to copartner his plan. Mark had been right all along about Isaac having another phone, and the messages between Isaac and Allen made my blood run cold. The shooting had been a suicide mission for Isaac, but it'd been a fun game for Allen. At least Allen's grandmother wouldn't remember what her grandson had done or that he was no longer with us.

All the boys carried out similar plots with similar plans—homemade pipe bombs and guns. I'd been shocked to discover that Isaac hadn't been spending as much time with Jules as I'd thought. Isaac had used his visits with her to cover up what he was doing with Allen. There was security footage of the two of them at Walmart buying bullets, and it made me sick every time I watched it. The whole reason they'd staged Isaac's kidnapping was to ensure that in two weeks, all the police and law enforcement resources would be directed toward patrolling backcountry roads and combing ditches. Nobody would be patrolling in town. Isaac's shooting was the signal for the others to begin, and that day had ended with more tragedy than anyone ever could have imagined. Allen and the other two boys had taken their lives at the end of their rampages. Two by police and the other by his own hand.

Once again, Isaac stood as the sole survivor.

Did he feel guilty?

Mark said he did now that the doctors were weaning him off the antipsychotic medication and he was becoming more coherent, but I wasn't sure. I wasn't sure about anything with Isaac anymore. I understood his reasoning and logic behind wanting to take his own life. As much as I didn't want to, I did. It all made sense—the survivor guilt, feeling like it was supposed to be you, the hopelessness, the loss of yourself and your old life. All of it. I did. Right up until the point where he hurt other people. That said something about him. Something different. Something horrible. Stuff no mother ever wanted to believe about their son.

He'd ignited a huge media storm over the effects of bullying on school shootings, and all the media outlets had been trying to get us on board with their platforms. To speak out against bullying and ask schools to take a stronger stance, but we hadn't done it, and we weren't going to. Kids were mean to Isaac, and unfortunately, for whatever reason, he'd always had a target on his back. Except it didn't matter how awful those kids treated him: none of them deserved to die. Lots of kids got bullied. Many of them way worse than his experience, and they didn't go to school and hurt innocent people. Even if people were mean to you, they didn't deserve to die.

I'd spent weeks throwing massive amounts of blame and responsibility on my shoulders for what Isaac did. Guilt was just one piece of my emotional chaos. Nancy Grace and all the other forensic psychologists weighing in on the case didn't help. All of them pointed to the accident with Jules as being the tipping point for Isaac. That was the hardest part for me because when all was said and done, I'd set the ball in motion by not being able to pick him up after the basketball game. But recently, I'd started remembering strange incidents with Isaac that had pricked at the corners of my consciousness. There was one in particular that I still couldn't shake.

It had been a completely regular day. Nothing out of the ordinary was happening. I had just gotten Katie together and sent her off to school with Mark since she had to be there early for choir tryouts. It was just Isaac and me alone in the kitchen. I walked by the table, where he sat eating his oatmeal, and noticed it looked a bit mushy and thick. He hated it that way.

I pointed at his bowl. "Do you want me to put more milk in that?"

He lifted his head and gave me a look of utter disdain and contempt. "No," he said, turning his nose up at me like I smelled bad.

It had stopped me in my tracks. For the first time since the accident and all Isaac's subsequent behavior changes, I had found myself questioning my role in it.

Was it possible Isaac would've turned into an angry, disgruntled teenager no matter what? Was that going to be his path all along? Could the accident have just been the thing to push him there quicker? The thing that tipped the scale in that direction? Put him over the edge?

Adolescence was a turbulent experience, and teenagers lost their minds during it on a regular basis. You never knew which ones were going to make it through safely and which ones were going to derail. How did we know that wasn't going to be the case with Isaac all along? Maybe he would've turned into a different person whether or not he'd been in the car on that fateful night.

I glanced at him in the front seat next to Mark, where he sat lifeless, and my breath caught in my throat like it did every time because I still couldn't reconcile the little boy whose hand I used to hold when we crossed the street with the one who'd committed such a horrible act. His body sagged in his seat like he barely had enough energy to hold himself up, and his gaze never wavered from the road. His expression was blank, like all the lights inside him had been turned off. It'd been three nights since we'd brought him home from jail, and despite how much I'd missed him, I'd counted every single minute until we could get him to Bridges, where he would be safe. Where we would all be safe. He couldn't be trusted, which was why he couldn't come home, but jail was no place for him either. He needed help.

The car slowed, and Mark announced, "We're almost here," as he took a right onto the long gravel road. He said it the same way he used to say it when we showed up at Disneyland or any other vacation spot, but this wasn't any kind of amusement park. Not even close.

Since I hadn't been able to visit Isaac while he was in jail, I'd channeled all my energy into getting him out of jail and into a residential facility where he could get the help he desperately needed. It'd been an almost impossible task. First, because of all the legalities and upcoming court cases that he was in the center of, and second, because nobody wanted to touch someone like him. Even mental health professionals, who were supposed to be nonjudgmental no matter what, didn't want to treat him after what he'd done, and I couldn't be mad at them for it. Detective Hawkins had pulled some strings to get him into Bridges.

I leaned over and put my hand on Isaac's shoulder as the gravel crunched underneath us. My mind searched for something to say. The right words. An inspirational story. A mantra that he could say to himself to help get him through whatever painful journey lay in front of him. But I kept coming up empty handed. Nothing would make this better. Nothing would take it away. There was only one thing I could say.

I gave his shoulder a tight squeeze. "I love you, Isaac, and it's going to be okay."

CASE #72946

PATIENT: JULIET (JULES) HART

My eyes scan the visitors sitting at each table as the guard leads me into the room. I spot Dr. Stephens immediately, and his eyes meet mine as he grins. I hold back the urge to run at him and throw myself into his arms. The guard must've felt my impulse because she tightens her grip on me. We zigzag our way through the other tables. The room is filled with other visiting families and spouses, so there are tons of screaming babies and fighting siblings. Just as many angry couples. One was being removed when I entered the room. Lawyers are littered around the room, dressed like they just came from court and wearing the most serious expressions of everyone.

I'm probably the only one with a therapist who comes to visit them. Dr. Stephens didn't have to do this today. My case is officially closed. It's over. All done. But he still came to see me, and I've been counting down the minutes ever since I found out.

As soon as we get close, he rises to meet me like a perfect gentleman. It feels so good to see him. I haven't seen him since our last session at Samaritan House before everything went down. Three months passed in a blur, but jail is like that. Each monotonous day bleeds into the next.

"Hi, Juliet," he says, using my formal name, and it dawns on me that he never used my name during all our sessions. And the first time he does, he chooses the formal one? Nobody ever calls me Juliet. Not even my parents when they're mad at me. I've been Jules since I came out of the womb. But I like the way it sounds rolling off his tongue. Maybe it's time for a change.

"Hi, Dr. Stephens. I'm so happy to see you." I can't help beaming. "It's so nice of you to visit." There are so many things we can talk about now that we don't have to keep secrets. It was tough not to just tell him everything before, and he worked just as hard dragging information out of me, but ultimately, I couldn't betray Isaac. I had to be true to him. After all, he's the father of my child. My miracle baby.

I instinctively rub my belly at the thought. They say you pop faster with your second one, and I'm sure it'll happen any day now. It's only a matter of time. I just need to be patient.

"I can't wait to hear everything," Dr. Stephens says as we take our seats, but there's not anything to tell that hasn't already been reported in the media ten times. He's here because he wants to see me, and I don't try to pretend I'm not happy about that.

We're on opposite sides of the table like how we sat in the therapy room, but this time we're surrounded by people. This place is a sea of visitors with absolutely no privacy, but I don't mind. I've got nothing to hide anymore. Everything is out in the open, and there's an indescribable freedom when you just get to live your life unabashedly naked and unafraid. Speaking of naked, Dr. Stephens looks good.

"You look really nice today," I say, hoping he knows how much it means to me that he came. "I mean, not like you looked terrible before, but you weren't sleeping much during the investigation, and I can tell you've gotten some rest."

"Thanks." He gives me a timid smile like this is an awkward first date, and I want to tell him not to be so nervous. "How's jail?" he asks, then quickly laughs at himself. "Can I ask that? Is that something you say?" He smiles, pretending to be innocent and naive, but he's been in jail plenty of times before this. Sometimes I forget he's a forensic psychologist, so he knows all the right things to say, but I like the way he plays with me. I wouldn't want him to treat me any different. It would take all the fun away.

"The food is terrible, like really, really terrible, but you know what? The people are less scary than the ones in the psych ward, and they are so much more reasonable too." I giggle.

"I imagine there's a difference." His mood is light and airy. Like a breath of fresh air into this place. I knew I'd missed him, but hadn't realized how much until I saw his face.

I sit back against my chair, trying to pull my shirt tight against me. These jumpsuits are so unflattering, but I do my best. I've got to give him something to think about until the next time he visits.

"How are things going with the case?" I ask, eager to get him talking. I missed the sound of his voice.

He shook his head. "My part is done. I was only called in as an expert witness in your case. I won't be involved in the others."

There are so many lawsuits happening it's hard to keep track of them all. Most of the time it just makes my head spin. Isaac's is the biggest one, of course. Two of the boys he shot didn't make it, and they're charging him with first-degree murder on top of everything else they can throw at the poor kid. I already wrote a letter to Amber and told her I'm willing to do whatever I can to help on his case. That didn't go over very well. Things with her never do. She still doesn't understand our relationship or the fact that I was the good influence in Isaac's life. She's the one who forced my pregnancy test and the subsequent charges. I'm the one who should be mad at her, but I was willing to put all that aside for Isaac. Still am. Because we should work together to help him. He needs to be punished for his actions, but he shouldn't be tried as an adult like they're attempting to do. That's too much. At first, they even tried to keep him in jail until the trial, but the Greers finally got him out last week.

He sits at the top of the legal pyramid with a cascade of cases underneath him. The parents of the murdered boys have filed a suit against the

Greers for failure to report terroristic activity. Apparently, Isaac had been playing a violent video game with other people from all over the country, and they'd acted out similar attacks online. A handful of kids came forward after the shooting at Falcon Lake High School and confessed to knowing about it. Some of them had played it. The problem facing the Greers is that they knew all about the game too. Amber's husband, Mark, actually played it with Isaac. Their trial doesn't even start until September.

Then there's all the parents of the boys who carried out similar attacks who have banded together to sue the video game creators. They're all suing *Dracho*, claiming it created the aggression in their sons and that the game wasn't being monitored closely enough. They also say the kids thought everything they were doing was all part of the game; that they didn't actually know it was real. It's all a big legal nightmare.

"Have you talked to Isaac?" Dr. Stephens asks.

I give him a sly smile. He knows better than that. I'm not supposed to have any contact with Isaac. It's part of the conditions of my release and parole. Signed and stamped by the judge. But I wasn't supposed to have any contact with him before, and we all know how that one turned out. "You know I can't do that."

"That's never stopped you before."

I grin. He's right. "This time is different. We're respecting the rules."

He nods, but I can tell he doesn't believe me, and since I don't want there to be any secrets between us, I lean forward and motion for him to come closer so none of the guards overhear. "We sent each other letters back and forth while he was in jail." I keep my voice low. "Of course we weren't dumb enough to send them ourselves. I had someone here send them for me, and they were all written in code, so if someone intercepted them, they'd never be able to figure out what we were talking about anyway."

Adjusting to jail hadn't been nearly as hard as I'd imagined it'd be. Turns out, people around here will do just as much for a cigarette as Hank would at Samaritan House.

I didn't fight at my trial at all. I pleaded guilty on all my sexual abuse charges. As soon as I knew for sure I was pregnant, I just wanted to get it over with as quickly as possible. Get in and get out, as they say. I'm lucky. Minnesota has one of the few prisons that has a nursery ward. So even though I'll give birth to my baby in jail, I'll get to keep her, and we'll get to live together while I serve out the last few months of my sentence. By then, I should only have about three months left, and all this will be behind me. I can finally move on. To bigger things. Better things.

I shift my gaze to Dr. Stephens. Those eyes. He doesn't turn away from the heat of my stare. He must've missed me too.

"Have you ever had a case that you just couldn't let go of because you had so many unanswered questions?" he asks after a few beats pass and neither of us has spoken.

"Absolutely." There wasn't a therapist who hadn't. We all had our cases that haunted us and kept us up at night. Ones that invaded our dreams even after we'd finally fallen asleep. You couldn't be a good therapist if you'd never had one of those moments. At least not in my opinion.

"I'm just hoping now that everything is said and done, you can tell me the truth about your relationship with Isaac." Hadn't he read the prosecutor's report? It was all there in black and white.

"What do you want to know?" I lay my hands flat on the table and try to look like an open book. I'm willing to let him read my insides.

"You swore to me that your relationship with him wasn't sexual."

"It wasn't."

He cocks his head to the side and points at my stomach. "I'm confused."

"There are other ways to get pregnant." Even though I'm not really showing yet, it's no secret that I'm pregnant or who the baby's father is. The Greers insisted on a paternity test. Dr. Stephens looks even more confused now, and it's hard not to giggle. "I told you our relationship wasn't sexual, and it wasn't. I promised you in the beginning that I wouldn't lie to you, and I haven't. I may have left out information and not been able to tell you everything, but I never lied to you."

"I'm not following you."

I reach across the table and pat his arm gently. I want to leave it there, but if I do, the guard will scream at me, so I quickly pull it back. "There are lots of other ways to get pregnant besides the old-fashioned way. There are cups . . . turkey basters . . ." That's as far as I'll go. He's a grown man. He can figure it out. I watch my words sink in as some version of the actual story registers and then give him another moment to recover before going on. "First, he kept me alive, and then I did the same for him. It's really that simple. We kept each other alive."

We'd stumbled upon our mission and our purpose the same way we'd stumbled on each other—by accident. "I'd never hurt Isaac. I told you that from the beginning. Just like I told Amber. Having sex with Isaac would've just been so confusing for him. It would've blurred the lines of our relationship, and I couldn't have that. That wouldn't have been good for us." I pause to look up at him. He's listening intently. "I don't need to tell you how important firm boundaries are in a relationship, especially one in which there's such a power differential." It was the entire reason they'd been able to charge me with felony sexual misconduct with a minor. The judge said I was abusing my position of trust and authority. I'd expected him to say just as much.

But I'll never forget the night I conceived and how magical it was no matter what anybody says or does to taint it. I've stored every single one of the details in my heart just like Mary did after she had Jesus. We read the story every season at Christmas, and I've never understood it more than I do now. My situation is no comparison to a virgin birth, obviously, but getting pregnant from one attempt after so many other heartbreaking tries in my life and at my age is pretty miraculous, nonetheless. That's why I know it's meant to be.

I gave Isaac his privacy in the bathroom so that he could accomplish what he needed to. He'd been so gracious in agreeing to help me even though it was such an awkward request, but that's how we did things. I helped him with his school project—he helped me with mine.

I believe in giving kids their space, so I only knocked at the door twice to check on him. I didn't want the magic fluid out of his body for too long before it was in mine.

"Isaac, honey? Everything going okay in there?" I wasn't sure exactly how to ask. I didn't want to do anything to embarrass him, and he'd been so incredibly touchy lately. He was such a moody teenager, but I couldn't blame him. He'd been through so much. I gave him the same grace with his intense and unpredictable emotions that he gave me. That's why we worked so well together.

"Everything's fine," he mumbled from behind the door. "I'll be done in a second."

We'd been planning tonight for weeks. I hadn't felt like this since I was a kid the night before Christmas. He wasn't nearly as excited as me and couldn't wait to get it over with so he could go hang out with the new friend he'd made, but that didn't matter to me as long as we got the job done. I couldn't wait to get him upstairs, and I'd quickly ushered him inside.

It wasn't hard to sneak him in. Girls snuck their boyfriends in all the time thanks to Hank. He worked overnights two nights a week and spent most of his shift sleeping. Also, there were plenty of people who worked the late-night shift and didn't get home until after midnight, so staff expected there to be a certain amount of activity around then. That was when all the overnight visitors made their way inside unseen. Isaac was no different that night. I explain the entire system to Dr. Stephens.

"It wasn't like the staff cared that much anyway," I say after I'm finished. "People were caught on a regular basis, and all they did was take their privileges away. Basically, grounded them for a week by making them stay inside the house. It was different for me, though. I didn't think they'd turn a blind eye to Isaac since he was a minor. Our stakes were higher, but it was definitely worth it."

"So, why'd you do it?"

"Because I knew it was the thing that would save us both," I explain. He's giving me one of those looks like I have two heads and one of them has a horn growing out of it. I wrinkle my face at him.

"Save you from what?"

"Ourselves." Hasn't he been listening to anything I've been saying? "Everyone needs a reason to live, or you can't stay alive. We kept each other alive. Our job was to create life, and in the beginning, that was enough." I pause for a second, remembering what it used to be like. "But after a while, it started to fade, so that's when we decided"—I rub my stomach and give him a huge grin—"to create this beautiful life. A reason for both of us to stay alive."

"Except Isaac tried to kill himself. Seems like the plan backfired."

Sadness tries to weigh down my face, but I won't let it. I've worked too hard putting myself back together. "Isaac made his choice, and everyone's entitled to them."

"Did you know what he was going to do?" It's a logical question. Everyone assumes I played a role in his disappearance and attack on the school no matter how many times I deny it. Despite my denial and the fact that there's no evidence to support it, nobody believes me. That's okay, though. His is the only opinion I care about.

"I swear I had no idea what he was planning. I was always worried about Isaac hurting himself, and so much of our relationship was spent just trying to keep him from going there. It's why I showed up at his house that day. I was there to save him. Not hurt him. I—"

Dr. Stephens cuts in. "The day you broke the window at the Greers? Is that what you're referring to?"

I nod. "Isaac was extremely angry and suicidal. He'd been that way since the first day he came to visit me in the hospital. So much of our relationship was me trying to save him from himself. It's like I told you before: that was the first time I felt like I had a purpose and a connection since Gabe died. I was determined not to let him do what I'd done."

That's what happens after you've put your car on the train tracks. You recognize the signs in others. "He'd taken pills from his doctor before, and his last message to me had been so cryptic and laced with threat that I knew he was planning something that day, and I had to stop him."

"Why not tell his parents?"

"He'd never trust me again if I did that, and I needed him to trust me. I was the only person he had. If I had known that his plans included trying to blow up his high school, I promise you that I would've said something. Not just to you. I would've told the police too. I had no idea he was capable of that kind of violence. I was always afraid of him hurting himself, but it'd never once occurred to me that he'd hurt someone else." I still can't wrap my brain around that one. Never in a million years would I have predicted that Isaac was capable of hurting another person on purpose and in such a violent way. I'm not going to lie; it makes me a little nervous about the life I'm carrying inside me since they'll have half of Isaac's DNA. Are violence and aggression inheritable traits? It's been so long since graduate school and my studies on psychopathology that I can't remember.

"How did you know Isaac was going to be there at the lake that day?"

He's trying to trip me up with a different tactic. He doesn't have to play these games anymore. "I told you—I didn't know anything about what he was planning or why he disappeared. I thought he was working on a school project with a friend. That's what he told me we were doing. Creating a 3D-printed design of the school." I laugh at myself. I can't help it. I feel like a naive teenager. I really had been so swept away by the magic of the experience that I'd turned a blind eye to so many things. "As soon as I heard he was the shooter, I just knew where he'd go. What he'd do. I told you already—we're connected like that."

Whenever Amber talks about that day and they ask her the same question, she always goes on about how it was maternal instinct that led her to the lake. But it wasn't the same experience for me. Instinct had nothing to do with it.

Isaac and I had talked about taking our lives numerous times before. That's most of what we did in the beginning of our relationship. We spent hours talking about different plans. Just the fantasy of it helped us feel better. Less trapped, as if we still had options. A piece of our life that was under our control. At one point, we discussed doing it together. In that exact same spot where he almost shot himself. I pulled up what was happening on my phone as soon as Dr. Stephens left that day, and I only watched half a clip before I was racing out of the door. I was so afraid I wouldn't get to him in time.

He looked like such a lost soul standing there in a blood-spattered jacket with a gun in his hand, trembling and shaking like he was in the throes of some strange seizure. The Greers don't know how lucky they are that I got there first.

Everyone credits Mark with saving Isaac's life. How he talked him out of it when Isaac pulled out the gun, and I'll admit, it was a nice move, but I got there almost fifteen minutes before the Greers, and Isaac was an absolute mess. He hadn't stepped over into the suicide part yet—he was still half in the rampage. I probably saved innocent lives that day.

Dr. Stephens props his elbows on the table and rests his chin on his hands. "So, after all that, how are you? How are you really doing?" He gives me a smile. That dimple.

"You know what?" I smile right back at him. "I'm actually doing really well. For the first time in a long time, I can say that I'm happy."

This is a fresh start. A new beginning. Isaac gave me a new chance at a life. A reason to live and get up in the morning. That's all you need. I rub my hand over my tightening stomach. And love. You need that too. You can't survive without love. I lock eyes with Dr. Stephens. Maybe it's time I call him Ryan.

What's that saying about second chances at love? Oh yeah. *Sometimes life gives you a second chance at love because you weren't ready for it the first time.* That one there. It's my favorite.

ACKNOWLEDGMENTS

Thank you to all of my readers for reading my twisted stories. I will keep writing them for as long as you keep reading them. Thank you for allowing me to have the coolest job on the planet. To everyone at Thomas & Mercer: my deepest gratitude. Another book in the books—ha! I love being on your team and can't wait to see what we do next. To Christina—you're amazing. Thank you for always having my back.

ABOUT THE AUTHOR

Photo © 2020 Jocelyn Snowdon

Dr. Lucinda Berry is a former psychologist and leading researcher in childhood trauma. Now she writes full time, using her clinical experience to blur the line between fiction and nonfiction. She enjoys taking her readers on a journey through the dark recesses of the human psyche. Her work has been optioned for film and translated into multiple languages.

If Berry isn't chasing after her son, you can find her running through Los Angeles, prepping for her next marathon. To hear about her upcoming releases and other fun news, visit her on Facebook or sign up for her newsletter at https://lucindaberry.com.